A Life Made of Lava

LISSA DEL

Cover design by Apple Pie Graphics

Edited by Catherine Eberle of WordWeavers

For my mom, because I haven't dedicated a book to you yet and you're probably the most deserving.

CHAPTER 1
Evie

"Thank you for coming," I say, bestowing a polite smile on the girl opposite me. The smile I use when I don't want my true feelings made plain. It hurts my cheeks. "I'll let you know as soon as I've made a decision."

She nods, all doe-eyed, painful shyness. She's not the one. I know it, she knows it, but we stick to the courteous formality that one expects in such situations. Until we reach the door. *Screw it.*

"Look, Darla, I'm going to level with you. You don't have the job. I'm sorry, but you're just not what I'm looking for."

She pulls nervously at her too-short skirt but nods anyway. "I kind of figured. Thanks for not keeping me hanging."

"I don't want to waste your time. For what it's worth, I hope you find something soon. Oh, and Darla?" She turns back. "I don't think you're cut out to be a nanny. I get the feeling you're not particularly fond of children at all. You should find something you're passionate about and do that instead."

She opens her mouth. Shuts it again, nods her head, the ripple of ebony down her back sending a pang of envy through my frail frame, and walks away. I shut the door and lean back against it, exhaling in a rush of breath.

"Well that was a complete waste of time." My best friend Kat raises her brow at me from the kitchen doorway. "I could've told you within seven seconds of her sitting down that she wasn't the one."

"I know. I figured I had to at least hear her out. She came all this way."

Kat rolls her eyes. "She came from Rushmore. It's not even five minutes away."

"It would've been convenient."

"Yeah. Plus, she had a cute ass."

"She had a cute everything." I follow her back into the kitchen. My fingers move of their own accord, slipping beneath the neon print of my scarf to scratch at my naked scalp.

"You've stopped wearing your wig," Kat announces, pulling a bottle of chilled *Dom Perignon* out of the fridge.

"It gives me a rash," I reply. "Besides, bald is the new black, haven't you heard?"

"I must have missed that." Her thumb skirts across the white-gold label, clearing the condensation in a smooth line. Over two thousand dollars' worth of limited edition vintage champagne sloshes around in that bottle. Kat sighs longingly. "I guess we'll just have to keep hoping," she says eventually, setting the bottle back and pulling out a carton of orange juice instead.

"God, you're a lousy cook," I tell Kat half an hour later. I prod the congealed mass lurking in the bottom of the pot. "How do you screw up spaghetti?"

She peers over my shoulder. "It's fine. Besides, they're kids, they won't even notice."

"My children aren't dogs, Kat. They have standards."

"That's not what I meant and you know it. As far as children go, yours are by far my favourites."

"What about your niece?"

Kat shudders. "Utter little bitch."

"She's five now, right?" Kat nods solemnly, oblivious to the fact that I'm pointing out the obvious – that one should not call a five-year-old an utter bitch. I scan through the pile of resumés stacked on the kitchen table and then set them down. I'm too tired to think anymore. "You know," I tell Kat, "if you actually liked children, it would make my job a lot easier."

"Well I don't," she says. Kat likes money, apple martinis and younger men. She's never been married and the only babies she's interested in are the spawn of her media conglomerate, which sprouts new offices every other month. She snatches up the pile and withdraws three resumés randomly. "Here, call these in next. If you keep reading them over looking for some sort of sign you're going to give yourself a brain tumour."

"Too late!" we cry at the same time. Technically, my specialist hasn't confirmed the presence of a brain tumour, but only because I won't let him look.

"Or you could ask Steph to help you out," Kat taunts.

"Ugh!" I give the spaghetti a sharp jab. "She's already been over this morning, all porcelain veneer smiles and telling me to stay strong and keep my chin up when we both know she can't wait for me to kick it."

Stephanie, or Steph, as she likes to be called, is Nick's new employee, a perky, twenty-something millennial with a crocodile smile and skin as thick as elephant hide. She's as gleaming as she is efficient. I quit working shortly after my diagnosis five months ago, and Steph is the shiny new me at Danvers Inc., the interior design company that Nick and I started twelve years ago.

"What excuse did she have this time, or did she come out and admit that she has grand designs for a new spa bath in the main bathroom?" Kat asks, venturing closer to the wine rack and trying to read the labels over her shoulder.

"Oh, you're going to love this!" I say, yanking the cork-screw from the top drawer and sliding it over to her. "She wanted to give me the name of her plastic surgeon."

Kat's jaw drops. "She what?"

"Yeah," I wave my hand in a perfect imitation of Steph's extravagant hand signalling. "You know, Evelyn, you really should consider cosmetic surgery. A healthy body image goes a long way to creating a positive mind-set, and you know how important that is when it comes to a disease like," I lower my voice to a conspiratorial whisper, "cancer."

Kat's hands are trembling with ill-concealed rage. "She didn't."

"She did." It's easy to shrug off because I'm used to it by now. When you're dying, people feel the need to help, to offer all sorts of sage advice, as if I hadn't tried everything. Twice. Cannabis on multiple occasions and in multiple forms, if we're keeping score.

"Nick needs to fire her, Evie. No, don't look at me like that, I'm serious. That little bitch needs to go."

"It's too late to train anyone else and you know Nick can't afford to lose her now. The business is already struggling with all my medical bills..." I trail off, melancholy tugging at my resolve. "Anyway, Nick's not going to fall for someone like that, he's not an idiot. Okay, well, he's a bit of an idiot," I concede, "but he's *my* idiot and I know he would never be attracted to someone like Steph. Besides, she couldn't handle my kids. I'd give it twenty-four hours and she'd be running from the house screaming."

"With all your jewellery shoved in her pockets, I bet," Kat points out, but my sense of humour died the second I mentioned the children. "Oh, screw it," Kat adds, pulling a bottle of red from the rack. "We're having a drink."

"You say that like you didn't already make that decision on the drive over."

Kat is gone by the time Nick gets home. He puts on his post-diagnosis smile as soon as he sees me, the one that doesn't quite reach his eyes. He's trailing kids, like the pied piper of parenthood because he picked them up from school this afternoon and went to watch Jesse's cricket match. Jesse, a ten-going-on-thirty preteen with a full-potato-sized chip on his shoulder, gives me a scowl as he passes. He heads straight to his room, no doubt to plug in the electric guitar I bought him as a consolation prize when I missed his football game last month. Radiation's a bitch.

"I guess that answers the 'am I forgiven' question," I say. "I sure hope he gets around to it before I keel over."

Nick winces. He hates my gallows humour. He preferred the Wonder-Woman, warrior-style smugness I adopted the first time around. The one that got me through chemo and defied my illness, sending it scuttling back to hell with its tail between its legs.

Dylan is almost six and still looks at me like I'm the only woman in the world who makes life worth living. As introverted as his brother is outgoing, Dylan is my secret joy.

Baby Casey is four years old and fearless, her cherubic face combining only the very best bits of Nick's and my own, as if God held himself up to a higher standard the day she was conceived. Nick's bold chin: check. Evie's single dimple: check. Evie's non-existent eyebrows, ah hell no. Eyes: let's throw in a shade of blue that we've never used before, shall we? Okay, now you're just showing off.

"Did you see Dr Moxley today?" Nick asks, arranging his features into an expression of polite interest.

"Oh, um..." I rack my brain trying to think of an excuse I haven't used yet. "I couldn't. I had to replace the batteries in my vibrator. Third time this week, would you believe it?"

Sex jokes are Nick's second worst kind, after death jokes. "Evie..."

"Oh, and Nick," I interrupt before he can build up momentum, "the floor's lava."

For the infinitesimal space between heartbeats, I think he's not going to react. It would be the first time in eighteen years and the flash of fear the thought induces almost brings me to my knees. Then, without another word, Nick leaps onto the kitchen counter, upending the cold pot of overboiled spaghetti and almost decapitating himself on the overhead pot rail.

And I smile. Because it doesn't matter if you're dealing with shitty diapers, or a failing business, or even stage four bone cancer, when the floor's lava, you get off it.

CHAPTER 2
Nick

EVIE'S SMILE IS A SUNRISE. HER EYES LIGHT UP WHEN SHE laughs, they always have, and the green gives way to blue. Her smile was one of the first things I ever noticed about her back in college. It was naughty enough to invoke wicked thoughts, nice enough to make me want to take her home to meet my mother. Back then she didn't have the crow's feet, but somehow they make her more, rather than less beautiful.

As I climb down from the kitchen counter she dazzles me with that smile. She still has the tiny chip in her front tooth, the one she claims gives her character, but which is really just proof of how shit-scared she is of the dentist. The kids haven't been for a check-up yet despite my mother's growing horror because Evie can't even walk into the dentist's room without hyperventilating.

"What is this?" I ask, scraping congealed pasta off my pants.

"Kat tried to cook," she says. She's still smiling. She's still so beautiful and I feel my heart twist, the way it does every time the possibility of a life without her sneaks up on me.

"You really didn't see Dr Moxley?" I ask, hoping that she'll deny it. She's been impossible since the diagnosis.

"I really didn't see Dr Moxley. I've been busy."

"What could possibly be more important than seeing your specialist?" I ask. "And don't even think about mentioning the vibrator you don't actually own again." I know Evie doesn't have a vibrator. I know, because I've always been enough. I wouldn't go so far as to say we were sex-crazed, but... no, actually, I would go that far. And then some.

Evie holds up a stack of papers. "I've been interviewing nannies."

"Can't you just go through an agency?" She's been at this for weeks. How hard can it be to find someone who can cook, clean and drive the kids around?

Evie shakes her head, the soft, smooth skin catching the overhead light. "No. This person is going to be living with us, Nick. I need to make sure I find someone I can get along with, someone who's the right fit."

"She's not a shoe, babe."

"Thank God. Can you imagine how much longer it would take if she was?" She mock gasps and I feel my stomach tighten again at the thought of having an Evie-sized hole in my life.

"How was your day?" she asks, as she sets about wiping down the counter with an ancient cloth that must have been blue once but is now the grey of dirty dishwater.

"It was okay." I avert my eyes as I add, "I um... I fired Steph."

Her hand freezes, cloth-deep in white pasta water. "What did you say?"

I make my way to the fridge to read the take-away menus. It helps, not having to look at her. "I laid her off."

"Why? Nick, you need her help at the office. You can't do it all on your own!"

"I caught her stealing." The words are acid on my tongue. I never lie to Evie. She falls silent and I resist the urge to look back at her. "I think I'll get pizza," I say. "Unless you feel like something else?"

"No," she says in a voice as small as I feel. "I'm not that hungry."

I draw in a deep breath and turn around. "I'll finish this up. Why don't you go and lie down? I'll wake you when the food gets here."

I watch her walk away with a heavy heart. I didn't catch Steph stealing. Instead, I caught something far worse. I caught the end of her conversation with Evie this morning. I popped home to fetch Jesse's boots which he'd forgotten and which I'd promised to bring to the match. I'd driven straight back to the office to draft her notice, my hands gripping the steering-wheel so tightly my knuckles had turned white.

"WHAT IS THIS?" Steph asked when I handed her the envelope. She'd smiled at me - she was always smiling at me. It made me uncomfortable, but I'd learned to ignore it.

"It's your severance."

Her perfect teeth disappeared and I tried not to enjoy the feeling of satisfaction.

Inside the envelope was a check. It was generous – too generous for someone like her – but I didn't need a labour dispute now, not with everything else going on. "I'm letting you go."

"Letting me go?" her eyes narrowed and she cast a furtive glance around the office as if looking for a hidden camera. "Is this some sort of joke?"

"No. I've paid you notice, but there's no need for you to work out the month. You can pack up your things."

"You're firing me? On what grounds?"

I could've given her any number of excuses – the expense of Evie's medical bills, the way she always found a reason to touch my shoulder when I was showing her something on my computer screen; the way she'd upset one of our biggest clients, not because she'd mistaken him for a delivery man, but because of the way she'd treated him when she'd thought that's what he was - but I didn't use any of those excuses. I wanted her to know the truth. Nobody spoke to Evie like that. Nobody disrespected my wife.

"On the grounds of marriage," I replied seriously, and then I got up and left, without another word. Jesse had played in a brand-new pair of boots because I'd been too afraid to go home in such a state. I had needed time to calm down, or Evie would've seen right through me.

I TAKE out my cell phone and call the pizza parlour and then I set about cleaning the kitchen. There are two wine glasses in the sink, one still half-full. Evie's tolerance isn't what it used to be. I watch the burgundy liquid pooling in the plughole. It looks like old blood and new pain.

"I'm hungry." Jesse stands in the doorway, his face set in a scowl. I don't know when he became this angry young man, such a far cry from the hot, pink bundle we brought home from the hospital. He'd slept through the night before any of the other babies in our ante-natal class, which Evie had boasted about every chance she got. A good student and an excellent sportsman, Jesse has always been a good kid. Until recently. Until four months ago when we came back from the hospital and Evie spent two days in bed, overwhelmed and terrified. She had roused herself on the third day and had gone on to act like nothing was wrong, but it was too late. Jesse *knew*. He knew that something was very, very wrong and no amount of damage control could undo it.

"I know kiddo," I tell him now. "I've ordered pizza. It'll be here any minute."

"I need someone to test me," he adds pointedly. "And mom's sleeping."

"She needs to rest, Jess. Bring your books in here, I'll do it."

By the time Jesse has unpacked what looks like the entire school library, Casey has waddled into the kitchen.

"Can I have a cookie?"

"After dinner."

"What's for dinner?"

"Pizza."

"Gross."

"Dad," Jesse growls, pencil hovering.

"Right!" I snatch up his words book and clear my throat dramatically. "Disappeared."

A puff of impatient air. "That was yesterday's. It's the next page."

"I want a cookie!"

"After dinner, Case. Problematic."

"I need one!"

"No. Gigantic."

Casey lets out an enormous fart and I burst out laughing. She grins and shakes her ass around.

"Dad!"

"Sorry," I quickly glance back at the page. "Gigantic."

His pencil slams down on the page so hard it leaves a blunt grey line through the date. "Don't worry about it," he says, gathering up his books.

"Jesse! Calm down!"

"No! I've got a test tomorrow and nobody has time to help me. If I fail, it's not my fault!"

"Give me five minutes. I'll put a movie on for Dylan and Casey and then you and I can go into the dining-room and do this together. How's that?"

He's considering it, his angry blue eyes slowly clearing.

Then Dylan steps into the kitchen. "The pizza guy's here," he announces innocently. Jesse storms out.

CHAPTER 3
Evie

I'm not sleeping, but I've closed my eyes and I'm pretending to sleep. I need time to think. Nick lied to me. He's never done that before and I can't help but wonder what it means. Did something happen between him and Steph? The thought is crucifying, but my mind doesn't play fair anymore. It always used to gravitate toward the best-case scenario but now it likes to fuck with me every chance it gets. Cancer doesn't just ravage your body. It takes everything else as collateral damage.

The first time I was diagnosed I had just turned thirty. Thirty, flirty and thriving, according to the birthday card Kat gave me that year. Thirty, flirty and dying, I corrected two weeks later.

The thing is, breast cancer isn't as scary as you might think. I personally know of seven friends of friends of friends who have had it, kicked its ass and gone on to live a healthy and happy life. Granted, I've never met any of these women, but when people told me their stories, I got on board. If they could do it, so could I. Better, even. I might even scare cancer so much that it would never raise its ugly head again, anywhere. I would be the universal cure for cancer and I would go down in history as the woman who had terrified cancer into remission.

My prognosis was good. There was a lump, it was malignant, it would have to be cut out. Doctor Moxley smiled. He told me that if there is any type of cancer one would want to have, this would be it. I'd asked him if his breasts had told him that and Nick had kicked my foot under the desk.

I spent seven years in remission. Six-month screenings proved that I had indeed kicked cancer's ass. Cancer doesn't come here, I told Nick in my best impersonation of that awkward-looking kid on *Twilight* who was replaced as soon as the producers realised that they'd hit pay dirt with the rippling naked torsos of the wolf-pack.

He'd pronounced the floor hot lava and I'd jumped into the broom cupboard.

Dylan and Casey were born during the seven years I spent in remission, each a miracle that reminded me of how life would prevail. I'd won two battles: I'd beaten cancer and my ovaries had beaten chemo.

Five months ago, everything changed.

"This is the cancer you *don't* want," Dr Moxley admitted. "It flies below all of our marker readings and spreads rapidly. I'm sorry Evie, we wouldn't even have picked it up if you hadn't complained of the pain."

Nick, being Nick, immediately went on the offensive, questioning treatment options and lambasting Dr Moxley for not having caught it sooner, while the kind doctor steepled his fingers and bowed his head. All I could think was that, after everything, I would die of back ache.

I didn't ask how long I had. It didn't matter if the answer was two weeks, two months or two years. Whatever answer they might give me wouldn't be enough. I wouldn't see Jesse become a father. I wouldn't get to celebrate Dylan's graduation. I'd never witness Nick walking Casey down the aisle.

I roll onto my stomach, burying my face in a pillow that has soaked up countless secret tears, tears that my family will never have to endure. I breathe slowly, listening to the rhythm of my heartbeat and letting it echo in my head, a steady countdown. I'm spiralling, being pulled under by the depression I fight it every single day, but sometimes the fear wins. I need a distraction and, mercifully, no sooner have I thought this when one is provided. From downstairs comes the sound of Jesse's raised voice and I open my eyes. I know that tone. I strain my ears and hear him clomping up the stairs. The sound of his bedroom door slamming only a few feet down the hall is deafening.

I sit up in bed and take a moment to wipe the pain from my face. I can hear the chaos of the pizza arrival downstairs, but behind Jesse's door it is silent.

"Knock knock." I keep my voice low and musical. Of course I don't wait for his permission before I open it - he's only ten and a long way from that sort of privilege. "Hey Jesse Knight, what're you up to?" I ask, slipping inside. Jesse Knight started when he was five. He was obsessed with dungeons, dragons, all things Arthurian. I dubbed him Knight Jesse, but he kept forgetting and called himself Jesse Knight, always in the third person. *Jesse Knight needs an ice cream, Jesse Knight never baths, Jesse Knight will save mommy from the dragon.* The dragon was always Nick, until Dylan got old enough to pull himself up and sent Jesse's favourite shield crashing to the floor. One look at the cracked plastic and Jesse had promptly dubbed Dylan the dragon and tried to stick his sword into Dylan's ear.

Jesse is coiled like a spring on his bed, his back pressed up against the denim-covered headboard, his legs drawn up to his knees. He's playing on his tablet, the one my mother-in-law bought for him after I expressly told her not to. For a woman who despises technology, she's remarkably adept at granting my kids whatever their hearts desire, so long as those desires are in direct opposition to what I want.

"Minecraft." It's a statement all on its own.

"Ah." I slip onto the bed beside him, ignoring the way he arches his body away from me. "What are you building?"

"A castle."

I peer over his shoulder. "Does it have a moat?"

A pause. "No."

"Can't be a castle then."

"It's a castle, Mom."

"What's this?" I jab my finger at a towering grey monstrosity.

"The tower."

"It needs a window."

"Mom."

I raise my hands in surrender. "I'm just saying, Jess, if it's a castle, it needs a moat. And that tower isn't really a tower until it has a window. How else does the damsel escape?"

"There's no damsel in this castle."

"There's *always* a damsel, Jesse Knight."

He doesn't argue, but I'm rewarded with a slight upward tug of his lips.

"You want to tell me why you're giving your dad such a hard time?" I ask.

"I wasn't..."

"Jesse." It's my warning voice, the bridge between my normal 'Mom' voice and the roar that finally gets their attention.

Jesse has the sense to look sheepish. He's always been a good kid, at heart.

"I have a spelling test tomorrow and Dad was testing me but he wasn't really trying. And Dylan and Casey always interrupt whenever I'm trying to do homework."

"Ah," I lean back on the pillows. "Well, to be fair, Dylan and Casey don't really understand homework yet so they wouldn't know how much stress you're under."

"When they start getting homework I'm going to interrupt them as much as I can."

"That wouldn't be very nice."

"They deserve it, Mom! They have no idea how hard it is, and they need to be taught a lesson."

"True, but still, that wouldn't be very nice." I hold his gaze and a silent communication passes between us. I know he'll see reason. Jesse is mature for his age. He gets angry quickly but it never lasts. "Why don't I test you now?" I offer. "While there are no distractions." His finger hovers over the screen of his tablet and I take it from him, setting it on the bedside table. "Homework first, Jess," I say firmly.

CHAPTER 4
Nick

By the time Dylan and Casey have finished eating and I've settled them in the living-room with a DVD, I'm exhausted. I never really appreciated how much work the kids are until Evie got sick. Even when she was initially diagnosed with breast cancer, she soldiered through it, not missing a beat. I put it down to our kids being easy. Now I know better. It's more to do with Evie being Evie. She's always marched through life with single-minded determination.

We honeymooned in the Bahamas. Evie dragged me kite-surfing, scuba diving and even to a night club called *Gutsy's*, where she drank four local fishermen under the table. She'd been tired on the plane ride back but I'd put it down to her recovering from such an action-packed holiday. When we arrived home, she'd spent three nights in hospital. It turned out she'd developed bronchial pneumonia. She'd been sick on our wedding day, but she'd refused to acknowledge it until we'd enjoyed our honeymoon. My mother had called it irresponsible, Kat had snuck a bottle of red into the ward and I'd just held Evie's hand and laughed so I wouldn't cry. I wasn't even surprised. It was just so Evie.

I glance up at the photograph on the mantel of the heart-shaped rock she'd discovered on the beach in Harbour Bay. She'd refused to remove it in case we were stealing someone else's sign. If I close my eyes I can still picture her face perfectly, the damp tangle of her hair falling over one shoulder, the almost transparent white shift-dress she wore over her bikini. Her skin had tasted of salt, and the sun had coaxed out a sweet canvas of freckles across the bridge of her nose. Her toes had been painted coral, but the black and white Polaroid doesn't capture that. Only our feet and the rock - proof that our love was forever, Evie had claimed at the time. I haven't thought about that day in ages. It seems that the closer I come to losing her, the more I'm determined to remember every memory we've ever shared.

I drag my feet up the stairs, two slices of steaming pepperoni pizza on a plate as a peace offering for Jesse. When I reach his door I hear voices and I peep inside.

"Beautifully," Evie says, her voice slow and deliberate. Jesse's dark head is bent over his writing book as they sit, shoulder to shoulder on the bed. "You're doing great, Jess." Evie is using the same voice she always has when helping him with his homework – the one that calms him and makes him believe he can do it, even when he's struggling.

He finishes the word and stares down at the page, waiting expectantly for the next.

"Olive juice," Evie says, but her tone has changed and I can see the dimple prominent on her cheek as she tries to fight a smile.

Jesse's dark head whips up. "That's not in my book."

"Olive juice," Evie repeats, her mouth exaggerated around the word. Jesse opens his mouth to argue and then she says it again, only this time, with no sound. Even from here, I can see that the shape of her mouth forms three little words. Jesse finally gets it, and even though he's trying to be cool, he is, after all, only ten years old, and the stupidest of jokes is hilarious when made by his mother.

He smiles up at her. "I love you too, Mom."

They don't move for a long time, Jesse's head buried under Evie's shoulder, his homework forgotten and I tiptoe downstairs to fetch more pizza.

"Dinner is served!" I announce, entering the room and depositing two plates on the bed.

They're under the covers now, doing something on Jesse's tablet. By the light of the bedside lamp, the shadows beneath Evie's eyes look almost black.

"There!" she announces happily, her eyes fixed on the tablet screen. "Now it's perfect."

"Mom says a castle isn't a castle without a moat," Jesse tells me, grabbing a slice of pizza and shoving it into his mouth.

"Well obviously. How else would you keep an invading army out? Here," I add, offering Evie her plate. She shakes her head and my stomach does the nasty twist. "Please?" I prompt, my hand still extended. Jesse looks between the two of us, and then at the cooling slice of pizza on Evie's plate. His face falls and he starts to set down his own, a gesture Evie doesn't miss. Quick as a flash, she snatches the plate from my hands, folds a slice of pizza in half and crams it into her mouth.

"I prefer *calzone*," she mumbles around a mouth full of food, "but I guess this'll have to do."

Ten minutes later we're still lounging on Jesse's bed while the faint sound of the kids' DVD filters up the stairs. I feel Evie's weight shift beside me as she sits up.

"I think I'm going to go and have a bath," she says cheerily, ruffling Jesse's hair so that it sticks up on end. "Do you think you two can survive without me for a few minutes?" She doesn't wait for an answer but, as I watch her leave, a voice whispers in my head: *a few minutes, yes, Evie. A lifetime, no.*

I know she's not coming back. I could see her wilting in those last few minutes in Jesse's room and I know that when I go through to our bedroom she will be curled up on her side, facing the window, with one hand tucked beneath her head and the other on my pillow. If

Jesse has noticed that no water has started running in the bathroom, he doesn't comment.

"Time for bed, kiddo," I tell him. "Go and brush your teeth."

"What about Dyl and Casey?"

"I'll go down and get them."

"Can I read for a few minutes?"

"Ten minutes," I warn, "and then lights out." I kiss his head and head downstairs.

Casey is already asleep. Her pyjama top has pulled up, exposing her rounded, pink belly. Dylan doesn't say a word, but he follows as I carry Casey up the stairs and into her room.

"Where's Mom?" he asks, once I've pulled Casey's bedroom door closed. He looks so much like Jesse did at that age, but his brown hair is a shade lighter and his blue eyes not quite as bruised.

"Mom's sleeping. You can go in and kiss her goodnight, but then it's time to brush your teeth and get into bed."

"Can I sleep in Jesse's room?"

"Let's ask him."

Dylan scoops up his pillow, assured of a good thing. I want to tell him not to be so sure but I don't have the heart.

I open Jesse's door to find him back on the tablet. "Jesse!" He jumps and tries to stow it under his covers but I cross the room in a single stride. "Hand it over." I'm starting to see why Evie was so set against my mother buying it.

"I'll put it away," Jesse insists.

"Give it to me."

"Dad!"

"Now, Jesse!" He shoves it toward me, the scowl firmly back in place. I already know what his answer will be, but for Dylan's sake, I pose the question. "Your brother wants to stay in here tonight."

"No," Jesse snaps. Dylan's face falls and I wish I could explain that Jesse's anger isn't directed at him, that he's simply an easy target.

"Sorry, Dyl, it looks like you're in your room tonight." I scoop him up, careful not to drop the tablet. "Goodnight, Jess," I say as I walk out. Jesse doesn't reply.

CHAPTER 5
Evie

It's two in the morning and I know before I'm even fully awake that I won't be going back to sleep. My whole body throbs. I curse in frustration as I recall that I forgot to take my pain pills before bed. I ease out from under the covers, taking care not to wake Nick. It's only after I've MacGyvered my way out of bed that I realise he's not next to me. A brief exploratory mission reveals him snoring softly in Dylan's bed. I smile down at the two of them, Dylan curled into the crook of Nick's arm, his legs thrown over Nick's stomach, before venturing downstairs.

I curl up on the sofa with a cup of tea and the three resumés Kat picked out. It'll take a while before the pain medication gets to work. A scraggy black cat sits on the windowsill, flicking his tail in disdain.

"Hello, you." The cat has been coming around more and more often lately. I have no idea who he belongs to, but he seems to have chosen our family to endure the most. "You look as bad as I feel," I tell him, which he interprets as an invitation to leap onto the sofa and make himself comfortable. I scratch his ears absent-mindedly. "I guess if you're going to be spending this much time around here, you might need a name after all," I say. The cat doesn't respond.

I read through the resumés carefully, trying to find something – anything – that stands out. Nothing does, save for the fact that two of the applicants are named Amy. Determinedly, I set their resumés aside and pick up the third. Julia. It's a nice name. Julia is twenty-nine, a psychology major, and, under health, she's listed excellent. Lucky Julia.

I frown at her credentials. Why would a psychology major be applying for a job as a nanny? At least the Amys have some childcare experience.

"Ouch!" I jump as the cat sinks his claws into my thigh. He glares at me through one slitted eye and I shove him off my lap.

"Evie?" Nick's voice is thick with sleep. "What are you doing down here?"

"I couldn't sleep."

"Are you in pain? Do you need anything?" The question ends in a yawn.

"No, I'm fine."

He joins me on the sofa and I scoot over, laying my head on his chest. He takes my hand, playing with my fingertips, like he always has.

"What really happened with Steph?" I ask.

"I told you, I caught her stealing. She borrowed money from petty cash without permission and there's no way of knowing if she would've put it back if I hadn't checked."

I want to call him out for lying but my courage fails me. "How are you going to manage without her?"

Nick pats my hand. "I'll manage."

"I could come in and help out until you find a replacement?"

"That's not necessary. In case you've forgotten, I'm more than just a pretty face."

"Your face isn't actually that pretty," I tease.

Nick and I met at college. He was a year ahead of me and graduated *summa cum laude*, with a degree in design engineering. I barely made it through finals, although it didn't help that I spent almost every night of my final semester out on the tiles. Nick played state football, I played a mean game of poker. On the spectrum of college social classes, we were polar opposites, but somehow, we clicked. I don't know who was more surprised to find that not only did we click, we *worked.*

"Do you remember the night we met?" I murmur into his shirt.

"How could I forget?" he chuckles. "You flashed your boobs at the entire football team."

"To be fair, Kat dared me to."

"I remember. I also remember thinking that I didn't want anyone else to ever see them again, except me."

"Nobody did. You stole my heart that night."

"If memory serves, you stole my beer."

It begins as a laugh, but I choke and bury my face in his chest. His arms come around me, pulling me closer so that our bodies are pressed together.

"I would've flashed my boobs more often if I'd known I wouldn't have them forever," I say.

"I still wouldn't have let you, even if you had known," he replies firmly, kissing the top of my head. "Besides, boobs are overrated. All they do is put a barrier between our hearts." He pulls me closer and our flat chests touch in all the right places. "See," he adds sleepily, "I couldn't do this before. Now I can touch all of you at once."

I raise my head and kiss him, because only Nick can make me feel beautiful, even after a double-mastectomy, even after losing my hair. To be fair, it did grow back after my first round of chemotherapy was over, but the waspish tufts were so far removed from the thick, bushy curls I was used to that I kept it shaved. I'd bought a lot of hats that first year. Now, thanks to bouts of radiation and chemo to slow the cancer down, I don't need to bother shaving.

Nick kisses me back, slowly, leisurely. It doesn't matter that we haven't brushed our teeth, or that my breath smells of tea, because things like that don't matter when you only have so many kisses left.

"I'm sorry." He pulls away and I know it's not because he wants to, but because he feels bad that his erection has risen like the leaning tower of Pisa to nudge suggestively at my hip.

I do a quick mental assessment of my body. The meds are working, the pain has receded to a dull ache and a tiny fire has ignited in my belly. It doesn't get much better than this.

"I'm sorry," Nick repeats, taking my silence for embarrassment, or worse, disappointment. I silence him with another kiss and then reach for his pants.

He stays my hands with one of his own. "Evie..."

"Shhhh," I whisper.

His hand falls away. "Are you sure?" he asks, his eyes heavy-lidded with desire.

My heart skips a beat and I reach for the hem of my night-shirt, pulling it up and over my head. "Less talking, more touching, Mr Danvers."

I fall asleep after, cocooned in Nick's arms. If only I could emerge beautiful again, like a butterfly, but I don't. Instead, I wake with a niggling spasm in my lower back and a dull burn in my lady bits, protesting such an energetic work-out.

Nick isn't on the sofa but I can hear the shower running upstairs. I pull on my pyjamas and go through to the kitchen to turn on the coffee machine only to find it's already been brewed. Typical, thoughtful Nick.

Caffeine-fuelled, I make the kids' lunches for school and set up their breakfast on the island.

Mornings in our household are chaos. I wish there was a better way to put it, but there's not. Three kids are the social equivalent of an army of adults, only they make more mess.

"Promise me you'll reschedule with Doctor Moxley," Nick says as the children rush off to brush their teeth.

I cross my fingers behind my back. "I promise."

By the time Nick has ferried them all out of the front door, planted a wet kiss on my mouth for good measure, and driven out of the garage, I feel like I've run a marathon. Not that I would know what running a marathon feels like, but I can only assume it's how I would feel if ever I did.

Before I clear away the breakfast dishes I phone the three applicants Kat picked out. Julia and the Amys can all come through for an interview after lunch so I schedule them forty minutes apart. I've just hung up the phone when it rings in my hand.

"Are you dressed?" Kat asks.

I look down at my wrinkled pyjamas. There's a Cheerio stuck to my thigh. "No."

"Get ready, I'll be there in fifteen minutes."

"Are we going anywhere special? Should I wash my hair?" I tease.

"No, it'll take too long to blow-dry."

I take a lightning shower and pull on a pair of faded jeans and a tank top. I look about eight from the neck down, with my androgynous body and jutting hip bones and I've gone up another notch in my belt. I don't bother with make-up, and by the time Kat's flashy silver Mercedes pulls up to the curb, I'm already waiting on the verge.

"Took you long enough," I say, sliding onto the leather passenger seat. "What were you doing, driving Miss Daisy?"

"I had to make a quick stop." She grins and points into the back seat, on which lies a *bona fide* 'For Sale' sign. I read the details upside down and burst out laughing

"Excellent!"

It's no secret that I don't get along with my mother-in-law. Mary-Anne Danvers had taken one look at the nineteen-year-old reprobate her son had brought home and decided that this girl would never become her daughter-in-law. Five years later she wore black to our wedding and cried quite sincerely into her silk handkerchief. Jesse's birth had resulted in a temporary ceasefire, but only for the duration of time it took for Mary-Anne to discover that my parenting style was nothing like her own, and so began a decade-long war of wills. I believe in letting children sleep when they're tired and eat when they're hungry. Mary-Anne imposes a rigid bedtime routine and follows a paleo lifestyle.

Mary-Anne believes children should be seen and not heard. In our household, whoever yells loudest, emerges victorious. When, during one of our very rare lunches at the country club where Mary-Anne has been a member for over twenty years, she claimed that no floor could ever turn to lava, I had promptly thrown myself to the ground and burned to death. It was vocal and dramatic, but necessary. My children had been present and I couldn't let her steal their magic. Mary-Anne has never forgiven me.

Every Tuesday my mother-in-law leaves home at nine o'clock on the dot and drives four miles to Grace Fawcett's house to play bridge with a group of women who, for all intents and purposes, detest one another. The bridge routine is simply another means for them to attempt to outdo one another – a pissing contest for old women, as Nick calls it. I peek at the clock on Kat's dashboard. It's 9.27. Nick's father, dear David, works tirelessly to afford Mary-Anne the lifestyle which she deems worthy, which means he's doomed to fail. It also means he's almost never at home.

"Where did you get it?" I ask Kat as she pulls into the street on which David and Mary-Anne live.

"I had it specially made," Kat replies. "Nothing's too much for my dear friend Mary-Anne."

I snort. If I am the thorn in Mary-Anne's side, then Kat is the ultimate pain in her ass. When Kat made her first million, the first thing she did was join Mary-Anne's country club. She claimed it was because it was good for business, but I knew better. Kat never forgave Mary-Anne for telling her, the very first time they met, and with no compunction whatsoever, that Kat would never amount to anything. When Mary-Anne got a young waitron at the club fired for 'being rude', when in fact it had nothing to do with his demeanour and everything to do with the fact that he was black, Kat promptly hired the young man in her emerging company and proceeded to take a slew of young African-American men on dates to the country club just to piss Mary-Anne off.

"You don't even like the food!" I'd teased.

"Yeah, but the look on her face is worth it," Kat had replied, without any trace of contrition.

"She mentioned you've reserved seven seats at the fundraiser next week?" I'd asked, knowing the exclusive event was costing over a thousand dollars per head and that Kat would never spend that kind of money on something so obnoxious. "Mary-Anne's positively orgasmic that she's sold more tickets than Grace."

Kat had burst out laughing. "She's going to shit her pants when she discovers I bought them for Jasper and his family."

Jasper was the young waitron whose dismissal Mary-Anne had organised and his immigrant family barely spoke a word of English.

Kat pulls the Mercedes over to the curb and peers up at the house. My in-laws have the greenest grass on the street and no self-respecting weed would ever dare trespass on the property.

"Right, let's get this done," Kat says switching off the engine.

"You know that's less than half the market value," I say as I follow her onto the verge.

"That's kind of the point," Kat replies. "Check the number, will you? I'd hate to have made a mistake."

I quickly scan the mobile number, printed in bright red and check it against the contact details stored on my phone. "Yes, that's definitely hers."

"Good." Kat plunges the sign into the lawn with a satisfying thud. Then she dusts her hands off on her designer trousers and gives me a devilish smile. "Our work here is done."

CHAPTER 6

Julia

I HEAR THE FAMILIAR SOUND OF A KEY IN THE LOCK AND A second later my dad calls out for me, as he does every time he enters the house. As if I might have disappeared during the short time it takes for him to walk that ridiculous dog. "Juju?"

"I'm here, Dad!" The soft drag as he limps down the hall and I cast a quick look around my room for any discarded underwear. I've just stashed a grey bra that used to be black under my pillow when he appears in the doorway.

"I wondered where you..." he trails off, catching sight of me. "Oh wow, you look nice! Are you going somewhere?"

I give him the benefit of a mega-watt smile, knowing how excited he'll be when he hears the news. "I have an interview!"

"Juju! That's wonderful news!"

"Yeah," I agree, sneaking another look at my reflection in the old looking-glass dresser I inherited from Grandma Soanes. "How does this look?"

"Very tasteful," my dad replies approvingly as he takes in the beige linen pants and white button-up shirt combination. It's one of the nicest outfits I own and the small stain on the front of the shirt is easy enough to hide with a matching scarf.

"What's the job?" Dad asks, leaning against the door frame.

I start picking up the clothes littering my bed so I don't have to meet his eyes. "A family in Oakland Park are looking for a nanny."

A pause. "Julia..."

"Dad, I know it's not exactly what I had in mind, but the pay is good and it'll keep us going until you find something new." I cringe at that last part. It's been three years since the accident - three years since he lost his leg - but even the slightest mention of it still brings back memories too painful to bear. My father isn't going to find another job. Nobody wants to hire an amputee jockey, not even to muck out stalls.

"It breaks my heart to see you throwing away your dreams because of me," he says now. "You were supposed to be a psychologist, not a nanny. What good is that degree if you don't finish your studies?"

"I'm not throwing away anything, Dad. As soon as I've got enough money saved, I'll start attending night classes and, with any luck, by then you'll be back on your feet. Financially, of course," I add, trying to lighten the mood. "Besides," I say as a miniature Yorkshire terrier bursts into the room and takes a flying leap onto my bed, "if I'm working we'll be able to buy Pepper all the jerky treats she can eat." I bury my face in Pepper's silken fur and wait.

"What time is your interview?" He changes the subject and I'm filled with gratitude.

"At two."

"Where is it?"

"In Oakland Park." It's less than a ten-minute drive, or it would be if we had a car.

"Oh yes, you mentioned that. Do you need money for the bus?" His disability pension doesn't stretch very far and I'm almost out of savings too. Fortunately, Oakland Park is only a forty-five-minute walk.

"No, I'm good, thanks Dad."

He nods. "I'll keep my fingers crossed for you," he says, holding them up as proof before limping back toward the kitchen. I can tell his prosthesis has been worrying him lately. He's developed angry red sores where the socket fits against his stump, and the more he wears it, the worse they get. I read recently that the newer, more expensive models come with an anti-allergy silicone coating, but there's no way we can afford one. I shove the clothes back into my wardrobe with a weary sigh. When my fingers brush against the softest silk, I pause. If I close my eyes I can picture the dress perfectly – tiny diamante spaghetti straps, a soft cowl-neck draped in chiffon and a long skirt which flows straight down. It was made in a happier time, before the accident; before my life fell apart. I know it so well because I designed every perfect inch of it and the delicate stitching was made by my mother's own hand. It was meant to be my wedding dress.

I still don't blame Aaron for calling things off. He had proposed to a girl who wanted to see the world. I had shared his dreams and his wanderlust. As soon as I graduated, we had booked tickets to Thailand and we hadn't stopped travelling for a long time. We had made love under a blanket of stars on the beaches of Malawi, explored the catacombs of Rome and had gotten high with a group of locals in a Mexican *estancia*. And that had only been the beginning. We had worked and travelled extensively, going from one adventure to another without responsibility or consequence. Our wedding had been planned and postponed three times, not because we didn't want to commit, but because we were so busy living we couldn't find the time to stop long enough to hold the ceremony.

And then the accident had happened. In a flash, my entire world had been turned upside down. There would be no more travelling, not while my father needed me. Aaron was wonderful. He offered to stay behind, to help, but I had declined. I would join him as soon as Dad had found another job. One month had become six. I'd seen Aaron twice since the accident and even then I had felt the distance between us. It wasn't only physical, there had been a disconnect between us on a much deeper level. We were losing 'us'.

Six months became a year and a new name started dropping from his lips. Moira. He had met up with her in India, a fellow traveller, and they would journey to Egypt together, sharing costs. It was nothing to be concerned about. In the fourteenth month, Aaron flew home, unexpectedly. Something had happened, he wanted me to hear it from him. His guilt had sent Moira packing. He had begged for my forgiveness, it was a mistake, I was the one he loved. I didn't doubt it. He needed me, would I join him so things could go back to the way they were? Never going to happen. I knew by then that my father would never be able to provide for himself. I knew that my place was now with him. I was done travelling. Aaron wasn't. There was only one logical conclusion, only I didn't have the guts to say it. Eventually, Aaron did.

I shove the silk away into the bowels of my closet and slam the door shut. Aaron got married a few months ago. I had heard through a mutual friend. He and his new wife had bought a house in her hometown. Aaron was putting down roots while I was still living in limbo in the unending space between the day my mother had died and the present.

CHAPTER 7
Evie

The cat is back. It weaves between the serviette holder and the spice rack while I wait for the coffee machine.

"Have you named it yet?" Kat asks.

I don't mention my moment of weakness last night. "Hell no! If I name it, I claim it, and the last thing I need is to be responsible for another living thing. And as for you," I tell the cat, lifting it off the counter and depositing it on the floor, "you need to stay down here. Nick will kill me if he finds cat hair all over the condiments."

"You know he can't actually understand you." Kat checks her phone for the tenth time in as many minutes. "Oh, Ian wants us all to have dinner on Friday night." Ian is a friend we've all known since college. Back then I'd had high hopes for an Ian-Kat pair up, which would have been perfect because two of our best friends falling in love had seemed like the ultimate plan, but sadly, neither Kat nor Ian had been remotely interested. They did get along famously, though, so we'd all kept in touch and spent a lot of time together, barring the two years Ian had spent married to a Goth hairdresser before he'd come to his senses and divorced her.

"I can't do Friday," I grumble. "It's David's birthday."

"Tell Mary-Anne you're too sick to make it."

"She wouldn't care if I was already dead and Nick and the kids would still have to go." I point out.

"I'll tell him Saturday then," Kat replies easily, jabbing at her phone with a plum-coloured fingernail.

"I need to check with Nick," I remind her.

"Nick's not going to say no."

"True, but I need to find a sitter."

"Stop being such a Negative Nancy. You're going to find a nanny after lunch." She flips her wrist to check the time on her Tag, even though she's holding her phone already. "Oh God, speaking of which, I have a meeting in twenty minutes. Cancel the coffee, I don't want to be late."

"Since when have you cared about keeping someone waiting?"

"Since the 'someone' is a delectable young executive from Parker Homes who hasn't succumbed to my usual charms," she replies wickedly.

I drink the coffee on my own while re-reading the resumés. None of these three applicants are ideal on paper. I just hope these interviews aren't going to be yet another colossal waste of my time.

I finally set them aside when my phone rings and Nick's name appears on the screen.

"Hey babe."

"Hey, how's it going?"

"Good. I'm just looking through the resumés for this afternoon's interviews."

"Do you need me to pick up the kids?"

"No, I'll get them. I should be done by the time they come out of school."

"Okay." He pauses, a sure sign that he's got something important to say and I quickly intercept him.

"Kat said that Ian wants us to get together for dinner on Saturday night."

"Don't we have my dad's birthday thing this weekend?"

"That's on Friday."

"Do you want to go? It won't be too much for you, two nights in a row?"

"No, Nick, it won't be too much for me," I tease.

"Okay, sounds good."

"Great, I'll let him know. I'll see you later."

"Evie," he says before I can say goodbye.

"Mmmm?"

"Did you speak to Doctor Moxley?"

I cringe. I knew he wouldn't let me off the hook that easily. My gaze falls on the cat, which is now trying to cough up a fur-ball on the sofa.

"I did," I reply confidently. "Just a few minutes ago."

"Oh good." He sounds relieved and I hold my breath, praying he won't ask for any more details. Either God is listening, or Nick is far more swamped without Steph than he's letting on, because he tells me he loves me and rings off.

I drop my phone onto the sofa beside me and reach for the cat. "Looks like you've got yourself a name, after all, Doctor Moxley," I tell him, scratching his mangy ear. "And I have a feeling you and I are going to be spending a lot more time together."

By the time Amy number one arrives, Doctor Moxley has left, leaving only the faint tang of cat piss and a slug-like, black fur-ball behind. I've just wrapped it in a paper towel and tossed it in the bin when the doorbell rings.

"Hi!" Amy number one yells cheerily as I open the door. It takes her about a nano-second to register my bald head and another twenty to compose her face into something suitably sombre. I'd take this girl for everything she had if we were playing poker.

"You must be Amy," I smile, the perfect blend of polite but professional distance. "Please, come in."

We sit in the living-room. My sofa has never looked as sophisticated as it appears with Amy draped elegantly over it, I think enviously. Then I remember that she's sitting where the cat spat up.

"So, why do you want to be a nanny?" I ask.

"Well, obviously I don't want to be a nanny forever," she admits. "I'm actually waiting for a lucky break in my acting career. Until that happens, I need something simple to tide me over."

"My children aren't simple. They have well above average intelligence."

Her eyes widen in horror. "Of course they aren't! I didn't mean..."

"I know, Amy, I was joking."

"Oh!" A relieved bubble of laughter is followed with another inquisitive glance at my head.

"You want to be an actress?" I prompt. I haven't even looked at my interview questions yet. I have an inkling I won't be needing them.

"Yes," her dark head bobs enthusiastically. "My agent says I have a very raw talent." I suspect the agent didn't intend this as a compliment, but I don't pass comment. "He's got a whole bunch of castings lined up," she adds proudly.

"I'm looking for someone who can be reliable," I point out. "How often do these castings occur during the day?"

Her smile slips. "Um... mostly they take place during the day, but I can be in and out in a couple of hours. You won't even notice I'm gone."

I set the sheet of paper in my hand aside. "Amy, I'm sorry, but at this stage I just can't afford to be without my nanny for any extended duration. As you can see, I'm not well," I add, when she looks set to argue her case, "and I'm not always available myself. My children need someone who will always be here if I can't be." Amy's mouth closes. No one argues with someone who has cancer. It's a cheap shot, but I'm not wasting her time, or mine.

"I understand, Mrs Danvers. I'm very sorry I..."

"Not at all," I say, waving my hand breezily in the air. "It's not your fault and I wouldn't want to stand in the way of your aspirations."

She gets to her feet a moment after I do and I walk her out. The entire interview took about four minutes, which leaves me with over half an hour before Amy number two arrives. I phone Kat.

"Aren't you supposed to be finding the world's best nanny?"

"I found the world's worst actress instead."

"Really? She's been already?"

"She's already left."

"Don't sound so down in the dumps. The next one will be the one, I can feel it in my waters."

"I haven't trusted your waters since they told you that Ricky Ferris was straight."

"Hey, that wasn't my fault. Besides, how many women do you know who can say they've snogged a gay guy?"

"Probably just me," I admit. "But I would've preferred not to spend six months chasing him around campus because your waters told you he was into me."

"My waters were wrong about that. They're right about this. Just you watch."

"If you're wrong you're buying my dinner on Saturday night."

"If I'm wrong, Ricky Ferris is straight," she says before hanging up.

Amy number two makes a much better first impression. Not only does she not baulk at my bald head but she notices the dark spot on the sofa and, before I know what's happening, she's blotting it with a paper towel dipped in vinegar.

"It's an old trick my mom taught me," she says. Even better, her short, pixie-cropped hair doesn't poke the jealous hair-bear that's taken up residence in my chest lately.

Everything is going perfectly until she spots the pictures of Jesse, Dylan and Casey on the mantel.

"Oh wow, they're gorgeous!"

I smile in the smug way that mothers do when someone praises their children before I realise I'm doing it, and then realise I don't care. "Do you want kids of your own some day?"

She sets Casey's picture back down and shakes her head. "It

wouldn't be right. I know a lot of same-sexed couples are taking the plunge, but Jacky and I just don't believe it's fair on the child. We both love kids, though."

I'm so surprised it's rendered me speechless.

"Are you surprised?" Amy asks, the corners of her lips tugging upward.

"No!" I scoff as if the thought is absurd.

"Then maybe you should tell your face," she teases.

I can't help myself and I start to laugh. "I'm sorry. I just didn't realise. You don't seem..."

"Gay?" she asks. "It doesn't roll off the tongue very easily, does it? But then again, I'm guessing neither does cancer." She gestures at my head. For a moment, I'm stunned, affronted and hopeful all at once. This girl is a dynamo. She's not being rude and she's not treating me like I'm dying. She's just that blunt. I think I'm in love.

"Amy, I'm going to level with you. You're not the right person for this job. I'm looking for someone very specific and you're not it. But," I snatch up her resumé with renewed excitement. "I see you studied business management?"

"Yes." The word is drawn out into three syllables, a question, not an answer.

"My husband and I own a design business and we recently lost our in-office manager. Please don't think I'm crazy, but I think you'd be perfect for that position. The pay is better," I add quickly, "and there's a lot of work, but to be honest, the kids are much more."

Amy stares at me for at least half a minute and then she grins, a face-splitting smile that is dazzlingly sincere. "When do I start?"

CHAPTER 8
Nick

THE PHONE DOESN'T STOP RINGING. THE SOUND DRILLS INTO MY temples and gouges out what little brain matter I have left. Steph was a bitch but she knew how to keep things in order.

The phone rings again and I snatch up the receiver. "Danvers Inc., Nick speaking."

"Hey buddy."

I breathe a sigh of relief. "Hey Ian."

Ian Harris is the closest thing I have to a best friend, or he would be if men had such things. He's also been madly in love with my wife for the better part of two decades, something I forgave him for a long time ago because he's never acted on it and, well, I understand just how easy it is to fall in love with Evie. What I've never understood is why she picked me when she could've had anyone. Evie is life incarnate, every inch of her bursting with energy and enthusiasm. Even now, with everything she's facing, she refuses to go quietly. Death, it seems, may take life, but it cannot subdue it, and my fearless, feckless wife is irrevocable proof of that.

"I wanted to check if you and Evie were free for dinner on Saturday night," Ian is saying now and I force myself to pay attention.

"Yeah, she mentioned it. Where do you want to go?"

"How about *Lapiz*?"

"That's the new pizza place downtown?" Pizza twice in one week, I think, is probably not the best thing for Evie's health, but I know better than to mention it to her.

"Yeah, they have a live band on Saturday nights," Ian continues, "I thought it could be fun."

"Sounds good."

"Awesome. How's eight o'clock?"

"Eight's good. I just need to check if Evie's found a sitter."

"If she can't, I'm sure Donna would watch the kids."

Donna is Ian's younger half-sister. A twenty-something collegian, Donna is always looking for ways to make extra cash.

"Great, I'll keep you posted." My phone lights up on the desk next to me. "Listen, I've got to go, Evie's calling."

"Tell her I say hi."

"I will, buddy. See you Saturday."

I hang up and raise my mobile to my ear. "Evie?"

"I found you the perfect assistant!" she practically squeals down the receiver.

"What?"

"Amy number two, the one who came for the nanny interview – she's gay, by the way – she has a degree in Business and she can start immediately!"

My shoulders sag in relief. "Oh, thank God." I know Evie and she wouldn't recommend someone if she wasn't suitable. She's half the reason Danvers Inc. made it through the recession of 2007. Actually, she's the sole reason we made it through. I was ready to foreclose but Evie wouldn't hear of it and, instead, she went through the phone book and scheduled meetings with every reputable developer in the greater area. One, in particular, had refused point blank to see her, but Evie had simply arrived at his office unannounced and demanded to be seen. She'd dragged me along against my will.

"Mr Tidwell is not available to see you, Mrs Danvers," the receptionist said when Evie handed over her business card.

"That's okay, Ingrid," Evie replied easily, reading her name upside down from her desk, "we can wait." Evie had smiled then, completely disarming the woman. Evie's smile was dynamite, it always had been, and I had yet to see anyone – man, woman or child, immune to her charms when she wanted something.

"Yes, well, I'm not sure if that will do you any good," Ingrid had muttered, less certain now. "He has back-to-back meetings for the rest of the morning."

Evie hadn't responded, she had simply taken a seat in one of the plush, overstuffed armchairs in the reception hall and had gestured to me to do the same.

We had waited for almost four hours until I knew every inch of the marble-tiled floor, until the swirls of paint on the abstract artwork adorning the walls had begun to spin from being stared at too long. One by one, we watched as stuffy, suit-clad businessmen and one stunning blonde in a red onesie, which Evie called a pants suit, filed past and were granted entrance into the office behind Ingrid's desk. Evie had glared at that polished oak door as if it had personally insulted her. I'd looked down at my beige pants and white, open-necked shirt and felt my anxiety rise.

My left leg had started to cramp by the time the last visitor had left and the unwelcoming oak door finally opened fully, to reveal a middle-aged man in a pair of faded jeans and a cream polo-neck sweater. Victor Tidwell almost didn't notice us as he passed, but Evie jumped to her feet and planted herself firmly in his path.

Victor gave a start and then shot a puzzled look back at Ingrid who had discreetly buried her nose behind her computer screen.

"Can I help you?" he had looked down his long nose at my wife as if she might bite.

"Mr Tidwell, I'm Evie Danvers from Danvers Inc." Evie's hand snaked out and snatched Victor's. "And this is my husband, Nick."

He shook my hand automatically. "I see. And what, exactly, can I do for you folk?" His eyes darted toward the door and then slid to his wristwatch. I had seen that look before. This was a man looking for an escape route. I sighed inwardly and placed a hand on Evie's back. She stepped out of my reach, closer to her prey.

"We wanted to chat to you about your interior design work. That's what we do." Like magic, one of our corporate folders found its way into his hands. "Danvers Inc. is a design company and we would like to work with you." She said with *rather than* for, *because she was Evie and she was slyer than a snake in the grass when she needed to be.*

Unfortunately Victor Tidwell was one tough customer. "I'm afraid I've already got three design companies on my books and I'm not in the market for another."

"Do you like sushi, Mr Tidwell?" The mega-watt smile flashed, brighter than a homing beacon.

"I beg your pardon?"

"Sushi," Evie waved her hands in the air. "We'd like to treat you to lunch."

Victor Tidwell had started to squirm. "Now?"

Evie made a point of looking at her watch. "Well, it is lunch time."

"That's very kind of you..." he floundered.

"Evie," she inserted helpfully.

"Yes, well, that's very generous of you, Evie, *but I'm afraid I have a previous engagement."*

Standing beside her, I marvelled at how Evie's smile faded, so slowly it was like watching the sun disappear behind a cloud. Victor Tidwell started to look more than a little alarmed.

"Look, how about I schedule some time to see you on..." he glanced back at Ingrid, who hastily flipped a few pages in what was, no doubt, his diary.

"Wednesday, 9 o'clock?" she offered.

"Wednesday, nine o'clock," Tidwell repeated, looking anxiously at Evie.

Evie, to my utter horror, frowned at me, as if trying to recall if that time would suit us. As if we might have a thousand other places to be on Wednesday morning, as if our company's very existence didn't depend on this meeting and a positive outcome.

"That sounds good," she acknowledged finally, while I gaped at her, uselessly. I could have sworn Victor expelled a sigh of relief.

"Well, I'll see you then." He shook our hands again and walked out of the door. Evie waved at Ingrid, who smiled.

"You weren't really going to take him to lunch, were you?" I had asked as we made our way to the car.

"God no! We couldn't afford it anyway. How horrendous if the card was declined?"

"Nick?" Evie's voice over the phone pulls me back to the chaos of my office.

"That's a relief," I say, "when can she start?" I can picture the smug smile on Evie's face.

"I thought you said you were coping just fine on your own," she taunts. She loves to be right.

"Shut it you little Minx. When can I expect her?"

"She's on her way," Evie tells me happily. "Oh, I've got to go, I think my next interviewee's here. Wish me luck!"

I set down the phone and look around the whirlwind front office. There are papers everywhere and three unwashed coffee cups on Steph's desk. I haven't even lifted a finger to try to clean up when the phone rings again. Oh well, she may as well know what she's getting herself into.

I'm still on the phone when Amy arrives. She shakes my hand with confidence and, within five minutes of talking to her, I know that Evie's done well. Amy is self-assured and assertive. Even better, when the phone rings mid-conversation, she picks it up. "Danvers Inc., this is Amy speaking, how may I help you?" She's already reached for a pen and pulled Steph's diary toward her. "Of course, Sir, we'd be happy to give you a quote." She pauses, glancing at the printed calendar on the desk, where, under our logo, our unique selling point is highlighted in red. "Yes, we do offer free quotations. Could you give me your name and number and I'll get someone to contact you as soon as they're available?"

"I'm impressed," I admit when she sets the receiver down.

She shrugs it off. "I like to use my initiative. Although I will have about a hundred questions once I really get into things."

"Ask away."

"Do you mind if I clean things up a bit first?"

I can't help but grin.

CHAPTER 9
Julia

There are three things I notice when I arrive for my interview ten minutes early. The first is that the Danvers have a truly beautiful home – it's classy but not ostentatious, the type of home that is filled with more love than money, but by choice. The second thing I notice is that there's a mangy black cat lying in the fruit bowl. The third is that Evie Danvers is dying.

She has the ghost of a once beautiful woman wrapped around her like a shawl, fuelled by the sparkle in her mischievous eyes. Those eyes belong to a girl, not to a woman at the end of her life.

"I'm Julia," I say, shaking her hand firmly. I don't avert my eyes from her face. I can tell she's expecting me to, that it's something she's become accustomed to, but there's nothing to be feared from a bald head or the dark shadows beneath her eyes. "You have a beautiful home, Mrs Danvers," I say truthfully as Evie leads me through the entrance hall and into the living-room. The sofas are a dark grey – the perfect colour for hiding spilled juice stains and muddy footprints, but the cushions which litter their surfaces are bold and colourful, a defiant middle finger to the practical restrictions of parenthood.

"Thank you," Evie says. "Can I offer you anything to drink before we begin?"

"No, I'm fine, thank you." I shift on the sofa, toying with the delicate silver bracelet at my wrist.

"Before we start, I need to ask, why do you want to be a nanny?"

I sit up straighter. "I adore children and it's something I know I'd be good at."

"How so?"

"I'm used to taking care of people." The answer springs forth without any thought.

Evie sits back in her chair, a small crease between her eyes. "Your resumé shows no previous experience in care-taking," she says, her eyes sliding toward the papers beside her.

"That's because I haven't done it formally. I... I take care of my father. He was involved in an accident three years ago and his left leg had to be amputated. He was confined to bed for months and then there were months more of physiotherapy."

"And you nursed him through it?" She sounds dubious. "Surely your mother..."

"My mother died," I intercept, before she can finish. "She didn't survive the accident."

Evie falls silent. I can't blame her – even as the words leave my mouth I feel bad about it. This woman is dealing with a lot, she shouldn't be made to feel guilty, but I felt the sting of her suspicion and I'd known what she was thinking – that my mother would have been the one to take care of my dad and that I was simply taking credit for her hard work. Not true. If only it were.

Evie slides my resumé away from her and leans forward, her bright eyes boring into mine, assessing, evaluating, searching – for what, I can't begin to guess. Then, inexplicably, she grins.

"Let's get to the interview questions, shall we?"

It takes longer than I expected, which I try to take as a good sign. At times, Evie doesn't even consult her notes, she just fires off a random question as if it only occurred to her right this moment. I answer everything as honestly as I can, even though most of her questions don't make much sense. I wonder if she downloaded them off some obscure website, or if she was on a cocktail of medication when she wrote them down and couldn't be bothered to check later. When the interview is finally over, Evie fixes me again with that unnerving stare. I try desperately to hold my own but, in the end, I blink first. Evie's grin is in danger of dancing right off her face. When she gets to her feet I exhale a disappointed breath.

"Would you like to see pictures of the children?" she asks from where she's stopped beside the mantel.

I nod, blinking in confusion, and move toward her.

"This is Jesse," she tells me, proudly showing off a photograph of a nine or ten-year-old boy who looks like he's keeping too many secrets for his tender age. "And Dylan." The second son is Evie in miniature, his hair a shade lighter than his brother's. His eyes sparkle just like hers do, but they're open and honest. This boy keeps no secrets. Casey is the only blonde, but her eyes are blue, too. A beautiful, blue-eyed family. I wonder if the husband has blue eyes, but then I catch sight of a close-up of the two of them and my heart flip-flops in my chest. His eyes are brown, but that's not what captures my attention. It's the way he's looking at Evie, laughing down at her, every single feature on his handsome face drawn toward hers. They are beautiful, even more so together than I imagine they would be apart.

"That's my husband, Nick." Evie catches me staring and I look away from the photograph in haste.

"You have a beautiful family, Mrs Danvers."

"Oh, call me Evie, please. And thank you."

She walks me to the front door. I can feel her eyes on me again and I flush under the intense scrutiny. I've been weighed, I've been measured and, by the polite way she's escorting me to the door, I suspect I've been found wanting.

A welcome breeze washes over me as she opens the door. I step out of it, desperate to get away from here so I can deal with the embarrassment of not being able to find a job, not even as a nanny. I should plead my case, but the bite of humiliation stiffens my jaw.

"Julia." Evie's voice is low and musical. I round on her slowly, not daring to hope. Evie's lips pull upward, reaching for the amused crinkle of her eyes. She regards me steadily for a second and then she opens her mouth to speak. I find I'm holding my breath.

"The floor's lava."

It's the last thing I expect, but something clicks inside my head anyway, an impulse that I don't for one second consider fighting. My mother and I played this game endlessly when I was a child. My eyes dart around as Evie starts to count backward from five, but there's nothing for me to climb up on to. I didn't bring a car and Evie's must be locked in the garage, not that I'd vault onto her car... not unless I was desperate, which right now I am. I briefly consider a terracotta pot filled with posies, but I'd never be able to balance on its brim, so instead, I lunge upward and grab the top of the door, lifting my legs and clinging to the wooden frame like a god-damned chimpanzee.

CHAPTER 10
Evie

"You can come down now," I say. I'm not sure if Julia can even hear me through my cackle of unsuppressed laughter. I've never seen anything so funny as Julia hanging from that door as if her life depended on it. Slowly, she slides back down to the ground, looking mortified and dusts her hands across her linen pants.

"I'm sorry," she stammers, her cheeks aflame, "I don't know why I did that."

I reward her with a smile. "So, when can you start?"

It was that final leap that sealed the deal, but I'd already made up my mind to hire her. Julia reminds me of... well, me. There's a light that shines inside of her that I recognise, that I miss. She is, quite simply, perfect, and exactly what I've been looking for.

"You... you're hiring me?" She looks up at the door as if it might hold the answer to her question.

"I am. That is, if you still want the job?"

"I do!" It's a breathless rush that hints at just how desperate she is.

"You do understand it's a live-in position?"

She nods.

"Will your father manage all right without you?"

"Yes. He's physically able and at this stage his needs are more... financial."

"Ah. He's not working, then?"

"He was a jockey," she says, a flash of defiance crossing her pretty face. "It's difficult to win races with only one leg."

"I can relate," I reply solemnly. "I was a hair model." She narrows her eyes, not sure if I'm joking or not and I can't help but smile. "I'm kidding, Julia. And I think your father is very lucky to have you. Now, can you start immediately, or do you need a day or two to sort things out?"

"I'd need to pick up my things, but I'm available right away."

I make a mental note to let Nick know I've found a sitter for Saturday night. "What do you say you start tomorrow? Around nine?"

"Nine is perfect."

"Good. I'll see you then." I pause, looking toward the deserted street. The absence of a car is only dawning on me now. "Where did you park your car?"

Julia looks flustered. "I don't have one," she stammers.

"You don't have a car?"

"No, I took the bus." A tense silence. "The advert didn't stipulate..." she trails off, looking like she might be about to burst into tears.

"It's okay. You can use mine when needed until we... we'll sort something out."

"I can get a car," Julia says shyly. "The bank said all they need is a letter of employment."

"I'll get Nick to mail one over immediately," I say, sensing her renewed embarrassment.

"Thank you, Mrs Danvers. I really appreciate you giving me this opportunity."

"It's Evie," I insist. "If you're going to be living here, please, call me Evie."

She tries it out. It still sounds stilted, but it's a start.

"Are you sure I can't give you a lift home?" I ask as she starts to walk away. "I'm picking up the kids from school soon so I can drop you on my way. It's no trouble at all."

"I'm fine, thank you." It's an attempt to cling to her independence and I hide a smile as I watch her departing figure. Then I glance at my watch and almost scream. I'm going to be late and Casey has a ballet rehearsal. Her first recital is in a few weeks and we've already missed two practices. I head back inside to snatch up my keys and my purse and shove my phone into my pocket. I'll call Kat from the car to let her know that, for once, her waters were right.

"I told you!" Kat is as smug as I expected her to be.

"I know. I don't know why I ever doubted you."

"Where are you now?"

"I'm on my way to fetch the kids."

"Good, I'll be over in an hour."

"Make it an hour-and-a-half. Casey has ballet.

"I'll meet you at home, I can get supper started." Kat has had a spare key since we moved in.

"Oh God, please don't."

"Very funny. You know what this means, right?"

"We finally get to drink the *Dom Perignon*?"

"It's about freaking time. Now hurry up, will you?"

"Put it on ice. I'll see you soon."

CHAPTER 11

Nick

I STICK MY HEAD INTO THE BATHROOM FOR THE THIRD TIME IN twenty minutes to yell at the distorted creamy figure behind the frosted shower glass. "We're going to be late, Evie!"

"I'm almost done," she replies, sticking her nose up to the glass and giving me a grin that isn't even a tiny bit apologetic. Her voice is muffled. She sounds like a mischievous mermaid. "Besides, who cares if we're late? It's not as if being on time is going to change your mother's opinion of me."

"You do this on purpose."

"Stop being so melodramatic. We'll just tell her I was washing my hair."

I stomp out of the bathroom without responding. I've been on edge for two days ever since I came home to find Julia Soanes mixing egg whites, her pert ass shaking prettily in time with the beater. The sight had jolted me. For a second she looked so like Evie that I was tempted to smack that ass and plant a kiss on the nape of her neck, where dark tendrils were flattened by damp sweat from the heat of the kitchen. It was the hair that brought me to my senses and, when she turned around, the differences between them became obvious.

Julia's brown eyes were narrower than Evie's, her lips fuller, her cheeks suffused with a healthy glow.

"You could've consulted me before hiring her!" I'd raged at Evie in a rare temper later that night.

"Why?" she'd asked innocently.

My justification that this woman would be living in our house didn't faze Evie in the slightest.

"She's going to be great," she'd replied glibly. "You wait and see."

I follow the sound of children's laughter downstairs to find Dylan and Casey doing Julia's face with Casey's Disney make-up palette. One of her eyes is blue, the other a glittering purple and pink streaks zigzag across her forehead. Her laughter dies on her lips when she catches sight of me.

"Come on, let's get your shoes on," she tells Casey, scooping her up and brushing past me on her way to the stairs. This is another thing that isn't helping. Julia seems to sense my annoyance and bolts like a frightened rabbit every time I enter a room.

"You ready?" I ask Dylan. He nods. "Where's your brother?"

"He went outside already."

I find Jesse slumped in the back seat of Evie's Ford sedan. "What are you doing out here already?" I ask.

"You said we were leaving at seven."

I glance at the clock on the dash. "It's only ten past."

"Grandma's going to be mad."

"Grandma will be fine." I settle into the driver's seat and we sit in companionable silence while I prepare myself mentally. Having Evie and my mother in the same room is never easy. The first time I bought her home to meet my parents, Evie was wearing an *I love Eddie Vedder* shirt, cinched at the waist with a studded belt, and little else. Her nails were painted black and she had a small piercing through her nose. She had another piercing too, though not many people knew about it. The nose ring didn't last long, but she kept the other for a few years, until I almost choked on it one drunken night after we'd been celebrating Kat's birthday. My mother hadn't liked the

Eddie Vedder shirt. Worse, she hadn't a clue who Eddie Vedder was, which was like waving a red flag in front of Evie. I'd made the mistake of leaving them alone for a few minutes while I spoke to my dad about my college fund. After I'd dropped Evie back at her dorm my mother told me that it was very inappropriate for Evie to wear the face of her ex-boyfriend across her chest.

"Eddie Vedder isn't Evie's ex," I had laughed. "He's the lead singer of a band called *Pearl Jam.* She was only messing with you, Mom." It turned out that when my mother had told Evie how inappropriate the T-shirt was, Evie had claimed she would only let go of her ex when she was one hundred percent certain it wasn't *his* child she was carrying.

We'd had a massive argument about that. Sometimes Evie could go too far and I had really wanted my parents to like her. The problem was that Evie simply didn't understand, nor did she feel the need for anyone's approval. She'd been orphaned since the age of three when her parents had been killed in a railway-siding accident and she had been placed in the custody of her paternal grandfather. While he had provided for her financially, the old man hadn't been the most suitable person as a role model for a young girl. When Evie was seventeen her grandfather had passed away and, rather than go into foster care, Evie had had herself legally emancipated. As an orphan living independently and financially self-sufficient, the process had been relatively simple. Evie had softened as she had grown older, and, ironically, spending time with my family had gone a long way toward teaching her how to curb her wild ways, but the damage had been done and her relationship with my mother would never overcome that initial first impression.

I'm roused from my thoughts when Dylan yanks open the back door and climbs into his car chair. He buckles himself up after only a few clumsy attempts. Evie arrives five minutes later with Casey bundled in her arms.

"I'm ready!" she sighs, once Casey is safely secured and strapped in. "Let's do this."

My mother is wearing her pearls, the ones my father got her for their twentieth wedding anniversary. She's worn them at every family occasion since and has a habit of twisting them around her fingers when she's irritated. Right now, the pearls are so entwined in her hands it looks like they might cut off the blood supply. The kids rush right past her with only a cursory "*Hello granny*" and her lips pucker in disapproval but I don't have the energy to call them back.

"Mary-Anne!" Evie cries enthusiastically, throwing her arms around my mother's stiff frame. "It's so lovely to see you, how have you been?"

"I'm very well, thank you, Evelyn."

Evie flashes me a grin as she turns around and, from the glint in her eye, I sense trouble brewing, but her smile is so infectious I find myself grinning back.

My mother greets me with far more warmth. "Nicholas, darling, you look exhausted. Have you been eating properly?" An accusatory glance at Evie's back.

"I'm fine, Mom."

"You need fattening up. I've made your favourite – roast beef, with apple pie for dessert."

"That sounds good." I try to speak over the frenetic yapping descending the stairs as my mother's Yorkshire terriers join the fray. "Where's Dad?"

"He's on the patio. Go ahead, I'm just going to check the potatoes. I know you like them extra crispy."

I wander outside and find Evie ensconced on the sofa beside my dad. They've always had a good relationship, unlike Evie and my mother. I've always maintained that no man is impervious to Evie's charms and my dad is no exception. His grey head is bent toward Evie's shoulder while she shows him something on her cell phone.

"You look good with rabbit ears," Dad says and, intrigued, I glance over their shoulders. Oh God, Evie's teaching him how to Snapchat. I grab a beer from the bar fridge and settle onto the single-seater across from them. Through the glass of the sliding-door I can see the kids arguing over the television remote and my mother striding through from the kitchen to veto any ideas they might have about watching anything.

My dad glances up and catches me watching. "She's been under a lot of stress," he says. "Some mix-up with a realtor. I'm sure she'll tell you about it. Also, the annual bingo evening at the country club is coming up next month and she's chairing the organisation committee."

Evie's head jerks up. "Isn't that on the 18th?"

"I'm not sure, I think so."

"But that's the same night as Casey's ballet recital! I told Mary-Anne months ago and she said she would try to be there."

"Oh, well, I'm sure she wouldn't miss it. I might have the wrong end of the stick. You'll have to ask her, Evie."

Evie's eyes narrow and she stuffs her phone back in her bag.

"Right!" my mother's voice at the door. "Everything's on track. We'll eat in half an hour. Evelyn, I've given the children a board game to play until we're ready to eat."

Evie doesn't even glance up. "Thanks, Mary-Anne."

"Mom, Dad says you're running the bingo evening at the club next month. Isn't that the same evening as Casey's ballet recital?"

"Oh, yes, I forgot about that. I meant to tell you, Evelyn, I won't be able to make it after all. I definitely want a copy of the recording, though, I'd love to see it."

"Surely the club can find someone else to help out?" Evie is making a concerted effort to restrain herself.

"Oh heavens, I wouldn't trust anyone else with it. It's the biggest event of the season."

"The recital is the biggest event of Casey's life up until this point." Evie's stopped trying.

My mother gives a tinkling laugh. "She won't even remember it, dear. Besides, all proceeds of this event go to a children's charity. I'm sure Casey wouldn't want me to abandon dozens of orphaned children."

"Casey's four, Mom." I intercept before Evie can really let loose.

"You need to stop treating them like babies. They understand far more than you give them credit for. David, sweetheart, how's your drink?" As always, my mother is a master at brushing off what she doesn't want to talk about, and, as always, my father is quick to get on board.

"It's fine," he says. "I was just telling Nick and Evie about the mix-up with the realtor."

"So unprofessional!" My mom seizes the change of topic. "There was some mix-up and one of their sale boards ended up on our verge. People thought the house was on the market, but they listed my contact number, so I've been inundated with calls from people wanting to buy the house!"

"Really?" I narrow my eyes in confusion, about to point out that if it was a mix-up her number would never have been listed, but then I catch sight of Evie's face. I know her far too well to miss the small upward tug of her lip. *Oh shit!* "Well, I'm sure these things happen all the time," I say, trying to keep my expression neutral. "And I doubt you'd have too many calls given the current market."

"Not when the sale price listed is less than half what the house is worth!" my mother replies indignantly. "It's been terribly stressful and some of these buyers have been threatening to take legal action against me for false advertising!"

"They won't do that, sweetheart," my father tells her gently, "they're just trying to intimidate you."

My mother sits up straighter, proving to all and sundry that she won't be intimidated. "Yes, well, it's still been a trying time."

Evie is bent over her handbag, rooting around inside it, but I suspect it's only because she's trying not to laugh. "I almost forgot to give you this," she announces finally, withdrawing a slim, badly-wrapped package and handing it to my dad.

"Evie, you shouldn't have!" he insists as he takes it from her. My mother eyes the wrapping as if it's committed a cardinal sin, but even she can't fault the gift itself. The slim, silver Montblanc writing pen, with my father's name engraved along the side, is beautiful. It was Evie's idea. My dad has had a career in investment banking his whole life, but he loves to journal and has been threatening to write a memoir for the past few years.

"How very thoughtful," my mother says, dabbing at her eyes and bestowing a rare look of kindness on Evie. "That's a wonderful gift, Evelyn."

"It's from all of us," Evie says, but she gives my dad a hug and I see her whisper something into his ear which makes him smile.

It's only once we're back home and the kids are sound asleep that I call Evie out.

"You did it, didn't you?" I ask her, lowering the book she's pretending to read, from her face. "The realtor sign – that was you?"

"What?" she tries to adopt an indignant expression and fails miserably.

"Have you no shame?" I ask, while she grins like the village idiot.

"None at all, Mr Danvers."

"You're terrible, you know that?"

"She was terrible first."

I kiss her nose and vault over her to climb into my side of the bed. "True," I concede. "She was terrible first."

CHAPTER 12
Evie

"Are you sure you're going to be okay?" I ask Julia for the tenth time.

"I'll be absolutely fine," she insists. "I have your numbers if there's a problem, plus your in-laws, the fire department, police department and you've already made them supper, so I won't even need to cook."

"Okay," I relent. "Just make sure they're in bed by nine and call me if you need anything."

"I will. Go and have fun."

I check my phone. "The Uber will be here in five minutes. I better say goodbye to the kids."

Julia watches as I tug on my wig. It's one of my favourites, the streaks of copper through the warm brown and the long shaggy cut almost identical to how I wore my hair before the chemo.

"Is it bothering you?" Julia asks, the gentle lilt of her voice expressing concern rather than curiosity.

"It itches." I ram my finger up and under the edge to scratch my scalp. "I think I'm allergic to the tape."

She doesn't tell me to leave it off or suggest I wear a hat instead. She must sense that tonight I want to feel beautiful again. Instead, she waits until I've stopped scratching and then gently places her hands on either side of the wig and adjusts it.

"You look lovely," she tells me. It makes me want to cry.

The sound of footsteps coming down the stairs reaches us and a small frown crosses Julia's face, but it's only Jesse. He grabs a bottle of water from the fridge and then I'm alone with Julia once more.

"Can I ask you something?"

She smiles. "Technically, you just did."

"You seem a bit uncomfortable around Nick. Has he done something to upset you?"

Her smile fades. "I... it's not that. Mr Danvers seems like a very nice man."

"But?" I prompt.

"To be honest, I get the feeling that he doesn't want me here."

Pretty and perceptive, I think. "He's worried about me," I explain. "He thinks having you here might make me feel worse about myself."

"He *said* that?"

"Of course not. But I know him better than he thinks."

"How would me being here make you feel worse about yourself?" The concern is back, mingled with guilt that she can't put her finger on because she *doesn't* know Nick.

"You're young, and gorgeous," I reply simply. "And you're not sick. None of which is your fault," I add teasingly, "but the bottom line is that I'm not any of those things. Not anymore. Please don't let it affect how you handle me or my family. And please don't feel you need to avoid my husband. He'll get over it, I promise."

"I'm not going anywhere," she vows, and I'm struck anew by her intuition because that is exactly what I did fear most. "And you're wrong, you know," she adds, brushing a wayward curl over my shoulder. "You are beautiful."

It's only a fifteen-minute drive to *Lapiz*. Nick's hand is warm on my thigh, stirring up memories of car-rides long past. My dresses had been shorter, the rising heat of bare-skin contact usually resulting in compromising activities that were certainly not advisable while driving a motor vehicle, but we hadn't cared. Back then, it had just been me and Nick against the world, blissful and oblivious in our own little bubble. Now our bubble is a Saab driven by a surly, middle-aged Uber driver named Edward.

"When are you seeing Doctor Moxley?" Nick asks, keeping his voice low.

"Next week," I reply confidently. The cat's become an even-more-frequent visitor since I started setting out bowls of tuna. Nick squeezes my leg fondly and I feel a stab of guilt. "How's Amy doing at the office?"

"Brilliantly," he says. "She's created order from the chaos in only a couple of days." A grateful smile. "It was a brilliant hire, thank you."

"Two brilliant hires in one week," I point out. Nick's jaw tightens. "It's true, Nick. I know you don't feel entirely comfortable having Julia in the house, but she's a godsend."

Still no response.

"The kids adore her," I add, looking out of my window. "And she's taken so much off my plate, I finally feel like I can breathe again."

"Evie, I keep telling you, I'm here. I can do more, if only you'd let me..."

"No."

"No?"

"No, Nick. You're not a nanny. And... well, when I get weaker, I'm going to need someone to help me with things I'd rather you don't see."

Quick as a flash, his hand leaves my thigh and he snatches up both of my hands in his. "Evie, I'm your husband. For better or worse, remember? In sickness and in health. I want to be there for you. We can get through this, together."

"There's no getting through this," I sigh softly. "There's only seeing it through to the end."

My hands feel cold and empty when he suddenly lets them go. "Don't talk like that."

"Nick..."

"No," he snarls, and out of the corner of my eye, I see the Uber driver glance up with concern to look at Nick in his rear-view mirror. "You're not going anywhere, Evie," Nick continues, not noticing, or not caring. "If Julia being there is helping, that's fine, she can stay, but only until you're well enough to handle things on your own."

I don't correct him again. Deep down he knows the truth, but he's not ready to face it. I can, however, press my advantage. "She might leave before then," I say in a small voice. "You're not exactly making her feel welcome. Please just try to get along with her. For me?"

Nick jabs his thumbs into his eye sockets and presses hard. By the time his hands drop away, his eyes are calm, his face composed. "I'll be nicer to her," he promises.

"Thank you."

I feel a rush of gratitude for this amazing, heroic man who would do anything to please me, anything I ask, if it means I'll keep fighting. The storm has passed and I face forward once more, but his hand doesn't return to my leg.

The restaurant is packed, bodies crammed onto every available chair, so I am pleasantly surprised to find that Ian has reserved a booth at the back.

"Evie!" he croons, getting to his feet and spreading his arms wide. I hug him, ducking my face as he plants a kiss on my cheek and then I slip onto the leather seat beside Kat.

Nick sits opposite, next to Ian, and he gives me the ghost of a wink.

"How's the nanny working out?" Kat asks immediately.

"Her name is Julia," I remind her, "and she's wonderful."

Kat gives me a smug look and then beckons the hovering waiter over. "Bring us a bottle of your best Cabernet, please."

"I can't drink red tonight, Kat," I murmur, trying to be discreet, but both Nick and Ian have heard me.

"Bring the red and a bottle of Chardonnay too," Nick tells the waiter smoothly. The young man bobs his head and disappears.

"You okay, Evie?" Ian asks, his face filled with concern.

"She's fine," Nick snaps.

Ian is taken aback. "I was only asking."

"I'm fine." I snatch up the menu and fix a smile on my face that hurts my cheeks. "What's everyone having?"

CHAPTER 13
Nick

I'm going to murder Ian. Kat has become a pro at hiding her concern from Evie, at keeping Evie's spirits up and going along with her example of pretending that everything is okay. It's what Evie needs and, no matter how hard it is, we suck it up because Evie is the one who matters. What Evie needs is *all* that matters. What Evie doesn't need, is the haunted, pained look that has currently taken up residence on Ian's face.

Throughout dinner I catch him sneaking lingering looks at her, wincing when she does, at a sudden stab of pain, closing his eyes briefly when she makes a joke, as if it's the last thing he'll ever hear, and I swear to God if those are actual tears shimmering in his bloodshot eyes, I'm going to punch him in the mouth.

Thankfully, Evie doesn't seem to notice. As a result of her low tolerance and the fact that she only managed to eat a third of the penne on her plate, she and Kat are now giggling like a pair of schoolgirls, although, in Kat's case, it's more likely because she's on to her second bottle of wine.

"You sure you don't want any dessert, babe?" I ask. She shakes her head and I nod, calling for the bill.

"Let's go back to mine," Kat says. There's a wicked gleam in her eye and, to my surprise, it's reflected in Evie's.

"What are you two up to?" I ask, not bothering to hide my smile.

"Nothing," Evie hiccups and she and Kat fall about laughing.

"We can share an Uber," Ian offers, and I nod, sliding my credit card back into my wallet.

Kat is incapable of giving the driver directions and Ian's attention is diverted when he pulls up, so I heave a sigh and climb into the front seat. Evie sits in the back, cushioned between Kat and Ian, her speech only slightly slurred - enough to be adorable, but not too much to have me worried.

"I think you two have had enough," Ian says. "I'll make you some coffee when we get to Kat's."

"Okay, fun police," Evie says in her best *Gru* impersonation. She's got the deep Romanian-sounding inflection to a tee. Ian, who has no children and has never had to endure endless repeats of *Despicable Me*, looks confused.

"I may have something better than coffee," Kat drawls, and then, with a very obvious look at the back of the Uber driver's head, she lowers her voice and whispers loudly, "I've got some of Evie's medicinal herbs."

"You mean my marijuana?" Evie screeches. The Uber driver grins.

Kat's house is a sprawling single-storey mansion atop two acres of prime land. Evie isn't the only one who's proud of what Kat has achieved. She's come a long way from the wild collegian who dared Evie to whip up her top, and she deserves everything she has. She's also never let it go to her head and her generosity knows no bounds. I couldn't think of a better friend for Evie.

We sit outside, on the terrace. Evie shivers against the faint chill in the air and I set about lighting a fire. Once the logs are crackling brightly I take a seat next to Evie. She smells of apples and night-time, and the faint, sweet tang of the joint they passed around while I was busy at the fireplace lingers in her hair.

Ian and Kat have finally gone inside to make that coffee but I can hear from their constant giggling that they're as high as kites.

Evie smiles up at me, her eyes only marginally bloodshot, and I kiss her forehead.

"Happy?" I murmur, running my hand down her bare arm. She snuggles closer and leans her head against my chest.

"Very."

I know from experience that the marijuana makes Evie sleepy, but it also relieves her pain, so if I have to carry her out to the car and then into the house later, it'll be worth it.

"Is she sleeping?" Ian asks, keeping his voice low but managing to trip over the patio rug.

"I'm just blinking," Evie mumbles, her eyes still closed.

"Ah, hell no!" Kat descends upon us like a crimson-lipped vulture and hauls Evie to her feet, dislodging her wig. Ian winces. Evie giggles. "We have a secret mission to attend to," Kat tells us. "We will see you boys shortly." And with that, she steers Evie inside.

Ian watches them go and I watch Ian. He's always paid Evie too much attention, but this is the first time I've really been angry about it.

"You mind keeping your feelings to yourself?" I ask as soon as the women are out of earshot.

That gets his attention. "What?"

"You know what I mean."

"No, actually, I don't."

"Evie wants to be treated normally, Ian. Your long, lingering looks and cringing every time you see evidence of her illness isn't helping."

"I don't-"

"You literally cringed when you caught sight of her head, Ian! She's bald, get over it!" I know I'm not being fair, but I can't help myself.

"Get over it?" he asks, incredulously. "Are you being fucking serious? Evie is dying, Nick. That's not okay and it's certainly not something I can ignore. I can't believe you'd even ask me to."

"I'm not..." I clasp my hands together and lean forward in my seat. "That's not what I meant."

"Really? Because from what I'm seeing, you're not in the least bit fazed by all of this. You're acting as if nothing has happened! How can you be so cold?"

I clench my fists to keep from reacting. A burst of Evie's laughter drifts through the door and I let it wash over me, an anchor of calm. "Ian," I begin slowly, "you've been my best mate since college. You were the best man at our wedding. You're as close to Evie as you are to me, and I respect that. But this is my business, mine and Evie's. I'm asking you to respect that, please."

Ian deflates. When he finally speaks, his voice breaks. "I just can't bear to see her like this."

"I know. I know how hard it is. But she's *still* Evie."

As if on cue, Evie stumbles outside. "Nick." She manages only my name before she claps her hand to her mouth, but I'm already off the sofa, scooping her up and rushing for the bathroom as she throws up all over both of us.

CHAPTER 14
Julia

I HEAR NICK CALLING MY NAME FROM THE FRONT DOOR AND I leap off the sofa. He's carrying a pale and softly giggling Evie and, for a second, I wonder why he sounds so panicked. Then the stench of vomit hits me. Under the light in the hall, Evie is so pale the mascara smudged below her eyes looks like stage make-up.

"What happened?" I gasp, rushing forward to help.

"She's fine, she just had a little too much to drink. I need you to open our bed. Please," he adds.

I fly up the stairs before him, but he stays right behind me, Evie's weight not hindering his progress in the slightest. I yank open Evie's side of the duvet and hurl her scatter cushions across to Nick's side. He's not even out of breath as he lays her down gently, turning her onto her side. "Can you fetch a bucket?" he asks, setting about removing her wig.

"Of course." I fly downstairs, my heart hammering in my chest. Thank God I rinsed the bucket after mopping Casey's spilt juice off the floor.

Nick sets the bucket down gently on the carpet beside Evie. She's snoring softly as he tucks her in.

"Can I get you anything?" I ask, not sure exactly what to do.

Nick drags his eyes away from Evie to look at me. I've never been this close to him before, but now I see there are tiny flecks of hazel in the brown of his eyes. He seems to be deliberating about something. I'm about to leave when he nods.

"Coffee," he says. "I'd love a cup of coffee."

My hand shakes as I stir the sugar into the mug of black coffee. It's past midnight, so coffee probably isn't the best thing for either of us right now, but I don't think I could fall asleep now if I tried. The house is quiet as I carry the mugs through to the living-room. Nick is slouched on the sofa, his head in his hands.

"There you go." I set the mug on the table before him.

His hands fall away to reveal a stranger sitting before me. *Is he... crying?* Gone is the perfectly controlled man I've seen until now and, in his place, sits a man who is broken – shattered.

"Thank you," he mumbles, reaching blindly for the coffee. His hands tremble as he lifts the mug to his lips, spilling coffee over his tan pants, but he doesn't seem to notice. If he was one of the children, I'd wipe it away.

I should go. Every instinct is screaming at me to leave, to go upstairs to my room and leave him alone, but my legs have turned to lead, resolutely refusing to budge.

"Are you all right, Mr Danvers?"

He doesn't answer. Again, he fixes me with that unnerving gaze. "Call me Nick."

"Nick." I nod. "Well, um... I guess I'll go and check on the children and then get ready for bed." I've barely swivelled when he speaks.

"Evie asked me to be nicer to you."

I keep my back to him, not sure how to respond to that.

"She says she wouldn't be able to cope without you."

"I think we both know that's not true," I say, "but I'm happy to help ease her workload."

"The kids can be exhausting," he admits, and then, after a

moment's deliberation, he waves me onto the empty sofa beside him. "Please, sit."

Reluctantly, I do.

"How were they tonight?" Nick asks. "The kids?"

I smile without meaning to. "They were so good. I was worried they might not be comfortable because they haven't known me very long but they were angels. Jesse's learning a new song and he actually let Dylan sing along for a change. Casey danced the whole way through. They were in bed by nine, although I suspect Jesse may have read a little longer." I realise I'm rambling so I stop.

Nick nods and then his face crumples. It's like watching a stone sculpture crumble into clay. "He's not dealing with any of this."

"Do you mind if I ask what you've told them?"

"That their mom's not well. That she needs to rest – the usual bullshit. How do you tell them what's really going on?" He is pleading, searching for answers, but not from me.

"You're doing fine," I say, "the best you can. There's no right or wrong way to deal with this." I pause, summoning up my courage. "I don't know much about Evie's diagnosis... is... is there a chance she could recover?" He doesn't reply for the longest time and I wish I could take the question back. "I'm sorry, it's none of my business."

"Evie's doctors say her cancer is terminal," he says, "but there have been cases of people with her condition making a full recovery. Case studies..."

He's still talking but I zone out. I know exactly what he's doing. He's praying for a miracle. Evie will die. As the realisation dawns, I feel a surge of anger toward her. This is too much. How can I continue working here, developing a connection with this family when she's not going to be here? I don't want to witness this, I don't want any part of it. But then, if I won't help her, who will? I know I can make her life easier. I know I can work harder. I might not be able to help Evie get better, but I can help her children. I can be there for them during the most difficult time of their lives, because, looking at him now, there is no doubt in my mind that when it happens, Nick Danvers is going to fall apart.

He's finally stopped talking, his short record of successful case studies run dry.

"How did Evie enjoy her evening?" I ask, deliberately changing the subject.

"She had a blast. We've been friends with Ian and Kat since college so it's always a hoot when we get together, but we do tend to behave like irresponsible teenagers. I should've kept a closer eye on how much Evie had to drink."

"Would you have stopped her?" I challenge, daring him to admit it.

A ghost of a smile lifts the corners of his lips. "No."

I give him a small smile. "I wouldn't have had the guts to either."

CHAPTER 15
Evie

"AAAAH." I ROLL OVER AND CLUTCH MY HEAD. A PIN-PRICK OF light finds its way between my eyelids and I wince, scrunching them more tightly together. I check the bed by feel to discover that Nick isn't beside me. I must doze off again because when I finally summon the courage to open my eyes my head is pounding less like a bass drum and doing more of a tentative conga. A quick peek at my bedside table confirms that my husband is still that guy who leaves pain pills and a glass of water next to my bed after a heavy night out. My mouth feels like cardboard. I stifle another groan in my pillow. I didn't even drink that much. *Curse you, cancer, you fun-sucker!* I swallow the pills, slug down the entire glass of water and wait the mandatory ten minutes before I hobble to the bathroom.

Twenty minutes later I'm clean, dressed and feeling marginally more human. Downstairs I find the house spotless but with no signs of life. No Nick, no kids. He must have taken them out to let me sleep in. I pad through to the kitchen. No Julia, either. She must be up in her room. I hope Nick didn't say anything this morning to upset her. *He wouldn't*, my conscience scolds. He promised to make more of an effort and Nick doesn't make promises lightly.

I'm on my second cup of coffee when the front door opens and I hear the jumble of voices. My ears perk up when Julia's mingles in with the rest. Curious, I tiptoe toward the hall and peek around the corner. My heart gives a violent lurch in my chest.

They must have gone for a walk together, because Nick and Julia are trailing children, looking like the poster family for an insurance commercial. Nick is stamping his boots on the welcome mat and he's smiling – genuinely smiling – at something Julia's just said. As I watch, he waves her inside first. His eyes dip, only for a fraction of a second, toward her ass as she walks ahead. I whip my head back and my hand goes automatically to my chest, grabbing a handful of T-shirt and crushing it between my fingers. I feel a dragon of envy erupt in my chest. They're getting along. *When did this happen?* I rack my brain, trying to recall if I saw Julia last night when we came home, but I can't remember. I don't know if it's the wine or the weed's fault, but I'm drawing a complete blank.

"Evie?" Nick asks as he rounds the corner to catch me thumping my temple with the base of my palm.

"Hmmm?" I ask, dropping my hand and abandoning any attempt to remember.

"What are you doing?"

"Oh, nothing." He gives me an arch look but we're interrupted by a mini-stampede.

"Mama!" Casey throws herself at my legs.

"Hey baby!" I scoop her up and give Nick an innocent smile before following Jesse and Dylan into the kitchen.

"What do you guys feel like for lunch?" Julia calls brightly as she steps into the kitchen a minute later. She stops dead at the sight of me, her expression a mix of surprise, delight and guilt. Guilt. What would she be feeling guilty about? "Sorry, I didn't think you'd be up," Julia apologises. "Do you want me to...?" she gestures toward the fridge.

"Oh!" *Oh*. Of course. She doesn't want to "mom" my children in front of me.

"No, you go ahead," I tell her, taking a seat at the island. Nick settles himself against the counter opposite while Julia rummages through the fridge. Seeing me sitting and accessible, Casey rushes off to fetch her crayon box and a colouring-in book that Mary-Anne brought over the last time she visited.

"Colour with me." She's not asking.

"Sure, baby." I lift her onto my knee and we go through the motions of choosing the perfect picture. After paging through the book twice, I finally settle on a picture of a basket of flowers. "This one!" I say. Casey promptly turns the page and starts colouring the ears of what I assume is a donkey, but could well be a basset hound.

"Who draws these things?" I mutter.

"You're not colouring!" Casey chides.

"How are you feeling?" Nick asks as I snatch up a broken brown crayon. "Does your head hurt?" His tone is teasing and I discreetly flip him the bird.

"Mommy naughty!" Casey gasps. Does this kid ever miss anything?

"Mommy very naughty," Nick agrees, still grinning. "Oh, sorry!" he shifts aside to let Julia reach into the cupboard behind him. For a second, with her head at waist height and her long, lovely hair trailing toward the floor, it looks like they've been caught in a compromising position and I raise my brows at Nick before jerking my head toward Julia and waggling my eyebrows.

Nick frowns, glances down and realises what it looks like and his face turns puce. I laugh out loud as Julia pops back up. She gives me a smile, no doubt assuming I'm laughing at something Casey did and Nick shakes his head behind her back. "You are terrible!" he mouths.

I mouth back Olive Juice.

We're distracted by a high-pitched mewling. Doctor Moxley has snaked into the kitchen. He gives us each an equally disdainful look before leaping onto the counter.

Julia spots him sniffing the sandwich ham she just laid out and she rushes across the kitchen on her long legs like a baby giraffe.

"No, Doc-!"

"Julia!" I half-shriek, cutting her off before she can speak his name. I accidentally let it slip the morning she moved in and I've been terrified she'll let it slip ever since. Doctor Moxley gives a hiss of terror and launches himself out of the room while Nick and Julia turn to gape at me. "Sorry, but I think I spilt some coffee over there earlier," I wave my hand in the general direction of the floor before her. "I don't want you to slip."

"Oh," she shakes her head. Nick's eyes are narrowed, never a good sign. Julia bends down to inspect the floor for any slipping hazard and I catch Nick giving her another quick once-over. The dragon in my chest hisses.

"You ruined it!" Casey snatches the crayon in my hand and I see that I've marked the page with a jagged brown line.

"Sorry, sweetheart." I pick up the eraser to rub it out. "See, all fixed."

She grins up at me, grey crayon hovering, and then scribbles in the top left-hand corner of the page with a gurgle of cheeky laughter.

"Casey!" I mock-gasp. "What are you doing?"

"I can do that," Nick says, stepping forward and seizing a red roll-up.

I grab the blue and wield it like a sword. "Me too!"

Dylan is quick to join in the fun, and, to my delighted surprise, even Jesse leans over to add to the chaos.

Within seconds the donkey-hound has vanished under a rainbow riot of colour and I'm tickling Casey under her chin. She squirms on my lap, shrieking, while Nick attacks her feet. By the time we've stopped laughing, I look up to find Julia gone.

CHAPTER 16
Julia

Safe inside my room with the door shut, I pick up my pillow and hurl it across the room. It's not fair! The Danvers are a beautiful family and this shouldn't be happening to them. I can still hear the faint sounds of Casey's infectious laughter from downstairs and I feel a sob well up in my chest. I left because I didn't want to intrude on such a precious and private moment. It's theirs, a moment to cherish when... I stifle a scream and the second pillow joins the first on the floor. I wait until the house is silent and I'm completely composed before I head back downstairs. I'm going to visit my dad this afternoon. Sundays are my official day off, but I hadn't wanted to leave Evie this morning - she'd needed the rest.

Nick and I had taken the kids to the park. After our talk last night all my reservations had been allayed. I'd imagined him to be a cold, angry man but that's so far from the truth it's laughable. I completely understand now why he was standoffish toward me in the beginning. He's terrified of losing Evie, and my presence is just another reminder that this might happen, that she's growing too weak to do what she used to. Nick is nothing like I thought he was. He's kind, considerate and utterly devoted to his family. It's no wonder Evie fell in love with him.

I find them nestled together on the sofa, watching cartoons. The kids are eating ham sandwiches.

"Sorry, I was going to do that," I say. Nick and Evie's heads swivel to look at me.

"Hey, I wondered where you'd disappeared to," Evie says.

"I had to use the bathroom."

Casey is lying with her head in Evie's lap, her tiny hand stroking Evie's thigh while Evie's fingers comb through her hair. Dylan is on Nick's lap, playing with Nick's phone.

"Where's Jesse?" I ask.

"He's eating in the kitchen," Evie murmurs. Something in her voice isn't right.

"I'll just go and say goodbye before I leave and grab my things from the fridge." I'd popped out to the store yesterday to pick up a few things for Evie and I'd bought my ingredients for Sunday lunch at the same time.

Jesse is straight-backed and serious at the island, a half-eaten ham sandwich on his plate.

"You okay, Jess?"

"We're not supposed to eat in the living-room. It's the rule."

"I don't think Mom and Dad are sticking to that rule today. It's Sunday. Maybe the rules don't count on a Sunday."

"They don't count at all anymore." He is so angry, I can feel the rage radiating from him.

"Jess," I put my hand on his shoulder and he shrugs it off so furiously that he knocks over his cup of water.

"I'll get that," I say, relieved to have an excuse to round the counter and get a proper look at his face. Jesse is a brave little boy but he can't stop the tears that course down his cheeks. "Do you want to talk about it?"

"No." An angry swat at his wet cheeks.

I pull at the roll of kitchen towel, my mind racing. I should consult Evie and Nick first, but right now, Jesse is the one who needs me. "Hey," I say, mopping up the water. "I'm heading over to my dad's. Would you like to join me? If your parents are okay with it, that is."

"You're going now?"

"Yeah. He used to be a jockey, I can show you his medals if you like? But, like I said, only if your mom and dad say it's okay that you come along."

"They'll say no."

"Let me check."

He shrugs as if it doesn't matter either way, but I can sense he really wants to come. It's only when I'm back in the living-room, facing the back of Evie and Nick's heads that I start to panic. I've only been working for them a little under a week. They're going to think I'm some sort of child-snatcher.

"Um... Evie?"

"Yeah?"

"Do you think it would be okay if I took Jesse with me. I mean, would you mind?"

Nick's head pivots toward me so fast I think he might have given himself whiplash, but it's Evie who speaks. "To your dad's?"

"Well, yeah. It's only Sunday lunch and it's not far from here, I just thought I could show him my dad's medals. He might like that. And I'll keep my cell phone on me the whole time."

"Julia, I don't think that's a good idea," Nick begins, but Evie cuts him off.

"What time will you be back?"

"Before seven."

"Evie, it's Sunday," Nick murmurs, in a way which implies that Sunday holds some special meaning for them.

"Yeah, but he's..." Evie stops, takes a deep breath, starts again. "Does he want to go?"

It takes me a second to realise she's talking to me. "I think he does."

Nick is looking at me, so he misses it, but I don't. Evie closes her eyes, just for a second, but the flash of grim determination is impossible to miss. *It's just lunch,* I want to say. *He's still yours.*

But I don't say anything because the moment is over as quickly as it comes and Evie is smiling up at me.

"Are you sure he won't be in the way?"

"I'm sure. My dad loves kids, too, so he'll be grateful for the company."

"Evie," Nick's voice is harder but she shifts Casey onto his other knee – the one not occupied by Dylan – and gets to her feet.

"I'd prefer it if you take my car," she says. Behind her, I catch a glimpse of Nick's face and I want to take it all back, but Jesse's depending on me. I can't bear the thought of letting him down now. Taking a deep breath, I smile at Nick.

"We'll see you later," I say. He doesn't respond.

The journey home is far quicker by car than it would be by bus. Jesse has fallen silent in the back seat, probably worried about meeting my dad, but I keep up a running commentary as we drive.

"Do you know I used to play on this street," I tell him, pointing down a side road as we pass. My friend had one of those above ground swimming pools and, for some reason, it was so much more fun than a regular pool."

"What's an above ground swimming pool?"

"You've never seen one?" I mock tease. "Oh, Jesse boy, you haven't lived until you've swum in a portable pool!"

He catches my eye in the rear-view mirror and shakes his head as if the very thought is beneath him, but secretly, I know he's starting to enjoy himself.

"We're here," I say as I pull up to the curb and kill the engine. "You ready?"

Jesse gives me a quick nod and follows me to the door. I let myself into the apartment and hang my key on the hook beside the door. "Dad?"

"I'm in here, Ju-Ju!"

I take a few steps down the hall only to realise Jesse isn't following me. "Come on," I beckon.

My dad is sitting on the edge of the bath, repairing the broken towel rail.

"Dad! After two years you finally got around to that?"

"I did," he replies evenly. "Turns out I'm a lot more productive without you hanging around and being all needy."

"Very funny. Dad," I add, drawing Jesse into the cramped bathroom. "This is Jesse. He's going to be spending the afternoon with us."

My dad lowers his head to peer at Jesse over his horn-rimmed spectacles. "Is that so?"

Jesse's throat bobs in time with his head.

"Well in that case, you better earn your lunch, Jesse. Hand me that screwdriver, will you?"

I hover in the doorway letting my dad do all the talking, until I feel that Jesse is comfortable enough to be left alone with him. "I'm just going to put lunch on," I say tentatively. Jesse barely notices, but he nods and I take that as an 'okay'.

By the time the chicken is sizzling in the oven and the potatoes are on the boil, Jesse and my dad have worked up an appetite.

"Munch on this," I tell them, setting out a plate of cheese and biscuits, "but not too much or you'll ruin your lunch."

My dad leans over and nudges Jesse's shoulder with his own. "What does she think we are, kids?"

Jesse grins and takes two biscuits from the plate. "Julia said you used to be a jockey," he says.

"I was indeed." My dad lowers his voice to a hush. "In fact, I was one of the best. Would you like to see some of my races?"

As they head into the living-room, I feel my eyes prickle. All Dad's races are on disc, neatly labelled and organised in date order, courtesy of my mom, who was his number one fan. He hasn't watched any of them since the accident. I wait until I hear the tinny voice of the commentator before I realise I've forgotten the potatoes and, such is my good mood, that I decide to mash them instead.

CHAPTER 17
Nick

"Why did you do that?"

"Do what?"

"Evie, please don't play dumb."

She sighs and shifts Casey, who has fallen asleep on her lap. Her legs must be aching. Automatically I set Dylan on the sofa beside me and lift Casey off her.

"Please pull that blanket over her," Evie says as I set Casey down on the sofa opposite. I pause. It's hot out. Casey is sweating, but, even as I think it, Evie wraps her arms around herself and gives a little shiver.

"It's not cold, babe," I say, keeping my voice neutral and covering her with the blanket instead.

"Oh." I hear the tiniest hint of fear and then she's reaching for Dylan. "All the more reason to snuggle!" she growls into his neck.

Evie falls asleep in front of the TV. Dylan is still watching, heavy-eyed, when I get up to start dinner. I open the fridge and poke around inside it, taking inventory. Eggs, mushrooms, ham... omelettes it is, then. I glance up at the clock while I'm beating the eggs. It's six o'clock, an hour until Julia brings Jesse home. I still don't know why

Evie went along with it. It's something we need to talk about, but these days I'm finding it more and more difficult to confront her. I feel as if any additional stress will make her even more sick.

"No, push off!" I hiss at the cat, which is weaving around my legs. He flicks his tail and regards me with intent cat-hate, the most visual kind. "You're getting far too comfortable around here," I add, pouring the beaten eggs into the pan.

"Who are you talking to?" Evie yawns from the doorway.

"The cat." I point down at my feet and she steps forward to lean over the island. "We can't keep calling him the cat," I add, chopping the ham into bite-sized pieces. "Maybe we should think of a name for him? He doesn't seem to be going anywhere anytime soon."

A pink hue creeps across Evie's cheeks. "Can I help?" she asks, coming to stand beside me at the stove and tossing the small pan of mushrooms so they sizzle anew.

"Yeah, can you set four places?" I move all the cooking paraphernalia off the island and wipe it down with a cloth.

"You're so domesticated," Evie teases, setting two ceramic and three plastic plates down on the granite top.

"Jesse's not here," I remind her.

"Oh, of course." She puts one back.

"Why did you let him go with her?"

"With Julia? She has a name, you know."

"Evie." I hate it when she tries to distract me.

Evie closes the cutlery drawer and gives me a long look before she answers. "I know you don't like to talk about it, but I might not always be here. I think it'll be good for the kids to form a bond with someone else."

"She's not their mother."

"I know that, Nick. I am their mother, but what happens if I'm not here?"

"You're not going anywhere."

"Death isn't the be all and end all of this. What if I have to be hospitalised?"

"Then I'll make a plan."

"You're already spending too much time out of the office. I appreciate what you're trying to do, but you can't do everything."

I slam the spatula down on the countertop. "Do you really think that if you're not here I'll allow Julia to continue living in this house?"

Evie seems to shrink in on herself, and her eyes dart guiltily from left and right. "Oh my God. You do. You actually do."

"If something happens..."

"Nothing's going to-"

"If!" she yells. "I said if! And *if* something happens, I would want someone here to help you with the children, yes. And since they're already bonding with Julia, it makes sense that she should stay."

"Julia isn't going to be here forever, Evie. She's a young, ambitious woman who's been dealt a bad hand and is still recovering, but once she gets back on her feet, can you really see someone like her sticking around? Your plan is ridiculous! All you're doing is setting our children up to lose another mother!"

The words have barely left my mouth but I wish I could take them back. They're like lava, a corrosive, acidic poison that threatens to expose the deepest, darkest, ugliest part of me. I've spent months convincing myself that Evie is going to get better, and I did it so well that I haven't even allowed myself to consider any other alternative. The fear and doubt were locked away, buried, but now the shadows have been exposed. It's like my very own cancer – creeping, crawling, consuming everything else.

Evie isn't unaffected either. As my words pour over her, she stumbles backward as if trying to escape them. Her eyes are wild, her mouth slack-jawed and her face drains of what little colour it had to begin with.

I reach for her, but she holds up her hands, a silent warning for me to stay away. We stare at each other, saying nothing, while the smell of burning eggs fills the kitchen.

"Evie, I didn't mean... I don't know why I said that. I'm sorry."

Her lips are pressed together so tightly they've gone white, but when she finally opens her mouth, a little colour bleeds back. "It's okay. It's the truth."

"No," I slide the pan off the burner and rush round the island to snatch up her hands. It's like holding two blocks of ice. "We are going to get through this. *You* are going to get through this. This is not about me and you, it's about Julia. She won't be here long - no, listen to me, please," I add as she opens her mouth to protest. "I understand that she's helping and taking a lot off your plate, but I don't think it's right that you encourage this relationship with our children. She's a nanny, nothing more."

Evie shakes her head, slowly, sadly, and then she takes a deep breath. "How do you propose we stop it, Nick? Julia is taking care of them, she's there for them. She's kind and caring and perfect. How can we possibly stop them falling in love with her?"

The question hangs in the space between us. I drop my eyes first.

Jesse and Julia arrive back home ten minutes before seven. Evie's taking a long bubble bath, one of her favourite traditions. Every few minutes I hear the geyser groaning as she refills the tub with hot water. She can do that for hours until she's used it all up.

"Dad!" Jesse is more animated than I've seen him in weeks, his face alive with excitement. He even holds my hand as he recounts stories of Julia's dad and how many races he'd won, who his fiercest competition was and how he had let Jesse try on all his medals.

"Sounds like you had a blast, champ," I tell him, trying to hide my delighted surprise. I didn't realise how much I'd missed this Jesse, the sweet, lively young man he had been before Evie's remission failed. I meet Julia's eyes over Jesse's head and give her a brief nod of thanks. She smiles shyly in return and Jesse races upstairs to tell Evie his tales.

I regard Julia for a moment, recalling my discussion with Evie and my promise to be nicer to her. "Do you mind if I ask you a question?" I ask.

"Yeah, sure," she shrugs.

"How are you still single?"

"I beg your pardon?"

I laugh, thinking of the obvious conclusion she must have drawn. "What I mean is, you seem really nice, you know? And you're pretty," I admit, "and obviously smart. I'd expect you to be dating at least."

She hesitates for a minute and then drops onto one of the chairs at the kitchen island, her voice is so soft at first that I have to strain to hear her.

"I was engaged. We broke up about two years ago."

"What happened?" I find I'm genuinely curious.

"We grew apart."

I can't hide a smile. "You know, I've heard that expression at least a dozen times and I've always said it's complete bullshit." Julia's too surprised to answer so I save her the hassle. "You don't just grow apart, not unless you allow it," I explain. "Do you think there haven't been times in the past eighteen years when Evie and I started to drift apart? Staying together is hard work, but you either want to, or you don't."

"My mother died."

Oh fuck.

"Julia, Christ, I'm sorry..."

"Don't be, I wasn't finished! I probably shouldn't have opened with that statement. Anyway, my mom died in the same accident in which my dad lost his leg. Aaron and I had been travelling but I had to come home, to take care of my dad."

"And... Aaron, did you say his name was?" She nods. "And Aaron didn't want to stay with you?"

"I didn't want him to put his life on hold for me."

"He didn't think it was worth it?" *Sounds like an idiot.*

She smiles and I'm struck by the thought that I might have said that out loud. "We thought that it was a temporary situation. The plan was that I would join him again after a few months."

"But that didn't happen?" I vaguely remember Evie telling me that Julia's father couldn't find work.

"No." She doesn't elaborate. She tilts her chin, just like Evie does when her pride is pricked. I know from experience not to push a woman who sets her jaw like that, so I let it go.

"Well, I'm sure you're better off without him," I say.

Julia smiles, a dazzling flash of teeth that lights her up from the inside. "You know, I've heard that expression at least a dozen times and I've always said it's complete bullshit."

CHAPTER 18
Evie

When the doorbell rings at 8 o'clock on Monday morning I assume it's Kat. Julia left just a few minutes ago to do the school run and Nick left early to get started on a new bid.

"It's open!" I call as I pass by the door on my way to turn on the coffee machine. Except it's not Kat who walks into the kitchen. It's Ian.

"Hey you! What are you doing here so bright and early?" He looks good, all decked out in his smart blues for work. Navy pants, blue and white checked shirt, black shoes, and his sandy hair has been cut since we saw him on Saturday night. It's shorter than I'm used to, but it suits him.

Ian gives me a hug, practically lifting me off my feet. "I just wanted to check up on you. You looked a little out of it when you left on Saturday."

He's got that look on his face, the one he gets sometimes when he thinks no one else is watching. I know it well, it's an expression of my own making. Ian and I had kissed, once, a few weeks after Nick and I started dating. I adored Nick, but I was nineteen years old, and nobody knows what they want when they're nineteen and have had three quarters of a bottle of tequila.

NICK HAD GONE *on a trip to Greece with his parents, who I hadn't met yet, and Ian, Kat and I decided to go clubbing one Saturday night. Truth be told, we'd been clubbing on the Friday night too, but that's not the point. Nick and I hadn't been together long enough for our awesome foursome to have really bonded, and it was nice to hang out with Kat and Ian, who I'd known for some time already. To this day I'm not sure if it was me or Nick who became friends with Ian first. I think we both knew him, separately, which had worked out well when we got together. That particular night Kat had hooked up with a foreign exchange student who was two years her junior and didn't speak a word of English. Apparently he spoke in literal 'tongues', because Kat's face was glued to his for most of the evening, leaving Ian and I to our own devices. For me, that meant tequila. For Ian, it was the perfect opportunity to get months' worth of built-up sexual tension off his chest.*

We were outside getting some air when Ian dropped the bomb. "I love you, Evie."

I threw my arms around him, sloshing beer over his shirt. "Aw, I love you too!"

"No, Evie." He pushed me gently away. "I love you. I am in love *with you."*

"Ian..." I leaned back warily, suddenly feeling awkward. "I don't think you should..."

He cut right across me. "Let me get this out, please."

I fell silent.

"It kills me to see you with Nick. He's not a bad guy, but he's not the one for you. I know you, Evie, I know what makes you smile and I know what makes you cry. I also know I should've said something sooner, but..."

"Then why are you telling me this now?" I didn't like him

speaking badly of Nick and my tone carried a warning that he completely ignored.

"Because if I don't, it might be too late. It's not too late, Evie. You've only been with Nick a couple of weeks, it's not serious."

I had been thinking along the same lines but hearing him say it annoyed me. It also made me realise that Nick and I might be more serious than I'd been willing to let myself believe. "Ian, I really don't think..."

He seized my shoulders. "Stop thinking! That's exactly the problem. Just listen to your heart for once. How does this make you feel?" His voice had dropped, so low I had to strain to hear him as he ran his thumbs slowly down my bare arms. My stomach did a little wiggle-jerk-jump, which, I have since learned, it does whenever someone tickles my bare arms, but which I thought, at the time, meant there was something I must have missed between me and Ian.

His smile was smug. He'd felt my shiver and mistaken it for something deeper. Hell, I mistook it for something deeper. It was only when his lips touched mine and his tongue swooped triumphantly inside my mouth that I realised it was a mistake. Nick's kisses left me breathless and desperate for more. I'd cling to him like a drunken dryad. Ian's kiss was polished, practised and left me cold. We were going through the motions, nothing more.

"Ian!" I gasped into his mouth, pushing his chest and arching my body away. Rather than let me go, his arms pulled me closer, crushing me to him. "Ian!" I shoved harder, breaking the lip-lock. "No!" I shook my head. "I'm sorry, but I don't want this."

It took him a moment to gather himself. "You're lying. You felt that too."

"I didn't, Ian. I'm so sorry, but this isn't going to happen."

He was distraught, I remember that clearly, but I promised that we would always be friends and that Nick would never know.

A year later I broke half of that promise. I told Nick, when I realized that he was forever and not just for now. It turns out he knew. He didn't know where, or when, but he knew. It was never mentioned again. And we did all stay friends.

"Evie?" Ian's voice brings me back to the present moment. "Are you okay?"

"I'm fine!" I say brightly. "I had too much to drink on Saturday night and I had a bit of a hangover yesterday, but I'm perfectly fine now."

"Are you sure?" The look again. It had gone for the longest time, especially after he had met his wife, Carmen, but had reappeared after my first diagnosis, not long after his divorce.

"I'm positive." I turn my back on him so I don't have to endure the look any longer. "Do you want some coffee?"

He's at my side in an instant. "I just had some, but let me make that for you."

I swat his hand away. "My machine, my rules!"

Nick would've laughed. Ian doesn't.

I hear my car pulling into the garage and a moment later Julia walks through the kitchen door. I'm so relieved I could kiss her, but if she finds my exaggerated welcome odd, she doesn't comment.

"Ian, this is Julia, Julia, this is Ian. Ian is a very old friend of ours."

"Hello," Julia smiles politely and extends her hand. Ian takes it, not before giving her an appraising once over, and then cocks his head to one side. "I'm the nanny," Julia explains.

"*You're* the nanny?" His jaw drops. He looks to me for affirmation and I nod.

"She's the nanny," I repeat. I try to see Julia through Ian's eyes – her slim, but curvy figure with calf muscles to die for, which I assume she got from having to walk everywhere, dark hair naturally high-lighted by all her time spent outside in the sun, blue-green eyes. Julia is pretty - exceptionally pretty, if the look on Ian's face right now is anything to go by.

"Well, it's nice to meet you, Julia," Ian says, oozing private schoolboy charm. "I've heard only good things."

Julia laughs politely, but I can tell she feels uncomfortable.

"Thanks for taking the kids in this morning," I tell her. "Nick had to go into the office early," I add, for Ian's benefit, "so Julia dropped them off."

"Where's Kat?" Julia asks, busying herself making the coffee I've forgotten about. "I thought she'd be here by now."

"Did I hear my name?" Kat drawls from the doorway. "You do know your front door is open," she adds, stepping onto the hardwood floor as if it was a runway.

"Ooh la la!" I exclaim as she air-kisses Ian on both cheeks. "Where are you going looking like all of that?" I wave my hand up and down, indicating her woollen dress and tights combination. The heels of her boots are lethal.

"A meeting."

"Does it happen to be with a delectable young executive from Parker Homes?"

"His younger, more delectable assistant, actually," Kat replies, dead-pan.

"God help him," Ian tuts, accepting a cup of coffee from Julia.

"Your phone is ringing," Kat tells me as my iPhone vibrates across the island. I scoop it up.

"Hey babe."

"Evie." Nick sounds furious. "Please tell me, in the name of all that is good and holy, that you did not sign my mother up to Tinder." In the silence of the kitchen his voice carries.

"What?" I glance up, wide-eyed, to find Kat grinning like a Cheshire cat and a flashback of Saturday night blooms in my head. *Oh shit.*

"She's going berserk," Nick continues. "Apparently her phone has been ringing non-stop with propositions that she calls – and I quote – most inappropriate."

"I didn't even know you could list a number on Tinder," I say, and then I slap my hand over my phone as Kat starts to laugh.

Nick sighs. "Look, I'm not going to come out and say it was you and Kat, but I seem to recall that you two disappeared on Saturday night for a while and it sounded like you were up to no good. As usual," he adds, for good measure. "So please, if by chance this is your doing, could you delete the account. For me. *Please*."

"Got it."

"And Evie."

I cringe "Yes?"

Nick chuckles. "I love you."

"I love you too."

I end the call and look over to Kat, horrified. "Tell me we didn't."

"We didn't," she replies immediately, following the instruction without any care for the truth. Ian looks amused, Julia is simply lost.

"We have to delete it."

"It'd do the old bag some good."

"No, Kat. We have to delete it."

She sighs as she pulls her phone from her bag. "Fine." She jabs at the screen, "but you know, some of these older men are pretty hot."

"How did they get her number?"

"I added it into her bio."

"Kat!"

"What? You told me to!"

"Wait, what did you two do *now*?" Ian asks, with the emphasis on *now* because, let's face it, Kat and I are always up to something.

"We signed Mary-Anne up for Tinder." I say, trying to keep a straight face. Julia starts to giggle.

"Don't let them corrupt you, Julia," Ian warns. "They're incorrigible."

"There," Kat announces, setting her phone down, "all done."

"We're never drinking again," I tell her.

"If I had a dollar for every time you've said that," Ian muses.

"You'd be as rich as me," Kat grins wickedly.

CHAPTER 19

Julia

"Son of a bitch!" That's the second time I've pricked myself in as many minutes. A droplet of blood wells up on the pad on my finger and I pop it in my mouth, sucking the blood away. I'm not used to hand stitching. Sadly, my dad had sold my mom's industrial machine after she died to pay the water bill, so this is as good as it gets. Evie doesn't own a sewing machine. When I asked, she laughed. Literally threw back her head and laughed, as if it was the funniest question she'd ever heard. I had taken that as a no.

I finish off the last few stitches and hold up my masterpiece. It doesn't look like much, but it should do the job. It's been a week since Evie came home drunk and giggling. The drunk and giggling was a good thing. The rash that had developed on her scalp the next day wasn't. I hadn't noticed because she'd worn a beanie on Sunday and I'd spent most of the day at my dad's with Jesse, but by Monday morning the angry red welts were still visible.

I pack away my meagre sewing basket and wander downstairs. The house is so quiet without the Danvers family living loudly within it. Nick and Evie have taken the kids ice-skating, so I wash the few dishes left over from breakfast and straighten up the sofa cushions before settling down to read.

"We're back!" Evie calls, completely unnecessarily as she opens the front door.

"Hey, how was it?"

"Hilarious. Nick fell on his ass, twice."

"I didn't fall, I tripped."

"Tell that to the five-year-old you took down with you."

"That was your fault! And it wasn't even logical – how can ice be lava?"

Evie giggles.

"Did you have fun, Dyl?" I ask, as Dylan jumps onto the sofa next to me.

"Yes."

"And you, Jesse?"

Jesse grins. "Dad really did fall twice. Although the second time he was trying to get off the ice too fast because Mom called lava. Are you going to visit your dad tomorrow?" The question catches me completely unaware and I'm super conscious of the fact that Evie and Nick have fallen silent.

"I am."

"Could I come with you?"

"Jesse," Evie begins gently, "Julia might want to spend some time alone with her dad. She doesn't see him very often."

Jesse's face falls, but he takes it on the chin. "Yeah, I guess."

I want to reassure him but it's not my place to counter Evie's opinion.

"Why don't you ask your father over to supper one night next week?" she proposes suddenly.

"Here?"

"Yes, why not? I'd love to meet him. You could pick him up and drop him off after."

"You're sure?"

"Julia. I wouldn't offer if I wasn't."

"Okay, sure. I'll ask him."

"Awesome!" Jesse fist-pumps the air. "I'm going to show him my guitar!"

"He'll love that." I smile, ruffling his hair. He waits exactly three seconds before he combs it back with his fingers.

"I'm going to change Casey," Nick says, lifting her up and flying her around like an airplane. "She's soaked."

"She fell about ten times," Evie tells me as they disappear up the stairs.

"While I've got you alone," I say, pulling the poorly-stitched, elasticated cap out from between the sofa cushions. "I made you something."

Evie takes it and starts to turn it in her hands. "What's this?"

"It's a cloth cap," I rush to explain. "You wear it under your wig. I Googled it, and apparently it helps with the irritation. I'm sure you could buy a better one, but I thought you could try it to see if it works before you go and spend money on..." I trail off helplessly because Evie has gone still. She's staring at the elasticated cap intently, her fingers tracing the neat, if irregular, stitching.

"You made this?" she asks eventually. She looks up and I see that her eyes are filled with tears.

"I'm sorry! I didn't mean to upset you. I just thought – well, I know you like wearing your wig but it irritates you and I thought..." I trail off, because for the life of me I don't remember what I was thinking when I started making it. "Forget it, I shouldn't have..." I try to snatch the cap back but Evie jerks it away and clutches it to her chest protectively.

"Julia, thank you. It's..." she takes a deep breath and gives me a watery smile, "it's just so thoughtful."

"It might not work,' I say, suddenly terrified that I'll let her down.

"Only one way to find out. Come on!" she grabs my hand and pulls me up the stairs after her.

"What are you two giggling about in here?" Nick asks a few minutes later as he enters the room. He has Casey wrapped in a fluffy pink towel on his hip and an amused smile on his face. He catches sight of Evie wearing her wig and his smile falters. "Babe, take that off. You don't want to have another reaction."

"I won't!" Evie interrupts, giddily. "She whips the wig off and holds up the soft cotton cap. "Julia made this for me! I wear it underneath the wig so my skin is protected."

Nick takes it from her and rubs it between his fingers. "What is this?" he asks, looking directly at me.

"It's a cap," I reply shyly. "I read about them online. I'm sure you probably already know about them, but I figured Evie could try it out and if it works, you can order a new one."

"Stuff that," Evie says, taking it back from Nick and pulling it over her head. "This one's sentimental."

"What does it say?" Nick asks, leaning closer to get a better look. "Lin? What's lin?"

I blush. "*Zepplin.* I used one of my old T-shirts. I washed it first," I hasten to add, "but the website I found recommended old T-shirt material because it's thin and has already been softened.

"*Zepplin?*" Nick looks like he's trying not to laugh.

"You don't like *Zepplin?*"

"It's perfect," he says, and the smile he gives me is only marginally less warm than the one he bestows on Evie a second later. "It couldn't be more perfect. Unless it was *Pearl Jam,* of course."

Evie wears her wig for the rest of the afternoon. She even puts on a little blusher and, although she won't admit to anything else, her eyelashes look fuller than they did this morning.

When Nick offers to read the kids their bedtime story, Evie wags her finger at him. "It's my turn."

"Don't encourage her," Nick tells me when I chuckle. "The only reason she's offering is to get out of doing all these dishes."

"I've always told you, I'm not just a pretty face!" Evie's voice calls back to us from the foot of the stairs.

I giggle again and start clearing up the dishes. I scrape the left-over food into the bin and start running hot water into the sink. Nick hasn't moved.

"Julia..." he says, getting my attention.

"Yeah?"

"I don't know how to thank you, for what you've done for Evie."

"It's nothing," I insist. "I just cut up an old T-shirt."

"It's not nothing." He holds my gaze until I look away.

"It's just an elasticated cap," I mumble.

"It's a chance for her to feel beautiful again without the fear of pain," he corrects.

I scrape the last of Casey's mash into a plastic bowl so she can have it for lunch tomorrow. "Please don't say that yet. You're going to jinx it. For all we know, she's going to wake up tomorrow with welts all over her head."

"Don't do that."

"Do what?"

"Brush it off. Look at me." I do and Nick smiles. "If only my kids were that easy to control," he teases, before he turns serious once more. "What you did today was kind and thoughtful and I want you to accept my appreciation without making out like it was nothing."

"Okay," I nod self-consciously.

"Good girl. Now, let's get these dishes done."

CHAPTER 20
Nick

I OFFER TO DRY. I KNOW IT'S THE SHITTIER OF THE TWO JOBS and, after what she did today, Julia gets to wash. I glance over at her when she's not looking and wonder how such a sweet girl ended up with such a raw deal. Losing her mother, then her fiancé and becoming financially responsible for her father. It's heart-breaking.

"What did you want to do?" I ask, taking the next plate from her. "If you could've done anything, what would it be?"

"Well, I'm a psych major, so it would've been nice to continue with that."

"Private practice?"

"No," she hands me another plate, "I think I would've gone into social work."

"Why don't you finish? It's never too late to follow your passion."

"I was actually thinking of taking a couple of night classes next semester. It won't interfere with my work here," she adds quickly.

"I didn't say that it would. And, if it did, we'd work around it."

I'm not paying her lip service. I want her to achieve her full potential. Over the past two weeks Julia has become a part of the family. I found it easier to be nice to her than I had expected, once I let my guard down. And, with this one act of extraordinary kindness, she's secured a soft spot in my heart and somehow become an extension of Evie and my children.

Which is why, when Julia bends down to retrieve the milk bowl Evie had set out for the cat, revealing an ample amount of cleavage and the edge of a budded, rose-pink nipple peeking over the lace of her bra, the swooping sensation in my chest is so unexpected. I am so taken aback by my body's reaction that I drop the bowl I'm holding. It lands with a soft splash in the sink, sloshing sudsy water over my pants but, before Julia can ask what happened, I've bolted.

I find Evie curled around Dylan's body like an eel. Dylan's room is decorated like a pirate ship. Evie had painted the mural of the Jolly Roger on the wall herself but I'd drilled the ship's wheel into the wall. Dylan spent the first month turning it constantly, pretending to be the ship's captain. No one else was permitted to touch it although we were all invited aboard. Now it just hangs there, an abandoned helm. Dylan moved on to airplanes and neither Evie nor I had had the energy to keep up. They grow up too fast I'd told Evie, to which she'd replied that the sooner they left home, the sooner we could run around naked again.

I lift the edge of the duvet and curl myself around Evie. She wriggles backward until she's pressed up against me like she always does. She senses me, no matter how deeply she's sleeping.

When we were first married we hardly bothered with clothes at night. Nine times out of ten they'd end up in a discarded heap on the floor anyway, and Evie hates doing laundry even more than she hates doing dishes. We'd always had an incredible sex life. Evie was as uninhibited in bed as she was in everything else she did and I wasn't about to argue, not when I considered myself the luckiest man on earth for having a wife whose physical needs matched my own. We'd made love while driving through the gorge on our way home from a trip to the mountains, made out in an airplane until the stewardess banged on the door and Evie had to tug out a chunk of her hair to free herself from my zipper. I doubt the numerous hotels in every city we'd visited had ever seen such passion.

"What if someone sees us?" I'd asked, when she insisted we sneak into the waterpark in a resort in Phuket to prove we could have sex while going down the lazy water slide.

"We'll tell them we're leading by example," she'd replied, pressing her lips to mine in a way that meant business.

Thinking of it now I feel the stirrings of an erection pressing up through the thin cotton of my sleeping shorts. I shift, uncomfortably and try to put some distance between me and Evie, but she only wriggles closer, following me in her sleep.

Men should have an off-switch, I think, as the pressure builds. It's been over two weeks since Evie and I made love on the sofa. Slowly, I ease myself out of the bed. I pull the covers over her and Dylan and leave her, the small, contented smile on her face at odds with the grimace on my own.

As the hot water cascades over me I touch myself with fumbling hands. I'm not used to doing this. I know most men are experts, but I've never had to sort myself out, not while married to Evie. I feel guilty, but the physical ache is worse. I think of her while I do it, of the way her hair used to smell of mandarin and freesias, how her skin tasted of soap and salt and the way her toes would curl at the moment of orgasm. When I'm done, I lean back against the cold tiles behind me and sink to the floor, head in hands as my throat closes up and tears mingle with the water running down my face.

CHAPTER 21
Evie

I'M DRIPPING WITH SWEAT. MY SHIRT IS DRENCHED AND THE back of my neck itches as trickles of perspiration dribble into my collar. Surely it's not that much work to make meatloaf?

Julia's dad, Ted, is coming for dinner tonight and I want everything ready well in advance. I know how the older generation loathes to be kept waiting.

"What can I do?" Julia asks, pulling an apron from the broom closet and tying it around her waist.

"Check the potatoes, please?" I groan, abandoning any attempt to refuse her help.

She does so, then removes the vegetables from the steamer and deposits them in a bowl which she sets in the warmer. She moves around the kitchen with prompt efficiency and her skin is dry and cool.

"You really didn't have to go to so much trouble," Julia says, her tongue caught beneath her front tooth. It sounds like an apology.

"Nonsense! It's the least I can do after everything you've done for me."

"You pay me," she points out.

"True. But I'd still like to meet your dad and it's worth it to see Jesse out of his slump."

"He's been practicing a Justin Bieber song all afternoon."

"I know," I groan. "Why couldn't he be a rock fan?"

"*Zepplin*?" she grins.

"*Pearl Jam*," I correct.

"He could learn both," she says, as the opening chords of *My mama don't like you* drifts down the stairs.

"Bieber," I sigh. "Justin Bloody Bieber. I've failed at parenting."

"My dad will love it," Julia says. "He hates rock."

"How can anybody hate rock?" I ask, bending over the oven to check the meatloaf. The gust of hot air that emerges engulfs me.

"Right?"

"Okay, we're just about-" I break off as a spasm of pain cuts through my lower back. I can't straighten my spine, so I crouch in front of the oven like a little old lady, my hand reaching desperately for my back.

Julia is at my side in an instant. "Evie! Evie, what can I do?"

"Just help me into the living-room," I hiss through clenched teeth. "And keep the kids away, I don't want them to..."

"Hold on," she flies out of the kitchen and I hear her telling Casey and Dylan to go upstairs to get dressed for dinner. "Now!" she scolds when they start to moan about missing the end of whatever program they're watching. I don't think I've ever heard her raise her voice before and the scampering of little feet a second later would imply my children haven't either. If I wasn't in agony, I would be smiling.

Julia is back and she slides her arm around my back. "Lean against me," she murmurs, "I've got you." By the time we make it to the living-room she's supporting most of my weight.

"You're stronger than you look." It's a pitiful attempt at humour, and tempered by the choked sob at the end.

"I spent a lot of time helping my dad get around before he got his prosthesis," she says. She lowers me gently onto the sofa, propping cushions up behind me as we go. "What do you need?" she asks, the second I'm sitting. "Your pain meds, where are they?"

I shake my head. "I already took them. There's a red bag in my vanity cupboard, it's behind the-" I break off. She's already gone, flying out of the room on feet as graceful as a dancer's.

Julia sits beside me as I open the red bag with trembling hands. I take out the clean plastic spoon and scrape a tiny amount of cannabis oil – about the size of a grain of rice – out of the jar. Then I open the pill bottle and remove one of the empty pill capsules.

Julia disappears. For a second I think she's offended by the sight of the drug, which I haven't mentioned to her before, but then she's back, holding a glass of water. "You'll need something to take that with," she says.

"Thank you." I swallow the blue pill and settle back onto the cushions.

"How long will it take to work?"

"Not long. I might not be in any state to finish dinner, though. I haven't built up much of a tolerance."

Julia gets to her feet. "I should call my dad. To cancel."

"No, please don't. I'll be fine, I promise."

She hesitates for a few seconds, torn, but then she slowly lowers herself back onto the sofa beside me.

"So, my dad's going to be meeting high Evie?" she tries to smile, but she's still worried.

"I'll try not to let him know."

"I wouldn't worry, he spent most of his career around the mink and manure of horse-racing. I doubt there's anything he hasn't seen. Or tried," she adds. She picks up the small jar and examines the contents. "I wonder if this would've helped with his pain after the amputation?"

"Best pain relief in the world," I say. The pain is easing, whether naturally or because of the cannabis, I can't tell.

"Where does it hurt?"

"The base of my spine."

"Here, shift forward, I'll rub it for you."

I don't have the heart to tell her that this pain isn't something you can massage away, so I shift forward and let her fingers go to work.

"Look who's come to visit," Julia says, after a while. Doctor Moxley has deigned to enter the room and he gives me a foul look before he leaps onto the sofa beside me and sticks his nose inside the red bag.

"Oh no you don't," I lean forward to zip it up, "that's mine."

"Why do you call him Doctor Moxley?" Julia asks curiously.

"After my specialist," I tell her, scratching Doctor Moxley between his flea-bitten ears.

Julia's soft chuckle washes over my shoulder. "Is that a compliment or an insult to the cat?"

"I'm still undecided. And Nick doesn't know," I add, "he doesn't like to be reminded, so I'd appreciate it if you don't mention it to him."

"Cat's the word," Julia promises without hesitation.

The cannabis is working by the time Nick gets home from work. If he knows I'm a little high, he doesn't say anything.

"How was your day?" he asks. We're in the bedroom, getting ready for dinner. Julia will be back with her dad any minute and I'm putting on my wig while Nick gets dressed. I sneak a peek at his naked body reflected in the mirror. At thirty-seven, Nick is in great shape. His stomach is flat, a trail of dark hair tapering down his belly, and his legs are lean, but muscular.

"What time is..." he catches me staring and raises a dark brow at my reflection. "You see something you like?"

"How are you coping?" I ask, swivelling round to face him.

His mouth straightens. "What?"

"Without sex. I mean, I know men have needs, and I'm not exactly meeting those needs at the moment."

"You meet my needs just fine."

"Nick..."

"No, Evie. You're not allowed to feel guilty because you got sick. Besides, it was your mind that attracted me first."

"I thought it was my boobs?"

He cocks his head to one side as if trying to remember. "Okay, they helped."

"Do you think you'd ever get married again?" I ask. I try to look him in the eye but my courage fails me so I turn back to the mirror as I wait for his response.

"I'm not into polygamy."

"Seriously, Nick. Say I left you-" I catch sight of the look on his face and add, "for a Brazilian football player. Would you ever remarry?"

He knows I want to talk about it. He doesn't, that's as clear as day, but he can't avoid every single conversation about life after Evie.

"No," he replies after a tense silence, and, for just a second, I think he might actually give me a straight answer. Then he speaks again, and his voice has taken on the teasing tone that means the conversation is closed. "I'd fight to get you back. Those football players are renowned for their infidelity, you know. It would only be a matter of time before you realised, and then you'd come crawling back, begging for my forgiveness."

CHAPTER 22
Julia

Evie's recovery is remarkable. Her eyes glitter, but other than that there are no signs of her earlier pain, and if she's slightly more maniacal than usual, it's nothing like the high I expected. My dad is wearing his best suit. It's brown, with a thin grey stripe and the pants are straight cut, completely disguising his prosthesis.

"We're so glad you could join us, Mr Soanes," Evie says as we gather around the table. I'm sitting on Dad's right. Jesse insisted on sitting on his left.

"Call me Ted, please," Dad replies, "and I'm glad to be here. I wanted to thank you in person for offering Juju this job."

"You must miss having her around," Nick says.

Dad waves his hand in the air. "Please, I'm getting up to all sorts of mischief without my chaperone."

Everyone laughs politely and we begin the rigmarole of "please pass the salt" and "would you like any peas?"

We make it all the way to dessert before my dad informs the Danvers that my birthday is next weekend.

"Oh!" Evie blushes. "I should have checked – I know it was on your resumé."

"It's not a big deal."

"Not a big deal?" Dad stops dabbing at his mouth with his napkin and rounds on me. "How many times do you turn thirty, Juju?"

"Probably as many as you turn twenty-nine," I tease.

"Don't you sass your old man."

Jesse snorts and I can see Nick trying desperately to keep a straight face behind his own napkin. Evie is grinning outright.

"We should do something!" she announces, "for your birthday. Let's have a barbecue."

"Evie," Nick murmurs, "Julia might already have made plans."

"No, actually I haven't." It's the truth. I don't exactly have a strong social network, so I figured I'd just visit my dad as usual, only with cake.

"Well that settles it," Evie says. "We'll barbecue on Saturday, for lunch."

"I don't want you to go to any trouble," I mumble, recalling how her efforts this afternoon had taken such a toll on her.

"I won't." Evie's cheek dimples. "I'll invite Kat and Ian and Nick can cook. I won't have to lift a finger. You will join us, won't you Ted?" she adds.

"I'll have to check my diary," Dad teases, "but I'm sure I can make a plan."

"Is there anyone you'd like to invite, Julia?" Nick asks.

Dad clears his throat. I know what he's thinking – that I have no one to ask.

"Actually," I say, raising my wine glass, "I do."

"You do?"

"Don't look so surprised, Dad!"

"No, I'm not... it's not, I just didn't know you..."

"Had any friends?" I tease.

"No! Of course you have friends, I just haven't seen many of them around lately."

It's true. When Aaron and I had split, our social circle had too, but, one by one, those who had supported me had trickled over to team Aaron. It didn't help that he was throwing parties and inviting them all to his wedding while I was stuck taking care of my dad and always strapped for cash. Still, I'm sure Kylie and Angela would come if I asked them too.

"I'll let you know if they can make it," I tell Evie resolutely.

"Perfect." She raises her glass of sparkling water. "Well, cheers: to good food, good friends and good health." I don't know if she's taking the piss, but her eyes sparkle wickedly.

"To family," Nick adds, and then he leans forward to clink our glasses.

I'm stuffed by the time we finish eating. For all Evie's insistence that she can't cook worth a damn, dinner was delicious, but now I'm regretting that second helping. I get to my feet a moment before Evie does, and together we start ferrying the dishes through to the kitchen. Nick makes to stand, but Evie halts him with a look and, meekly, he sits back down again and engages my father in conversation.

"I still can't get over how the two of you can carry out a whole conversation without uttering a single word," I tell Evie as we move around the kitchen in perfect unison.

"We've had eighteen years to perfect it," she giggles. "And really, most of it is me bossing him around with my evil-Evie look."

I go out to retrieve the last of the dishes to find that my dad and Nick have been dragged upstairs to listen to Jesse's song. I smile as I recognise the opening chords.

I'm wiping down the island when Evie speaks my name.

"Yes?" I ask, standing on tip-toes to reach the other side of the granite top.

"I have something to tell you but I'm not sure how you'll take it," Evie confesses. I drop back down onto the balls of my feet and frown at her.

"Okay...?"

"I spoke to Kat, about your dad. You know she owns a whole bunch of companies, right?"

I nod. I did know that, or at least I had suspected. I've seen her clothes and her car. It's obvious she has money and her working hours are far too flexible for her to be reporting to a boss. Kat comes and goes as she pleases, and, while I've been out of the working world for a few years, I'm pretty sure drinking in the middle of the day and taking the rest of the afternoon off isn't usually permitted.

"Did you know she owns a racehorse? Three, actually."

I shake my head, too numb to speak because I think I know where this is going and I don't dare speak the words aloud in case it's not true.

"She bought them a few months ago," Evie says, making sure I know it was before my time, "but she can't seem to hold down a trainer." Evie laughs at herself and then admits, "Okay, she keeps sleeping with them."

I have a sudden vision of Kat and my dad going at it and I shake my head, trying to dislodge it.

Evie must read my mind. "Kat only likes younger men," she says. "Anyway, the latest just resigned yesterday and she really doesn't have time to look for someone new. I mentioned your dad and Kat would like him to come in for an interview."

My heart drops. "My dad can't ride anymore."

"Has he tried?"

"Well, no, but..."

"He's not going to be a race jockey," Evie points out. "And Kat has a couple of contracted jockeys who work the horses. What she's looking for is a trainer. I figure your dad's probably overqualified to do that, but he'll be around horses again and the yard's not far from here. You could probably lift him in when you take the kids to school and pick him up in the evenings. Or one of Kat's drivers could help out."

"He takes the bus," I whisper.

"I didn't catch that?" Evie looks nervous.

"Are you serious?" I ask. "I mean, are you being absolutely serious?"

"Yes, I'm serious."

"Oh my God." I collapse onto the stool beside me and cover my mouth with my hand. "You have no idea what this will mean to him..." I choke on the words and take a few breaths to clear my head. "He tried so hard to find work but nobody would see him. They wouldn't even give him a chance."

Evie moves closer, her hand brushing lightly across my back, the way I've seen her do countless times with the children. "He's got the interview," she says softly, "the rest is up to him, but everybody deserves a chance, right?"

I give a half-laugh, half-sob. "I think so."

"Do you want to tell him now, or..." she trails off and I shake my head, no. "He's going to be so overwhelmed and he'd be mortified if he broke down in front of everybody. He's still so proud... I hope that doesn't sound ungrateful."

"Not at all. Tell him when you take him home. I'll find out when Kat can see him and let you have the details." She picks up her phone and starts typing, as if it's nothing. As if she didn't just give me hope for the first time in three years. As if she didn't just change my life.

"I don't know how to thank you," I murmur.

Evie grins. "You can start by doing those dishes for me."

CHAPTER 23
Evie

"SHHH!" I HISS AT THE KIDS, WHO ARE 'WHISPERING' AT THE-house-just-caught-fire level. "She's going to hear you!"

"Hurry up, Mom!" Dylan whines. I shuffle forward more quickly until Casey steps out in front of me, unexpectedly, and the tray I'm carrying tilts alarmingly to the left. I right it just in time, before the *Spiderman* cup filled with freshly-squeezed orange juice and probably about a billion germs from the children's hands, tips over the edge.

The toast is only slightly burned. I left Casey in charge and she loves pressing the handle up and down, so what should have been a responsibility became a game. I'd finally noticed and hauled it out, but not before the edges had caught. After that, I'd made the eggs myself.

"Jesse Knight," I whisper when we reach Julia's door. Dutifully, he lets his guitar fall to waist height on its strap and raises his hand to knock.

"Come in!"

They don't need any further invitation. Jesse twists the handle and they fall inside. Casey trips over Dylan's foot and, seeing my hands full, Julia rushes to help.

"Happy Birthday!" I yell over the wailing. I set the tray down on the edge of the neatly made bed and straighten up. "Come on Case," I croon, taking her from Julia's arms. "It's time to sing Happy Birthday!"

Casey stops crying as quickly as if I had pressed a mute button and we all start to sing. Jesse plays along, only slightly out of tune.

Julia claps dutifully at the end. "That was amazing!" she says. I roll my eyes at her and she gives me an indulgent smile.

"We made you breakfast," Dylan announces proudly. "We squeezed the juice ourselves."

Julia takes a sip. "Yum!"

"You're going to get salmonella," I tease. "Nick's gone to the store to get stuff for tonight. Are your friends still coming?"

"I think so." She checks her phone. "They haven't messaged to cancel, so I assume they're still coming."

"Good. Kids," I raise my voice to be heard, "why don't you go downstairs and make Julia a nice card?"

"Can we use the poster paint?"

"Oh, you mean the paint I confiscated because you left it open with the brushes still inside?"

"Yes."

"Sure, go ahead." I wave my hand as they rush from the room.

"You know they're going to start arguing over brushes in about two minutes," Julia teases.

"That's all I need." I reach outside the door and retrieve the floral gift bag I left there earlier. "You'll get your real present later, but this is from me."

"Evie! You shouldn't have!"

"It's called *Happy*," I say as she opens the bottle of perfume. "I thought it suited you."

She lifts the lid and inhales deeply. I've been in Julia's room enough times to know that she doesn't own perfume, only a constant can of cheap anti-perspirant.

"It's beautiful!" Julia exhales.

"No, that's Estee Lauder," I tease. "This is Clinique. Now hurry up and come downstairs."

When Nick gets back Julia is painting with the children.

"Isn't it a bit ironic that she's making her own card?" Nick asks wryly after he goes onto the patio to greet them.

I shrug. "They wouldn't stop fighting. Besides, this keeps her away from the drive." I peek out of the kitchen window. "It's so cute!" I say.

"It's tiny," he grumbles. "I almost put my back out driving it over here."

"How did you get your car back?"

"Henry and his son followed me. They left together."

When one of our long-standing clients mentioned he was selling his son's little car, Nick had called me from his office and we'd agreed to get it for Julia. The mileage was low and, according to Henry, the fuel consumption was very efficient.

"Do you think she's going to like it?" I ask, suddenly nervous.

"I'm sure she will."

"A car is a pretty big gift. I hope she doesn't take it the wrong way."

"It's not like it broke the bank. Henry only wanted what was left on the loan. Besides," his gaze softens, "she deserves it. I can't imagine how hard it must be to be thirty and still taking the bus."

"Look at you, you big softie." I shove at his arm. "You're really starting to like her." I'm rewarded with a flash of something on his face that cuts me to the core and leaves me reeling, but before I can be sure, it's gone, replaced by his usual expression. *Did I imagine it?* I try to pretend nothing happened. "Should we call her now?"

"It's up to you."

I walk to the sliding-door feeling some of my excitement ebb away. "Julia."

"Hmm?" she looks up and there's a blob of green paint on her cheek. "Firstly, you have some, um..." I gesture at my own cheek and Julia rounds on a suddenly giggling Dylan.

"Oh, you didn't!" she scolds, tapping her brush to the tip of his nose. Dylan rubs it off, smearing blue paint across his hands.

"Wash up," I tell him as he follows Julia inside. I can imagine how thrilled Nick would be if he left blue fingerprints all over the car Nick had just had valéted.

"What do you need?" Julia asks, coming to a halt in the kitchen.

"Your present's arrived!"

"It has?" she looks around the kitchen helplessly.

"Yes. And before you freak out, our decision is final and you will not, under any circumstances, ruin this for the children by making a fuss, you got it?"

"Yes ma'am." She laughs.

"Right, then, step this way."

Thank God we didn't tell the kids or they would've ruined the surprise.

Julia's reaction is predictable shock. She follows me out onto the drive her eyes barely skimming over the little white hatchback as she searches for a package or a gift bag.

"You didn't have to get me anything else, Evie. The perfume is more than..."

"Oh, shut it. You promised not to make a fuss, remember?"

Julia's lips part, the semblance of a smile forming, but it fades as her eyes slide back to the car and her lips open, her mouth forming a perfect little 'o'.

She turns, slowly, to face us. "The... car?"

I nod enthusiastically.

"You bought me a car?"

"It was an excellent deal," Nick quips, sensing her mounting hysteria, "and to be honest, it's so small I don't even know if you could classify it as a car – it's more like a..."

He doesn't finish. Instead, he takes two strides forward and catches her as her legs buckle, because he saw it coming before I did.

Julia is sobbing. Not in a pretty girl way, but the real, body-wracking ugly cry that results in puffy eyes and fat lips. Nick has whisked the kids inside and left me to deal with her, not wanting Jesse, Dylan and Casey to witness such a monumental breakdown.

"You know, I saw this coming weeks ago," I croon, stroking her hair and trying not to think about the snot that's streaming onto my sleeve. "You hold everything in. No one can be that strong forever." Julia hiccups so loudly that it rocks us both and I giggle. "Let it out, Julia. You need to let it out."

And she does. Years' worth of pain and loss and heartbreak pour out of her, streaming down her face and onto her clothes while her body shudders and heaves, squeezing out every last drop, taking advantage of this opportunity.

My legs go numb and my knees start to ache but I don't move. I hold her until her trembling subsides and the only evidence of her breakdown is the occasional ragged breath.

"Evie." Nick's hand is on my shoulder and I look up to find him smiling down at me, a mixture of pride and concern. I wince as I become aware of how my body protests this extended cramped position, and I take his hand, letting him help me up. Julia is bent over like a snowdrop, her spine almost unnaturally curved. Pale hands and a cloud of dark hair conceal her face.

Nick gives me a questioning look. At my nod, he steps forward and crouches beside her.

"Julia?" She gives a start at the sound of his voice. "Come on, let's get you up." Without waiting for permission, he puts his hands under her arms and lifts her to her feet. I catch a glimpse of her tight mouth and the blotchy red of her cheeks before she wipes frantically at her face.

"I'm so sorry." It's a tiny admission, so soft we almost miss it.

I whip my head up as Nick starts to laugh. "For what? That's the single best reaction I've ever had to a gift."

A small giggle slips through Julia's lips.

"Don't you want to look at it?" Nick continues, and my heart swells with love. He's pretending like nothing happened, making Julia less self-conscious. "I mean, it certainly wouldn't be my first choice, it looks like it was made for kids, but maybe you like that sort of thing."

"I still can't believe you guys bought me a car." Her voice is hoarse, gruff from all the crying but I don't hear anymore. As Nick leads her forward to admire the little car, I slip away, back into the house, to check on the children.

CHAPTER 24
Julia

The wind whips my hair and dries the residue of tears from my face. I glide onto the highway and zip along, feeling lighter than I have in years. I didn't even realise I was carrying such a weight until I let it go. Evie was right. I needed to let it out. The fact that I finally did, in front of my employers, isn't how I would have planned it, but that's not the point. The point is, I feel liberated. I feel free. Evie and Nick have given me so much – a job, a car, a new sense of purpose for my dad - I wouldn't even know how to begin to thank them.

It was Nick's idea that I go for a drive to clear my head before the barbecue, so I'd paused only long enough to grab my purse and give the children a kiss before zooming out of the drive. My car isn't perfect. The pedals are slightly worn and there's a small hole in the fabric on the passenger seat that looks suspiciously like a cigarette burn, but it's mine and I love it.

I only go as far as the coast. I open all the windows and breathe in the salty air which brings on a flood of happy memories of my childhood. They're not as painful as they were before, and I find myself smiling as I remember hopping through my mother's footprints and ice cream cones dropped in the dirt. I indulge myself for a few minutes and then I turn around and head back.

It's only when I've pulled into my dad's street that I realise I no longer consider the little apartment I've lived in for three years home. If home is where the heart is, mine is well and truly ensconced in Oakland Park with the family I have come to love.

My father's astonishment is almost as great as mine had been. "They gave it to you?" he asks. "Just like that?"

"Yes! I couldn't believe it myself."

Then he catches sight of my face. "Have you been crying, Juju? Did they upset you? Did this car come with a price?"

I don't know what he could possibly mean and I suspect I don't want to. "Dad, no! They're just good people. *Really, really* good people."

"Well in that case, I owe them a debt," he says. "Two, if we're keeping score." I raise my brow and he grins. "I didn't want to say anything in case I didn't get it, but I had my interview with Miss Graham this morning."

"Dad! I said I'd drive you!"

"I took the bus," he scoffs. "You know I'm perfectly capable of getting around myself."

"And?" I ask, but it's only a formality because I know that he's got the job. He wouldn't have brought it up if he hadn't and I suspect that's why he didn't tell me when he was going. I should have known by the way he's sitting up a little straighter than before. He has the air of a man who has just had his pride handed back to him on a silver platter.

"There's a lot of work to be done," he says haughtily. "Those stables are in a shambles and the grooms, well, don't even get me started on how long they consider a standard lunch break to be, but I'll get it right for Miss Graham."

"I have no doubt about that, Dad," I say, my jaw aching from smiling so much. "You're the perfect man for the job."

Jesse hijacks my father the minute we walk through the door, determined to show off his new repertoire, which, to Evie's delight, includes an old Nirvana number. Kylie and Angela arrive half an hour early and Evie ushers us all outside. It's a perfect summer evening, a light breeze keeping the heat at bay.

"This house is gorgeous!" Ange hisses enviously, her long legs curled beneath her on the patio sofa. She's so tanned, her smoky copper skin is almost the same tone as the cushion beside her. "And I can't believe they bought you a car for your birthday!"

"Are you sure you aren't more than just a nanny, Jules?" Kylie adds, nudging me in the ribs.

I give a gasp of horror and raise my eyes to find Nick standing at the barbecue, his eyes on me. He looks away, but I'm almost sure I caught the semblance of a smile on his face.

"Right!" Evie steps outside, a platter of sausage rolls in her hands – slightly burnt if the faintly acrid tang is any indication. Evie is wearing a white cotton dress with strappy sleeves and she's pinned her wig so that half the hair is pulled back and the other half cascades over her bare shoulders. She looks beautiful, not even the dark shadows beneath her eyes can diminish that fact. "Julia, do you have a drink?" she asks, setting the platter down on the table. I hide a smile at the sight of the blackened corners of the pastry and hold up my glass of Sangria, which seems to be permanently filled.

"I do. Now stop stressing and come and sit with us, Evie. Please."

She glances at Kat, with whom my dad has been in deep conversation for the past twenty minutes. "I'll be there in a sec, I'm just going to toss the salad."

"Let me help." I start to get to my feet.

"Sit!" Evie barks in her sternest mom voice. "I may not be able to do a lot of things, but I can sure as hell toss a salad."

"She's awesome," Ange sighs the second Evie's gone.

"He's not too bad, either," Kylie adds, watching Nick flip burgers. I feel a strange sensation in the pit of my stomach at her words. If I didn't know better, I'd call it jealousy.

"So, what have you two been up to?" I ask, changing the topic.

They both start speaking at once. Kylie just got promoted, which is kind of a huge deal because she struggled at school and it really knocked her self-confidence. Ange has met someone, but it's still early days so she's not getting her hopes up just yet. Ange has had her fair share of boyfriends in the past, but they seldom make it past a few months before fizzling out.

"Are you still waiting for *the one*?" Kylie asks, making air quotes with her fingers.

"Hey, just because you don't believe in all of that, don't give me a hard time about it!" Ange quips.

"I don't believe in it," Kylie teases, "because I grew up and stopped believing in fairy tales."

"It's not a fairy tale!" Ange is indignant, but laughing. They start to argue among themselves, but I barely hear what they are saying because Casey has ventured close to the pool. Ian and Nick had a dip earlier and they left the net off in case anyone else wanted to swim. I listen to Ange and Kylie's conversation with only half an ear, watching Casey as she runs around the pool to fetch her push-bike.

I'm on my feet the second her foot slips and I jump into the water right after her soundless splash. I grab hold of her arms and haul her up. Her face erupts from the water in a volley of coughing and spluttering. I can't see much through the water dripping in my eyes and I can't wipe it away because I'm using both hands to hold Casey aloft. Which is probably why I'm so jolted when a warm, hard chest collides with my arm.

"Oh my God, is she okay?" Nick asks, reaching for Casey who is still screaming blue murder. I didn't even hear him dive in.

"I panicked!" I say, handing her over. "I know she can swim, but I panicked."

"I didn't even see her," he says, stroking Casey's wet hair and pulling her face into his chest. "I thought she was inside."

"What happened?" Evie's voice is about four octaves higher than normal.

"She's fine," Nick says, handing a still-screaming Casey up to

Evie. "She fell in but Julia got there just as she did. She was only under for a second or two. She's more shocked than hurt."

Evie is already crooning soothing words into Casey's ear. "I'll take her upstairs and get her changed. Will you put the net back on?"

"Yeah. I should've done it sooner. Ian, will you help me with this?"

"Sure." Ian is already reaching for the tangled web. I didn't even realise everyone else had gathered around the side of the pool.

"Are you okay, Juju?" Dad asks as I haul myself up the steps. My soaked clothes seriously hinder my progress.

"I'm fine," I insist, waving away the hands that reach for me.

"Um... Jules..." Kylie's voice is low and borderline embarrassed as I start wringing out my sodden skirt.

"Yeah?" I look up to find her gazing at my chest and, to my dismay, she's not the only one. Ian is grinning, staring unashamedly, while Nick is trying to look anywhere but at my blouse, which has become completely transparent.

"Oh!" I cross my arms over my chest. Nick is dripping beside me, also unable to go inside, so Kat comes to my rescue.

"I'll get you a towel." She's back in no time with one for me and one for Nick. I wrap the fluffy blue stripes around myself, quickly drying off most of the water and then I flee inside to change. I wonder how I'm going to recover from my embarrassment, but a few hours later I've forgotten all about it. The Sangria ran out shortly after the pool debacle and my fingers are freezing from being clutched around icy vodka tonics for so long.

On his way out Ian kindly offers to take my father home on his way. I've had far too many vodkas and Kylie and Angela aren't ready to leave yet, so the three of us sit around the fireplace under a sinking sun. I can hear Nick and Evie cleaning up inside, and the high-pitched squeaking of the minions coming from the TV room where Evie had settled the kids earlier.

"So, have you heard from Aaron lately?" Angela asks tentatively.

"No, but why would I? He's married now."

"I just wondered if you'd heard the news," she mumbles. Out of the corner of my eye I can see Kylie shaking her head, but it's too late to take the words back.

"He's having a baby?" I guess correctly.

Ange is relieved. "Oh, so you did know?"

I shrug, not wanting to hurt her feelings.

"I think it's a bit soon for them to be starting a family," Kylie interjects loyally. "I mean, they've only been married what – six months?"

"Seven." They both turn to look at me and I wish I hadn't just admitted to keeping track.

Kylie recovers first. "Yeah, well that's not very long, is it? And they're always arguing... it's just not..."

"I really don't think any of this is my business," I say pointedly.

Kylie looks shame-faced. "Yeah, I guess you're right. I'm sorry, Jules. It's just still weird to see him with someone else."

"What about you?" Ange asks. "Have you met anyone?"

"No. I haven't really had much time for dating."

"But you will now," she says, "I mean, now that you're not living with your dad anymore."

"Julia?" Nick's voice interrupts and I look up, grateful for the distraction. There's a strange look on his face and I wonder just how long he's been standing there.

"Yes?"

"Sorry to interrupt. Evie asked me to tell you goodnight. She's gone to bed. I think she's a bit shattered." I feel guilt flood through me but Nick raises his dark brows as if to tell me, *don't you dare.*

"Would you like to join us?" I ask. After all, it's his patio, fireplace. He shouldn't feel he has to hide inside.

"I don't want to intrude," he says, but I can tell he wants to. He deliberates for a minute. "I need a refill," he says. "Anyone need anything?" Kylie holds up her empty glass.

When Nick returns, he takes a seat. "I feel like the thorn among the roses," he teases.

Conversation is awkward at first but the four of us soon settle into an easy rhythm. Just after ten, Kylie orders an Uber for herself and Ange and Nick yawns widely.

"Thank you so much for everything today," I tell him, once I've walked my friends out.

"It was our pleasure. Did you have a good time?"

"I had an amazing time."

"Good," he smiles. "You deserved it. Goodnight, Jules."

It's the first time he's called me that, but I don't think he's even noticed as he wanders up the stairs.

CHAPTER 25
Nick

"I'm perfectly capable of going on my own," I insist for the third time. What I really mean is, *this feels awkward*, but that's not what comes out. I'm beginning to feel like a stuck record but Evie isn't budging.

"Why let a perfectly good ticket go to waste?" Evie says, and then, because she knows exactly what I'm trying to say, "I know you probably feel awkward going with Julia, but Casey adores her, and it might make her feel better about me not being there." She stops speaking as a hacking fit of coughing seizes her, and any further argument dies on my lips.

"You're going to the doctor tomorrow," I say. "You should've gone two weeks ago." Evie started sniffing a few days after Julia's party. By the time the coughing started I realised she hadn't shaken whatever bug had come over her, but she'd insisted she was fine. She was still attempting to downplay it.

"It's only a cold."

"No, it's not. You might've gotten away with that before, but we both know that it's not just a cold. Not anymore, anyway. If it was, there's no way you'd be missing this," I add pointedly.

That shuts her up. She'd been looking forward to Casey's recital for months. I know how devastated she is to be missing it, but she doesn't even have the energy to get out of bed.

"You promise you'll video it?" she asks in a small voice. "From start to finish – and the finale?"

I lean over the bed and kiss her forehead, letting my lips rest against the clammy skin. "I promise. And first thing tomorrow we're going to see the doc."

Casey cries when she realises that Evie isn't coming with us, but she perks up slightly when Julia takes her hand.

"I'm going to tell Mommy all about it as soon as we get home," Julia tells her. Julia's face is pinched and pale. I know she feels terrible about this, but she knows better than to argue with Evie and she wouldn't want to let Casey down.

I hold Julia's door open, standing awkwardly on one leg while she straps Casey into her chair. I've never known her to fumble with the restraints before, but Murphy's law ensures that tonight she does. I guess I'm not the only one who's uncomfortable with Evie's plan. I breathe a sigh of relief when she finally gets into the car and I close the door with more force than necessary. It's surreal – Julia sitting in Evie's place – but by the time I round the front of the car and reach the driver's door, I've composed myself.

Until I close my door and her scent assaults my senses. The fragrant citrus filling the confined space brings back memories of lazy Sunday sex and secrets whispered on breath and air. I feel something stir inside of me, and I open my window, as if the crisp night air might help me escape it.

Julia gives me a strange look and I feel an inexplicable urge to kiss her pink lips, to bury my face in her hair and trail my tongue down her neck, lower, lower and lose myself in the soft curve of her breasts. *Oh God, what is happening to me?* I've never been a particularly religious man, but I pray now. I pray for release from the sudden desire that has seized hold of me and I pray for forgiveness - for being weak when I should be strong.

We sit two seats apart, with Dylan and Jesse between us. I notice a few of the moms from Casey's school giving Julia and I strange looks but I grit my teeth and ignore them. Evie can't stand most of them, so what do I care what they think or say?

"I can't see!" Dylan hisses, as a large man in jeans and a ridiculously loud bomber jacket settles into the seat in front of him. His wife sits in front of me, half his size, with a short pixie crop of white-blonde hair. I'm about to switch places with Dylan when Julia pulls him onto her lap. He settles back against her as the lights dim and I face forward, determinedly, while Jesse slouches beside me.

Casey's performance is second to last in a line-up of no less than twelve dance routines. Still, the wait is worth it. Her yellow-and-black bee costume is adorable, complete with bouncing black feelers which fall off halfway through her act, and which she stops to collect, sending seven other bees into a confused frenzy. I laugh until my sides hurt and almost drop my phone which I'm using to record the entire debacle. Even Jesse can't stop giggling beside me. I meet Julia's eyes over his head to find tears of laughter streaming down her face. I grin at her, forgetting for a second that she's not Casey's mom, that she's not supposed to be here, that this is wrong... just so wrong. The thought sobers me instantly and I whip away from the gleam of mirth in Julia's eyes so fast I could've given myself whiplash. For the rest of the concert, I keep my eyes firmly on the stage.

Evie is sleeping when we get home. Julia puts the boys to bed while I try to explain to Casey that Mommy will watch the recording in the morning.

"You don't need to show Mommy," Casey yawns, showing her pink tongue. "She saw me."

"Okay, baby," I murmur, not bothering to correct her. She's so tired she's probably already dreaming. I pull her blanket up to her neck, kiss her forehead and switch off her nightlight.

Downstairs, Julia is making coffee.

"You're not going to be able to sleep," I tell her.

"I don't think I'd sleep anyway," she admits. "I keep remembering how her headband fell off and they all knocked into one another like buzzing little dominoes."

"It was pretty funny."

"It was hysterical." She waves her mug at me and I nod.

"Why not."

She pours the coffee and we settle into a comfortable silence.

"How's Evie?"

"She's sleeping."

"I'm worried about her," Julia admits. "That cough doesn't sound good."

"I'm taking her to the ER tomorrow. It's the only place open on a Sunday." It occurs to me that Sunday is Julia's day off. "Would you be able to watch the kids? I'm sure I won't be long."

"Of course. Don't rush. Worst case, I'll tell my dad to come over here, or I'll take the kids with me to lunch."

"Thank you."

Julia looks at the dishes stacked neatly by the sink. "I'm going to wash up before bed," she says.

"I really need to get the dishwasher fixed." The ancient machine leaks and neither Evie nor I have gotten around to getting it repaired.

"I don't mind washing, it's therapeutic."

I join her at the sink. "You wash, I'll dry," I say, folding up my shirt sleeves.

"I can manage."

"I know you can, but I think I need this therapy you speak of."

Julia laughs. "Joke all you want, but it works."

"If you say so."

She turns abruptly to pick up the pasta pot and a waft of that scent hits me, bringing with it another wave of nostalgia, but I'm relieved to find my body doesn't react as physically as it did earlier.

"You're terrible at rinsing," I tell Julia as she hands me a plate with suds dripping from the brim.

She gives me a wry look, but takes the plate back. Her fingers brush mine, the barest whisper of a touch and I come undone. I meet

Julia's gaze and my eyes are drawn to her lips, pale, pink, perfect. It all happens within the space it takes for Julia's startled inhalation of breath – I smell her, sense her, yearn to taste her, to touch... and then, before I can act on any of it, I drop the drying up towel, pivot on the spot and march right out of the room.

CHAPTER 26
Evie

I SMOTHER ANOTHER PAINFUL BOUT OF COUGHING WITH MY pillow, which is damp with sweat. It stinks, so I toss it aside, burying my head beneath the duvet instead. I feel like shit and am guilt-ridden above that. I shouldn't have gone to Casey's rehearsal. I'd vowed to stay home, to stay in bed where I should be, but the longing to see her on stage in her adorable costume, to watch my beautiful ballerina, was too much. I'd snuck into the back once the lights were out, unnoticed and invisible to the legion of proud parents who faced forward. I'd caught a glimpse of Nick and Julia in the second row, watched as their heads turned toward one another after Casey's performance. I'd seen the flash of Nick's smile, the one that is almost always directed at me and I'd felt the agony of a splinter pierce my heart.

As she dipped into an adorable and rather clumsy curtsey, Casey had looked right at me. Her dimple-cheeked smile lit up the auditorium and she'd raised both hands to wave at me, knocking the feelers off the startled bee beside her. By the time Nick glanced around to see who she was waving at, I had pulled back into the shadows, invisible once more.

I'd made it home just in time. If Nick had stopped to place his hand on the hood of my car, he would've felt the warmth, known that I hadn't been in bed all this time, but he didn't. And by the time he came upstairs to check on me, I was feigning a deep sleep, curled in on myself, trying to ease the ache that lingered in my chest.

I could hear them in the kitchen, the low murmur of voices trying to keep it down so as not to wake anybody. Running water, soft splashing, a deep chuckle. I shut my eyes against the sounds, willing myself not to cry, but then, suddenly, the bedroom door burst open and Nick stalked in, his breathing ragged. Through slitted eyes I watched as he ran his hands through his hair, and then, with a quick glance at the bathroom door, dropped his clothes. Almost subconsciously, his hand strayed to cover his erection as he passed the bed on his way to the bathroom. A minute later the hiss of the shower stung my ears.

I knew what he was doing in there, and I knew why. Nick may be the world's best man, but he is still only a man. A part of me wanted to get out of bed to go to him and ease his need, but I couldn't bring myself to do it. Instead, I pulled my pillow over my head and blocked out the sound of life going on without me.

When I open my eyes in the morning, Nick is sitting on the edge of the bed, fully dressed.

"Good morning." His smile is so bright that it dulls even the radiant sunlight filtering through the window as he hands me a steaming cup of coffee.

"I love you," I sigh, taking it from him and leaning back against the headboard.

"You didn't cough as much last night," he says, sounding pleased.

"Are you keeping track? Do you have a record book somewhere?" I dip my chin and put on my best commentator's impersonation: "Friday: Evie coughed forty-seven times. Saturday: Evie coughed thirty-two times then fell into a death-like sleep. Began to worry, but she farted at eleven p.m."

"Something like that," Nick says, his eyes twinkling. "Only you actually farted at midnight."

"Ha-ha. So, does this mean I get out of going to the ER this morning?"

"Nice try."

I sip my coffee. "How was the rehearsal?"

"Beautiful. Here," he hands me his phone and I watch Casey's performance. I smile, waiting for the moment that Casey's feelers fall off and I laugh out loud at the ballerina pile-up, which hurts my chest, but it's even funnier the second time around. Of course, I don't tell Nick that.

Nick is watching over my shoulder as the view swings around to catch Julia in mid-laughter, wiping tears of mirth from her cheeks. I feel him stiffen beside me, sense his discomfort, and I hand the phone back.

"It looks like she had fun, too," I say slowly, deliberately.

"I think so." He brushes it off. "I wish you'd been there."

"I know. I'm sorry."

"Julia made oatmeal for breakfast. Can I bring you some?"

"No, I'll come down. I'm just going to get dressed."

"Okay." He kisses my cheek. "I'll see you downstairs."

I let the water cascade over my face. My eyes are closed but I can still see Julia's smiling face, see the way her arm was curled protectively around Dylan. A sigh escapes my lips and morphs into a sob. I don't often let the depression consume me but I know already that it's going to be a bad day.

I eat only a small amount of the oatmeal. Julia is conspicuous by her absence but I don't ask where she is. I spotted her car through my window when I was getting dressed, but Sunday is her day off and I know she's been busy – the spotless kitchen and cooling pot of oatmeal on the stove-top are proof.

"Done?" Nick asks, gesturing at my bowl. I nod. "We should get going."

"Do we really have to go? The doctors are open tomorrow. I'm sure one more day isn't going to make a difference."

"We really have to go, Evie."

It's pointless arguing. I know if I do I'll earn myself a lecture about being irresponsible concerning my health. With my compromised immune system one day can make all the difference. I sigh my acceptance and get to my feet, when a thought occurs to me.

"Are we taking the kids with us?" I ask Nick as he plays peek-a-boo with Casey.

"No. Julia said she'd watch them." Her name sounds so easy on his lips now, compared to when she first came to live with us.

"Doesn't she visit her dad on Sundays?"

"She said she'd take them with her if she goes."

"That's nice of her."

"Yeah, it is."

Julia comes downstairs as we're preparing to leave. "How are you feeling?" she asks, eying the suitcase in Nick's hand with trepidation.

"It's just in case," I assure her. "If they want to keep me overnight for observation it would be pointless coming all the way home to pack."

"Do you think they'll make you stay?" She's genuinely upset.

"With any luck they'll tell Nick to stop being paranoid," I tease, and even Nick smiles.

Neither of us are smiling an hour later.

"You've developed mild pneumonia," the stern-faced doctor at the emergency room says. "It's not too serious, but with your already compromised immune system, I'd like to keep you in for a day or two. We can't afford for it to get any worse."

"What can you do here that I can't do at home?" I ask.

"I'm going to administer the antibiotic through an IV," he says, "and we need to get some fluids into you – you're slightly dehydrated as well as being underweight. With your condition, it's only natural," he adds, as Nick's face flushes with guilt and I know he's wishing he'd forced me to eat more oatmeal this morning.

"I'll be in touch with your specialist," the doctor – Riggs, according to the name badge on his chest – continues. He rifles through the file on his desk. "Doctor Moxley, is it?"

"Yes." Nick replies while I examine my shoes. "Evie saw him just this past week."

"Well I'll leave a message for him to contact me, but I doubt there's anything he'll want to add with regards to treatment. Pneumonia is fairly common and you're in good hands, Evie."

"Thank you," I mumble.

Nick helps me to my ward and settles me into the creaking hospital bed. He averts his eyes as a smiling nurse hooks up my IV and checks my vitals.

"What would you like for lunch?" she asks pleasantly, indicating the menu on the trolley table. "Surprise me," I say, not bothering to pick it up.

Her smile doesn't falter. "The chicken seems to be popular this week. I'll be back to check on you shortly. Just buzz if you need anything." She bustles out, her soft moccasins making no sound on the gleaming tiled floor.

Nick hands me the remote for the TV. The dividing curtain emits a screech as he yanks it open, revealing a large woman in the bed opposite mine.

"You sure you don't want me to reserve a private room?" Nick asks. The woman is snoring softly, her lower lip resting on a jowl.

"No," I insist, "the company will be good for me."

Fumbling for something to do, trying to act as though this is an entirely normal situation, Nick fills the glass tumbler on my bedside table with water and hands it to me. The perfect patient, I drink it all before settling back on the pillows. I'm already bored. The large woman across from me gives a snort, then falls silent. We hold our breaths but a second later she resumes her soft snoring and I fight the urge to giggle.

"I bet she's a farter," I whisper.

Nick only smiles as he takes my hand in his own, a dry,

comforting warmth against my clammy skin. His thumb traces lazy circles on my palm but I can hear the gentle, persistent tapping of his foot against the tiled floor, a symptom of the distress he is hiding so well. He stays far longer than necessary, but I don't tell him to leave. Hospitals frighten me now, more than before. Every time I enter one I wonder if it'll be the last time. Thankfully, my brain doesn't have much time to conjure up the worst. I don't know what that nurse snuck into my IV, but I feel myself becoming sluggish, my eyelids too heavy to hold open. Finally, I doze off.

'Evie," Nick whispers, his hand still holding mine.

"Hmmm?"

"I'm going to go."

"M'kay."

"I'll be back soon," Nick promises, through the haze of medication. "I'll bring the kids through at visiting hours."

I try to smile, but I'm not sure if it shows.

CHAPTER 27
Julia

THE KIDS ARE QUIET, WHICH IS NEVER A GOOD SIGN. THEY'VE been subdued since Nick and Evie left for the hospital and I found Jesse crying in his room shortly after. He won't open up about it, though, well at least not to me. I feel helpless and my cheeks hurt from trying to fake-smile the children's fears away. I've made hot chocolate and popcorn, offered to play board games, and, in desperation even brought out Evie's secret stash of candy, but although they eat and drink everything, it doesn't rouse them from their melancholy.

It's that much harder to reassure them because I'm worried about Evie, too. It's been four hours since she left. If everything was fine, surely she'd be back by now? Thinking of Evie brings a nasty serpent of guilt to life in my stomach. I've been trying to figure out a way to get things back to normal, back to when Nick and Evie were just two good people I adored equally, two people who I admired and respected and would do anything for. So far, it hasn't worked. Nothing seems to be able to dull the inner monologue that has been on a constant loop in my head since last night.

What are you doing, Julia?

It had been an innocent mistake. Nick had offered to help me with the dishes and somewhere between teasing me about my inability to rinse properly and finding a roach in the bottom of the pasta pot, his hand had brushed against mine. That contact had jolted me, far more than it should have. He'd seen it, too, I know he had. His eyes had widened at the sight of my face and he'd dropped the drying-up cloth and stalked out without saying another word. Whether it was out of pity or anger, I don't know, and I don't know which would be worse.

Or maybe he didn't notice and my guilt is messing with my head. Either way, I can't understand why it happened. Why did his touch jolt me so violently? *Because you like him*, the inner voice whispers evilly, and I flush with shame and despair because what kind of monster could have feelings for a man whose wife is dying? All in all, this has been a shitty day.

When Nick gets home, his face is grey beneath his suntan.

"How did it go?" I whisper, conscious of the children in the next room.

"She's got pneumonia. They're keeping her in for observation."

"For how long?

"A day or two. She'll be fine," he adds for my benefit and the snake in my belly twists painfully. "She said to tell you she's sorry but you'll have to cook and clean while she binge-reads Jilly Cooper."

Typical Evie.

"God broke the mould after making her," I say without thinking, but Nick smiles.

"No doubt about that."

I'm infinitely relieved that things don't seem to be weird between us. As Nick plays games with the children to keep their minds off Evie's absence, I wander around the house, picking up stray toys and straightening beds that I've already straightened. I've almost managed to convince myself that I imagined what happened last night when Kat and Ian arrive.

"We were just on our way to see her," I hear Kat telling Nick, "but we thought we'd pop in to see how you were doing? Do you need anything, is there anything we can do?"

"I'm fine, Kat. Julia's here and she'll do the school run tomorrow as usual. Thanks though."

"Where is Julia?" Ian's voice is sharp, pained.

"Upstairs, I think."

I move away from the top of the stairs so they won't see me.

"Hey kids!" Kat must have entered the living-room, but her voice carries to where I stand, clear as day. "What are you guys doing?" I hear mumbled replies before Kat continues. "Sounds like fun." A pause. "No, I don't really know how to play that, but you carry on."

I smile to myself. Kat really is awful with kids but I like her because she's honest and direct.

"Nick, can I talk to you for a second?" It's Ian's voice, closer than Kat's, and then the sound of retreating footsteps. They must have gone into the kitchen. Kat comes upstairs and I nip into the bathroom so that she doesn't catch me eavesdropping.

I flush the toilet and then wash my hands before opening the door. Kat is standing right outside it.

"I thought I heard your voice," I say. Her painted lips split in a knowing smile that makes me wonder how discreet I'd been entering the bathroom. "I've been meaning to thank you," I say quickly, before she can question it, "for putting my dad on the company's private health benefits."

Kat shrugs. "It's standard for all employees."

"Yes, but not all your employees are in desperate need of a new prosthesis."

"I noticed his limp is becoming more pronounced. Is it bothering him?"

"A bit," I admit, then quickly add, "not enough to interfere with his duties, but it's not comfortable. He endures it, but a replacement would do wonders for his quality of life."

"I'll make sure our policy covers it," Kat says. "And if not, I'll upgrade his plan."

"You don't have to do that."

"Your dad's turning my yard around. It's the least I can do. Besides, he's already saved me so much money it'll pay for itself."

She looks set to say something else, when the sound of raised voices interrupts.

"Is that Nick?" I ask, horrified. Without even thinking I rush down the stairs.

"You don't get to have an opinion!" Nick is roaring as Kat and I skid to a halt at the kitchen door. "Now get out of my house before I throw you out!"

"Nick!" I hiss, casting a concerned glance over my shoulder to where the children are sitting at the table, their eyes round with fright. Nick seems to come to his senses, but he's shaking with rage.

"Don't threaten me," Ian warns.

"It's not a threat, Ian," Nick murmurs, so the children can't hear. "It's a promise. Now get the fuck out of my house."

I turn my back on the cold fury that is so out of character and smile at Jesse, Dylan and Casey.

"Let's go and play outside!" I announce brightly.

Kat catches my eye. "That's a fabulous idea!" she says, "come on boys, you can teach me how to kick a ball."

Jesse skulks out, but Dylan pauses, eyeing Kat's stiletto-heeled boot with dubious suspicion. Casey takes my hand as we go, her small fingers clutching at mine for security.

"Daddy said 'fuck'," she whispers.

"Yes, he did," I tell her, crouching down so my face is on the same level as hers. "But I'm sure it was an accident."

"It's a grown-up word," she tells me conspiratorially, as if I might not know.

"It is a grown-up word," I say, "but it's not a very nice word. I don't think you should say it."

"I don't!"

"Good girl." We've reached the patio. "Why don't we sit here and watch aunty Kat play ball with Jesse and Dylan."

Casey giggles.

"What?"

"She's not our aunty."

"Well, not technically, but she's like an aunty, don't you think?"

Casey looks over at Kat as if trying to decide and we both jump at the sound of the front door slamming. I resist the urge to check on Nick, but I notice Kat throwing dark looks inside while she tries to keep up with Jesse's impressive footwork.

When Dylan scores his third goal, the ball rolling so slowly between Kat's feet that I probably could've sauntered over and stopped it myself, Kat throws up her hands in defeat.

"You win!" she says. She leaves the game to the boys and flops onto the sofa opposite me. Casey is playing on my phone, but I reach for it anyway. I know it isn't good for her to spend too much time on electronic devices, even if it is the easiest way to distract her when we need to.

"Case, why don't you go and get your brush and a hair-tie and I'll do an Elsa braid in your hair," I tell her when she opens her mouth to protest.

"Okay." She hops down and toddles off. I watch her go, craning my neck to see if I can catch a glimpse of Nick.

"I suspected that might happen," Kat says, following the direction of my gaze. "Those two have been circling a blow-out for years, it was bound to happen. It's also why I told Ian to bring his own car," she adds, smug in the knowledge of being right, even under the current circumstances.

"Do you have any idea what it's about? I've never seen Nick lose his cool like that."

Kat leans forward. "What do you think it was about?" She fixes me with that cool stare as if daring me to act ignorant.

"Evie," I answer, without any hesitation. "Ian's in love with Evie."

Kat sits back, her fingers picking at a loose thread on the cushion beside her. "He's always loved her," she confirms. "Since the very beginning – before she and Nick even got together, I think."

"Does Nick know?"

"Of course he knows. Anyone with eyes can tell how Ian feels about Evie, even Evie."

It's no surprise that Evie knows. Shrewd and smart, she doesn't miss a thing.

"How does Nick stand it?"

Kat glances at the sliding-door. Nick is somewhere beyond the glass, in what mood neither of us know. "He knows she loves him," Kat murmurs. "It's only ever been him. He's never had any competition. And neither has she." She holds my gaze at that, and I feel like there's a hidden message in her words. Never have I been so happy to see Casey as she toddles up to me with her pink hairbrush and a handful of colourful hair-ties.

"Is this the first time they've come to blows over it?" I ask, pulling Casey's hair back and brushing it out.

Kat sighs. "Yes. Sadly, I think the time is coming for our little foursome to part company. The sicker Evie gets, the more desperate Ian becomes. Somehow, in his head, he's convinced himself that he would be better for her – that Nick isn't doing enough." She laughs, and it's a hollow, brittle sound.

"Nick would do *any*thing for Evie," I snap, filled with anger at Ian for thinking otherwise.

Kat smiles, a sad smile filled with pity. "I know he would," she says. "And so does Evie."

CHAPTER 28
Nick

Evie is awake when we arrive for the evening visiting hour, and her colour is already much improved. She makes the usual motherly fuss over the scraggy bouquet of flowers which Casey picked herself and which Julia saved from being utterly awful by tying it together with a pale pink ribbon.

"Did you pick these yourself?" Evie asks, as if such a thing couldn't possibly be true. Casey nods proudly. "They're beautiful!" Evie announces. Evie's never cared if the kids denuded every plant in the garden so long as they were having fun. *Flowers are for picking,* she insists.

"This is my friend, Mrs Hinchcliff," Evie adds, gesturing at the large woman still occupying the bed opposite. Mrs Hinchcliff is smiling, her treble chins curved softly upward.

"It's wonderful to meet you," she says, in a voice like gravel. "I've heard so much about you children already, from your mom. Now, let me guess." She taps her topmost chin with a podgy finger before pointing it at the kids in turn. "Jesse. Dylan. Casey?"

Casey giggles.

"How did she know?" Dylan whispers, his eyes wide.

"Maybe she's magic?" I mock-whisper back.

Jesse sniggers.

"Are you sick?" Casey asks from the safety of Evie's lap.

"I was," Mrs Hinchcliff replies, "but I'm better now. I'm going home tomorrow."

"Speaking of going home," I say, turning my attention back to Evie. "Did the doctors say when you could come home?"

"Probably on Tuesday or Wednesday. Unless you want to break me out?"

Dylan narrows his eyes and peers around, as if contemplating how to do just that.

"You stay here until you're one hundred percent well," I tell her. "We'll be fine."

The arrival of Mrs Hinchcliff's family – two sons, one daughter-in-law and an impish-looking child who is so stick-thin it seems impossible that she could be any relation to the titanic woman – results in curtains being drawn to afford both families some privacy.

"What happened?" I ask, jerking my head toward the closed curtain in the direction of Mrs Hinchcliff's bed.

"Gallstones," she whispers back. "She had her gall bladder remo-" she cuts off abruptly. The kids are all listening. "Anyway, she's fine now," she finishes lamely.

It's only well after the other visitors have left, and Casey and Dylan have upended a bottle of sanitizer all over the floor, that the nurse insists we leave.

"I'll see you tomorrow," I tell Evie, squeezing her hand. I hate leaving her. She looks so small in the stark white bed, I want to pick her up and whisk her home like one of Jesse's knights, raise the drawbridge, draw my sword and challenge anyone who tries to take her from us. Still, she looks better than she has in weeks. The fluid IV must be giving her a lot more than just antibiotics and there's a rosy sheen to her cheeks that's been missing for some time.

I turn back as I reach the door. "I'll miss you," I say softly.

Evie's face splits into a devilish grin. "Speak for yourself. I get time to myself to binge-watch *Game of Thrones* while you and Julia deal with the kids. It's like a mini getaway, and I don't even have to cook."

"Yeah, well you better not get used to it," I tease. Evie gives me a cheerful wave and then I'm out in the hall, the kids trailing behind me.

The kids are more cheerful on the drive home now that they've seen Evie and know she's okay. The chorus of three high-pitched voices all trying to be heard is welcome, but I still heave a sigh of relief when I pull into the driveway. Julia comes out to the car to help bring the children inside.

"I've made something super special for dinner!" she sings, trying to lighten what she has assumed will be a far more sombre mood. The smell hits me the second I walk into the house. I'd recognise the smell anywhere – the smell of perfectly roasted beef. It's one of my favourites. I peek through the glass door of the oven.

"No way! Are those Yorkshire puddings?"

Julia smiles. "They are."

"I haven't had Yorkshire pudding in years!"

"What's a your-sure pudding?" Casey demands.

"A piece of heaven, Case." I lift her up so she can see.

She side-eyes me. "It's a muffin?"

"It's not a muffin. It's so much better than a muffin. You'll see. I haven't had roast beef since my dad's birthday," I tell Julia. "And my mom always overcooks it."

"No pressure," she laughs.

"They're definitely muffins," Casey sniffs, unimpressed.

"How's Evie?" Julia asks, pouring an entire jug filled with stock into the pan of meat juices. The kids love gravy.

"She's fine. She might have to stay an extra night, but she looks better already."

"Oh, good. I'm so pleased to hear it."

Knowing that Evie is doing better, that the kids are in a good mood and the prospect of enjoying my favourite supper has raised my spirits but I must stink like a pole-cat with all the running around I did today.

"Do you mind if I take a quick shower before dinner?" I ask, giving Julia an apologetic look. "Of course." She doesn't turn around, but waves the wooden spoon over her shoulder. "Go ahead."

As I bound up the stairs I hear Casey remarking that Julia's muffins are enormous and the sound of Julia's laughter echoes my own.

We sit at the table. I pour myself a glass of wine and one for Julia.

"Evie always says that it's the least the chef deserves," I tell her when she hesitates. "Although, in Evie's case, it's a bottle, not one glass."

The Yorkshire puddings disappear faster than Jesse's sense of humour on chore day, and, to my surprise, Julia keeps the conversation flowing easily. She really is remarkable with the kids, I find myself thinking. I should know by now that Evie is always right.

In the time that it takes to read the kids their bedtime story, the kitchen is spotless.

"I would've done that," I tell Julia, who is packing away the last of the dishes.

She ignores me. "Are they sleeping?"

"Yeah. Jesse's reading, but he's tired. He'll be out soon."

I refill my glass and look up to find Julia staring at me. Her brown eyes look black in the artificial light, all pupil. It's unnerving. "What?"

"I… I wanted to know if you were okay. You and Ian, well, things got pretty heated today and I know it's none of my business but Kat mentioned how he feels about Evie."

I take a liberal sip of wine. "He's always loved her. He kissed her once – a long time ago, but other than that he's kept his feelings to himself."

"Until now?"

"Until now."

She seems to steel herself. "What happened?"

I press my lips together. I don't know if I should be discussing this with her before I've even mentioned it to Evie, but the truth is, I might not mention it to Evie at all.

"Truthfully?" I ask. Julia nods.

"He doesn't like you being here. He thinks..." I trail off, shaking my head. "He thinks it's inappropriate."

She turns scarlet. I know, without a shadow of a doubt, that she's thinking about that moment last night. I know, because I'm thinking about it too.

"But Evie's the one who hired me. What could he possibly think...?" It's her turn to trail off as I smile at her and the penny drops. "Oh. He thinks that you... that you and I..." She blinks, rapidly, in succession.

"Yeah," I say, taking another slug of wine and feeling the anger mount again. "So there's that."

"I'm glad you told him to fuck off," she announces, so suddenly that I almost spit out the wine.

"It did feel good," I admit. A small frown creases my forehead, one that Julia doesn't miss.

"But?" she asks.

There's no point in denying it. "But a part of me wonders if he might be right."

She recoils as if I've physically slapped her. "You don't think I should be here?"

"I think that my wife is very ill and I'm drinking wine with a beautiful woman who isn't her."

I don't know what makes me say it. I don't know why I'm tempting fate when my whole life is in tatters. All I know is that, in this moment, I feel drawn to Julia in a way I never expected to be and I crave oblivion.

Julia's glass stops midway to her lips. Her eyes are wide, a deer caught in the headlights with nowhere to run, as she processes my words and tries to decipher their meaning. Without warning, she sets her glass down on the counter beside her, her fear giving her feet wings as she slips past me. She almost makes it. Almost. If I had just an ounce more self-control, I would've let her go, but I don't. At the last moment, my hand snakes out to grab hers, halting her in her tracks.

We stand, shoulder to shoulder, Julia's hand trembling in mine. Her head turns back toward mine, questioning, confused, and I know I have about two seconds before she bolts. Right now, there is no Evie, there is no illness - there is only me and Julia. It is heartbreak and bliss, grief and joy, all at once.

It takes only the barest dip of my head to bring my lips down onto hers, another tiny movement to prod them open with the tip of my tongue and bury it inside her warm, sweet mouth. Julia gasps and I fill her mouth with flesh and heat and breath, until I know nothing but the honeyed taste of her and the long-dormant fire that bursts to life inside of me.

When Julia pulls away I don't stop her. The empty space she leaves behind is cold and lifeless, but I don't follow her, even though my body aches to do so. Instead, I clench my fists at my sides, and let the reality of my shame wash over me in waves. The heavy burden of what I've done presses down on my chest until I forget how to breathe and I can't help but think it's the least that I deserve.

CHAPTER 29
Evie

I'M WATCHING THE TV ABOVE MY BED ON SILENT WHEN JULIA pops her head around the ward door. "Hey you!" I glance at my watch. "How did you get in here, it's not visiting hours yet?"

"I snuck in," she admits, handing me a small gift bag. I peek inside. Chocolates and a shiny new paperback book. I recognise the cover immediately. It's *The Book Thief,* but I don't tell her I've already read it, because there are unshed tears shimmering in her kind eyes and her long legs are trembling like a new-born calf's.

"Julia?" I jab at the remote and switch the TV off. "What's wrong?"

Her throat bobs as she tries to swallow, but she licks her lips, summoning her courage. "Evie, I'm so sorry to do this but I can't work for you anymore."

My heart beats faster, speeding up so quickly I feel like a hummingbird has taken flight in my chest. "What are you talking about? Why?"

Her head droops like a wilting sunflower. "Something's come up. I've had another job offer and I can't afford to turn it down."

She's lying. She's lying, and she's so bad at it that I want to laugh, but the situation is anything but funny. "What salary did they offer you?" I ask briskly.

"What?"

"This offer that's too good to refuse. How much money are they offering?"

"Evie, this isn't about..."

"You just said it's an offer you can't refuse. I'll match it."

"I don't expect you to do that. I can't take any more of your money."

"Oh, nonsense. You're worth every penny and you know it."

Her face crumples and it hits me between the eyes. The reason she wants to leave has nothing to do with money, not that I really believed that to begin with. Something's happened. Something serious enough to make her flee.

"I'm not going to change my mind," she whispers, her voice cracking under the strain.

I steel myself to pull the cancer card. I don't want to do it, but there's no way she's leaving now. My family needs her. I need her.

"I'm dying, Julia." Her tears blossom into a fully-fledged sob, but she doesn't contradict me. She's the only one who never has. "I can feel myself slipping away, a little piece of me every day and I don't know how much longer I can hold on."

"Evie, please..."

"No." I take her hands and will her to look at me. "I need you, Julia. My family needs you. Please, I'm begging you, don't abandon us now."

She meets my gaze levelly, not so quick to break. "That's blackmail, you know."

I smile despite myself. It's easy to forget how alike we are in so many ways. "I know. Doesn't make it any less true. You know my kids, Julia. You know what this is going to do to them. I need to know they'll be okay."

"They have Nick," she whispers.

"How do you think Nick's going to deal with it?" I ask. "He's going to fall apart. You know it and I know it. He's using up every single ounce of his herculean strength to get through this, to keep our family together and to be strong for me, strong for the children. He can't sustain that forever."

"He's going to fall apart," she whispers, echoing my words.

"And you aren't."

A watery smile. "How do you know that? I love you too – so much..." Her voice breaks and I pull her toward me, wrapping my arms around her.

"Then stay, please. For me?"

She doesn't give me an answer, other than to tell me she won't accept any more money and, by the time she leaves, I still don't know if I've convinced her. When she's gone I turn the TV back on, trying not to think about what could've happened to make her want to leave. I stare at the screen, unseeing, as tears stream silently down my face.

Nick arrives mid-morning, at formal visiting hours. He's quieter than usual but I don't hold any punches.

"Julia came to see me this morning," I tell him. "She wants to resign."

"What?" he's genuinely oblivious. "She said that?"

"Yes. She said she had another job offer. For more money. I offered to match it."

"You what? Evie, why would you do that?"

"Because we need her, Nick."

"Maybe we don't! I can take care of things at home until you're..."

"Don't!" He jerks back as I fling my hand up, my finger pointing right in his face. I'm grateful that Mrs Hinchcliff was discharged this morning and no one is around to witness me losing control, but I don't think it would have stopped me. "Stop saying things like that, Nick! Stop trying to delude yourself that I'm going to get better, that I'm going to make a full recovery. It's not going to happen. I know it and deep down so do you."

"So, what?" he snaps, sounding disgusted. "Julia is your idea of a replacement?"

"Of course not! I know that nothing will make any of this okay, but right now she's good for our family. For our kids."

Nick draws in a deep breath, his face hollow, haunted. "If she wants to go I think we should let her go."

I smile sadly down at him as he slumps in the plastic visitor's chair. I don't ask the question that burns in my mind because I don't know if I want to know the answer: whether he's really willing to let her go. Forcing down the sour taste in the back of my throat I place my hand over his. "I have a feeling that if she really wants to go she'll be gone already."

CHAPTER 30
Julia

Somehow, I blame the beef. The beef and those blasted Yorkshire puddings. I feel like if I hadn't made that dish, none of this would've happened. It wasn't even my idea – it was Kat who had suggested it. That's the last time I listen to her. I shove my clothes into my suitcase without any consideration, balls of tangled fabric filling it far more quickly than I'm ready to accept.

The perfume Evie gave me is on my dresser but it feels wrong to take it with me. Evie has been nothing short of wonderful to me and I repay her by kissing her husband. I don't deserve any of her kindness.

I slump on the bed in the room I've come to call my own, in the house I've come to call home, while tears splash onto my lap. There isn't time for self-pity. The kids will be coming out of school soon and Nick will no doubt be at the hospital visiting Evie. I need to make a plan for someone to collect them, or, I could pick them up and wait for Nick to get home before I leave. There's a six o'clock bus I could take, if I hurry. I certainly can't take the car. I haven't stooped that low yet.

Around and around, my thoughts crash and collide in my head, a spin-cycle that won't stop. How did I get to this point? How did I allow it? I've ruined everything. I kissed a married man, and worse, if I'm being one hundred percent honest with myself, I would do it again.

I ball my hands into fists and press them against my temples, trying to make sense of the two parts of me that have split down the middle. On one side, there's Evie: Evie, and the children, and this beautiful family that I've come to love as if they were my own. This side claims my morality, my guilt, my pain. And on the other side, there's Nick. Nick, who, despite everything, I'm falling in love with. Evie's side doesn't exclude Nick and Nick's side doesn't exclude the children, and the two halves are so blurred and so entwined that I cannot condone or deny either one, because to do so would be to deny the other.

"Oh God," I sob, reaching blindly for my pillow. I clutch it to my chest, trying to ease the aching in my heart.

"Julia!" I sit bolt upright, my heart hammering as I hear the front door slam. "Julia!" Nick yells again. His footsteps pound up the stairs and I don't have any time to act before he bursts into my room, not bothering to knock. The door slams against the wall and rebounds, almost knocking him senseless, but he stops it with lightning reflexes. I can tell by the expression on his face that he didn't expect me to be here. I must be imagining the flash of relief which crosses his furious face. I brace myself for his rage. Then he catches sight of my own swollen eyes and the tears streaming down my face, and his face crumples.

"Oh fuck, Julia, I'm sorry." He crosses the room in two strides, pulling me up onto my feet and crushing me against his chest. "I'm so, so sorry." His hands stroke my hair, my back, as I've seen him do to console Casey so many times. "I thought you were gone," he mutters into my hair. "This is all my fault."

"No," I sniff, pushing him away. "It's not your fault. I'm sorry I didn't tell you I was going to see Evie but I couldn't face you after what I did."

"After what *you* did?" He steps back and opens his arms, incredulously. "Julia, I kissed *you*. I'm the one who screwed up. I'm the one who..." he gives a bitter bark of laughter. "I'm not worthy of either of you."

"That's not true."

He holds my gaze, levelly, for the longest time. "Will you stay?" he asks. "I swear to you, I won't ever do anything like that again."

"I can't, Nick." I press my lips so tightly together they start to go numb, but fresh tears prick at my eyes anyway because he has this so completely wrong. "You don't understand. I know I should feel nothing but guilt about what happened, but I don't. There's a part of me that wants it to happen again – that wants you."

Nick sucks in a rush of air between clenched teeth and I feel the heat of shame rise to my cheeks.

"How can I stay if I have feelings like this? I'm a terrible person."

"Then we're both terrible people," he croaks. I raise my eyes to his and his face is tortured. "I don't know how this happened," Nick continues. "Never, in eighteen years, have I ever so much as looked at another woman. Never," he iterates, as if I might not believe him. "I love Evie. I love her to the depth and breadth of my soul, and then some. But there's something about you..." He reaches for me, his fingers edging toward my cheek, then remembers himself and his hand falls away. If I close my eyes I could imagine his touch on my skin, but I don't. "I don't want you to go," Nick admits through a ragged exhalation of guilt. "And I hate that I don't want you to go."

We face each other, neither of us budging. My chest rises and falls in time with his – too fast, too laboured. When he finally speaks I feel my resolve slip. "Will you stay?"

CHAPTER 31

Nick

"How was Evie?" Amy asks as I step into the office. It smells of wood varnish and tile cleaner. Amy is obsessive about cleaning. I could probably eat off the floor.

"She's good. Much better. They said they'll probably discharge her tomorrow."

"Oh, that's awesome news! You must be so relieved." A snap of guilt because, right now, Evie isn't the only woman on my mind.

"I am," I force a smile. "Any messages?"

"Just one, for a quote down in Bridgestone. It's a new development. I told them you'd probably only get there tomorrow."

"Thanks, Amy."

"No need to thank me," she teases. "It's what you pay me for."

"True." My eyes fall on the half-full coffee mug on her desk, the one that says *I don't work here*. It used to be Evie's.

For so long it had just been the two of us: Evie and me. We had worked together, lived together, raised our family together. Over the past seven months my life has literally been turned upside down. Steph, Amy, Julia – it's as if the universe is determined to cast Evie into the shadows, as if she's fading away and, in her place, a line of not-Evie's are stampeding through my life, wreaking havoc, making me question everything I've ever known. The floor isn't lava – it's quicksand, impossible to escape and collapsing beneath me.

"Are you okay, Nick?" Amy gives me a strange look and I pull myself together.

"I'm fine. I'll be in my office if you need me."

I closet myself in my office, wondering if I might be having a nervous breakdown. My heart is racing, a thunder in my chest that reverberates through my skull. I try to focus on work and the outstanding quotes I should've sent out this morning, but I can't concentrate. I'm terrified that Julia will leave. I'm even more terrified that she'll stay. And, most of all, I'm horrified that I'm thinking of her at all.

Maybe I should take Evie on a holiday – get us away from all of this and find a way to get back to where we were before... *Before what?* The taunt echoes in my mind. *Before Julia? Before the cancer?* There's no going back, there's only here and now and what we do with it.

Hours must have passed when Amy raps on my door.

"Come in."

I blink in astonishment as Kat pokes her head through the door. The look on her face is one of sympathy. A second later my children erupt into the room and it hits me like a ton of bricks. *Julia is gone.*

I set my face into a smile and listen while Dylan and Casey bombard me with stories of their day. Jesse hangs back, near the door, and Kat watches everything with her hawk-like eyes. When the children finally start to run out of steam, she asks Amy to keep an eye on them and shuts the door.

"I'm guessing you've worked out by now that you no longer have a nanny," she says, draping herself over the chair opposite me. "And I'm guessing, by the look on your face right now, that you might be part of the reason for that."

I close my eyes. "What did she say to you?"

"Nothing. She called and asked me to fetch the kids, said that she's resigned."

"I think she had another job offer..."

"Bull shit."

The weariness has crept into my bones. "What do you want from me, Kat? Do you want me to admit I'm a shitty husband? Fine, I'll admit it! I betrayed my wife and my family. Believe me, you can't think any less of me than I think of myself."

"Did you screw her?"

"What? No!"

She fixes me with that unnerving glare that must have intimidated even the most ruthless of businessmen over the years.

"I kissed her," I admit.

I wait for the hammer to fall but Kat astonishes me by laughing. "So?"

"So? Did you hear what I just said? I cheated on Evie, Kat!"

"No, you kissed a girl that you shouldn't have. A very nice girl, if I'm being honest."

"You can't seriously be okay with this. You're Evie's best friend for shit's sake."

"I'm your friend too."

That takes me aback. "Well, yeah, I mean I know that, but..."

"No, I don't think you do, actually." Kat leans forward to pick up a piece of stray paper on my desk, which she rolls between her fingers until it looks like she's holding a bizarre white cigarillo. She taps it on the wooden desktop. "I've known you for nearly twenty years, Nick. No one knows better than me how much Evie means to you – how you've always put her first. You're a rare breed, hell, half the reason I haven't found a husband yet is because I hold everyone up to the standard you've set, and no one comes close." She sets the paper down, but I'm too stunned to speak. "You're human, Nick. You've had the weight of the world on your shoulders these past few months and you haven't given a second's thought to your own needs. It's admirable, but did you really think you could keep it up forever?"

"Being under pressure is no excuse to cheat on my wife!" I hiss, hating that she's letting me off the hook, hating that I'm soaking up her words like a junkie needing a fix.

"Do you remember that weekend you and Ian went to Vegas?"

The abrupt change in topic throws me. "What's that got to do with it?"

"Evie and I ended up down at *Bar One*, remember? We called you from the payphone because Evie lost her phone?"

I remember it clearly. It was a few months before our wedding.

"She left it on the bar," I say, "and someone took it."

Kat smiles. "She left it in the backseat of a '93 Mustang. We hitched a ride down to the point with a pair of CU alumni. And before you freak out, no, Evie didn't screw anyone. She did, however, spend at least four minutes in a lip-lock with a young man named Peter."

Kat lets that sink in as the world falls away beneath me.

"Why?" I don't know what else to say.

"Because I dared her to," Kat answers simply.

I feel a dark, angry rage rise in my chest. "Why are you telling me this? What the hell are you trying to do to me, Kat?"

"I'm telling you because you think Evie is perfect. You believe it so deeply that you think nothing you do will ever be good enough. Every mistake you make, every action you take that doesn't meet the standard you've set for yourself, you perceive as a failure, because you've never believed you deserve her."

"I don't deserve her," I whisper through parched lips.

"Yes, you do, Nick. I've always known it, Ian's always known it – why do you think he never tried to take her from you? Because he knew he could never compete with you." She answers her own question.

My stomach twists. "I think I'm going to be sick."

"Even Evie knows it, Nick. You've spent your life believing you weren't good enough for her, but the truth is, Evie was always the lucky one."

I can't listen to her anymore. I lurch forward, snatching up the wastepaper basket beneath my desk and throw up.

Kat gets to her feet and moves to the door. She sticks her head through it and speaks to Amy in muted tones. I have no idea what she's saying, but I suspect Amy's taking the kids outside.

When I'm sure I'm not going to be sick again, I sit upright to find Kat back in her chair. "Feel better?" she asks.

"I don't know why you're saying all of this," I croak.

"I'm saying all of this because Evie is going to die."

"Don't..."

Kat ignores me. "And I don't want you to spend what time you have left trying to live up to your ridiculous expectations. It's time to enjoy what you have, without pressure, without second- guessing yourself every single minute of every single day."

"I don't do that."

"Yes, you do."

"I have to tell Evie about Julia."

"No, you don't."

"I can't lie to her, Kat!"

"Do you really think she doesn't know?"

It takes only a second for her words to sink in. *Oh Jesus!* I clap my hand to my mouth, dragging it over my unshaven chin. "I have to explain."

"You're not listening to me. You don't. Evie wouldn't want you to."

"How do you know what Evie wants?"

Her smile is smug. "Because I'm her best friend."

I'm so tired, so very tired and my head is pounding. "What do you expect me to do?" I croak.

"Enjoy your life, Nick." She waves her hand in the air. "Live, laugh, love. Spend time with Evie, make memories and, when the time comes, let her go. Most importantly: forgive yourself."

I nod bleakly. "For what happened with Julia?"

Kat shakes her head. "For not being able to save her."

CHAPTER 32

Evie

IAN ARRIVES ARMED WITH ROSES, MY LEAST FAVOURITE FLOWER, and, even worse, they're red. Still, I smile as I set them down beside Casey's messy bunch. It looks even sadder now that the flowers have wilted, but it's still infinitely more beautiful than Ian's bouquet.

"You didn't have to come," I tell him. "They're letting me go this afternoon. You could've come around to the house."

He averts his eyes and I know immediately that something's happened. "Ian?"

"I don't think I'm welcome at the house right now."

"What happened?" I ask. What happened, not what did you do, which is what I really want to ask.

"Nick and I got into an argument the other day. We haven't really spoken since."

"Nick didn't mention anything to me."

"Yeah, well, it wasn't pretty. I didn't want to bring it up, but since you asked..." He wanted me to ask, I can tell, but I nod politely and repeat the question.

"What happened?"

"He kicked me out of the house."

"Nick wouldn't do that."

He sits down on the edge of the bed. "Evie, how well do you know this nanny of yours?"

"Julia? As well as you can know someone who spends every minute of every day in your house. Why?"

"It's just – look, I don't want to start anything here, but I think something might be going on between them."

"Between who?" I know exactly who he's talking about, but if he thinks he's going to disrespect my husband like this, I'm damned well not going to make it easy for him.

"Nick and Julia."

"Why would you say that?" Calm, curious, no hint of the anger roiling inside me.

"I don't know, it's just a feeling. She shouldn't be living there, Evie. And Nick shouldn't have allowed it."

"Julia has been an amazing help to me, Ian. She's my friend."

"She's not your friend."

"What did you do?" I ask. "Why did Nick kick you out?"

"I told him exactly what I'm telling you. That I think he's developing feelings for Julia and that it's not right that she's staying in your house while you're... while you're here."

"Let me get this straight," I say, smoothing the blanket over my legs. "You think that something is going on between Nick and Julia, and that she shouldn't be there when I'm not?"

"Well, I don't think she should be there at all, but certainly not alone with Nick."

"And if something was going on between them, how do you think me being there would make any difference?"

He gapes at me, lost for words.

"If Nick and Julia are set to have an affair I'm pretty sure they'd make it happen whether I'm around or not. I'm not omniscient, Ian, I can't be everywhere at once."

"You don't seriously mean that? You can't be okay with this?"

"Okay with what?" I ask innocently.

"With your husband lusting after another woman!"

"I don't believe he is. I'm just pointing out the flaw in your logic. The thing is, Ian, I trust Nick. And if he kicked you out of our house then he must have had a damned good reason."

Ian recoils but recovers quickly. "Evie, you're sick. And what is Nick doing? Nothing! He's not making the tough calls, he's not making *any* calls. Instead, he's letting himself become distracted by a newer, shinier model. If it was me, I would've turned this country upside down to get you better. There are specialists, new treatments..."

"Stop!" I yell. "Just shut up and listen, for once in your life! Nick isn't making the calls because they're not his to make! This is my life, my body, my decision! Do you really think Nick wouldn't have dragged me to every oncology specialist across the country if he thought for one second I would go? Do you think he hasn't begged, sobbed and screamed at me for exactly that reason? Because he has. He has, Ian, and he only stopped when he realised that all it was doing was killing me faster."

Ian's face is a mask of pain, but I don't care.

"You've never understood us," I continue more calmly, "because you've never known what we have. You think that Nick's screwing up, but he lets me be me. He lets *me* decide." My voice breaks but I push forward. "He loves me that much."

"I can't listen to this." Ian gets to his feet, but I'm not finished, and I hurl the words at his back.

"And the fact that you have the nerve to come over here and try to turn me against him after everything *you've done*, is disgusting."

He whips around to face me. "After everything *I've* done?"

"Do you think Nick doesn't know how you feel about me?" It's a sucker-punch, right to his gut. It's also the first time I've ever brought it up and Ian is gobsmacked. "He *knows*, Ian. He's always known. And yet, he's never said anything, never done anything to make you feel uncomfortable. Because he's a better man. A better man than you could ever be."

Ian's jaw clenches, his eyes narrow and I can see he's trying to salvage a scrap of self-respect. "I don't want to fight with you. We're both overwhelmed right now. We should talk later."

"By all means," I gesture at the hall, "there's the door. And Ian," I add, as he walks toward it. He turns back, his expression a blend of righteous indignation, shame, and hope. "Don't ever badmouth my husband again or Nick kicking you out will be the least of your worries."

As if by speaking his name I had summoned him, Nick walks through the door, right into Ian. Their eyes meet. I can't see the expression on Ian's face, but Nick's is smug satisfaction, with a hint of amusement.

"What she said," he tells Ian, before Ian stalks out.

Nick's eyes find mine, warm, loving, vindicated. "Wow," he says, stepping closer to the bed.

"It had to be done," I say simply. "How long were you listening?"

"I followed him down the hall," he grins. "I wanted to witness his big reveal." He sits, taking my hands. "About what he said – about me and Julia... there's something you need to know."

I lift my finger to his lips. "Do you love me?"

He nods, the truth molten in his eyes.

"Then get me out of here."

Ten minutes later, with all my discharge paperwork taken care of, we walk, hand in hand, out of my ward. I spot Doctor Moxley coming down the hall and I pick up the pace, hoping he won't see us before we round the corner. Only when we're safely out of sight do I release the breath I've been holding. Nick is still smiling. There's something different about him, something I can't put my finger on, but I like it. He's standing taller, his shoulders relaxed, as if a weight's been lifted from his shoulders, as if he's discovered a new strength.

"Well, this is a disaster," I say, as we round another corner and an open empty hallway beckons, nothing but gleaming tiles stretching on forever.

"What is?" he asks, all curiosity and not concern. My heart does a giddy backflip.

"What would we do if the floor was lava?" I tease, squeezing his hand. I give a startled cry of delight as, without any warning, Nick scoops me up into his arms and continues onward, one arm beneath my knees, the other supporting my back. I feel safe, and loved, and strangely, a little bit shy as he carries me determinedly all the way to the car.

When we get home the children are still at school. I make my way upstairs while Nick brings in my bags. Julia's room is empty. Not a trace of her remains, save for the bottle of perfume on the dresser. I reach for it and bring it to my nose. The citrus and freesia lingers in the room, but other than that there is no sign she was ever here. I hear Nick moving around in the kitchen downstairs and I quietly exit the room, closing the door behind me.

We don't mention Julia. From what I gather from Dylan, Nick has told the children that she's gone away for a while, but he didn't say when she would be back. Dylan seems to think she's gone on vacation. Casey insists she can't perfect her princess drawing without her and leaves her book open on the page to pick up when Julia returns. Jesse says nothing, but his glittering eyes follow us around the house as if he's searching for answers. The house is strangely silent, as if a piece of us is missing, but the change in Nick fills the void. We get through the first day, and the day after that. Kat is helping more with fetching and carrying the kids, as, to my utmost surprise, is Mary-Anne. Mary-Anne still annoys me, but we've come to a mutual truce and she doesn't hang around, for which I'm grateful. As the days go by, Nick and I discover a new-found peace which is built on truth and acceptance and taking each moment as it comes.

CHAPTER 33
Nick

I NEVER THOUGHT I'D SEE THE DAY THAT KAT INTRODUCED A man as her boyfriend, or that she'd gaze up at him with such adoration. It's so out of character that I'd almost feel uncomfortable if she wasn't so ridiculously happy. It's a balmy Saturday afternoon and the barbecue is hissing merrily, a dozen burgers on the go. The kids are splashing around in the pool, Casey's luminous pink water-wings providing a splash of colour in the clear blue. Evie is in a one-piece costume, soaking up the last of the day's sun on her favourite lounger, the one with the cup holder in the side. Kat is perched on the single chair beside her, a ridiculously floppy hat protecting her face from the effects of a gentle sun.

Evie's eyes are closed and I don't know whether she's simply content, or if the dull drone of Kat's endless monologue has put her to sleep.

"So," I ask Jack, the "boyfriend" who is helping me at the barbecue, "how did you and Kat meet?"

I expect him to say through work. Kat meets everyone through work, not that anyone has lasted beyond the first date – the second, if they happened to be spectacular in the sack.

To my surprise, Jack tells me they met at a singles club. I choke on my beer and he laughs.

"Believe me, no one was more surprised than I was. I've heard so many horror stories about those sorts of evenings."

"It's not that," I say, giving Kat a sideways glance. She can't hear us, but, as if she knows we're talking about her, her sun-shaded face turns toward us. I angle away so she can't read my lips. "I just never thought Kat was the type to go to things like that. She's always working and... well, no offence, but she's never seemed that interested in a relationship."

"Really?" his blond head rises. "That's weird."

"Weird how?"

"She seems ready to me. In fact, I was the one who asked if it might not be too early to meet her friends. She called me right out, asked me if this was just a fling or whether I saw something serious between us."

"Wow."

"Yeah," he laughs again. "I was a bit taken aback, but it made sense, what she said. That life is short and that she didn't want to waste any more time with someone who didn't want anything more than sex."

Life is short. I turn back to where Kat is now refilling Evie's drink. Unnoticed by Evie, she swivels her chair so that it shields most of Evie's bald scalp from the sun. I've done a lot of thinking since Kat came to see me that day in my office almost a month ago. I've come to realise that Kat is a true friend to both Evie and I, and that Ian was neither. I also took heed of her words, letting them fill me with faith and forgiveness. I had decided that day that I would accept what was happening and that none of it was my fault. All that was left to do was enjoy what time I have left with Evie, and to make the most of every precious second. It was easier than I thought it would be and, for the first time in a long time, I feel content.

Sensing the absence of sun, Evie opens one sleepy eye to glare at Kat, but the returning grin is unapologetic. So much love, so much consideration, all cleverly disguised by sarcasm and trickery. All along, Kat was the only one who knew what Evie really needed. She alone understood, and, in her own way, she made it happen. *How did I never notice it before?*

"Kat is a remarkable woman," I tell Jack, as I flip the burgers. "You better hold on to her."

"I intend to," he replies evenly, and I can't help but smile at the territorial tone in his voice.

We eat on the patio, the warm breeze lifting the edge of the tablecloth lazily.

"Can we swim again?" Jesse asks through his last mouthful of food.

"No, it's getting cold," I tell him. "Why don't you guys go and play upstairs for a bit and leave the adults to talk?"

"Can we play X-box?" Jesse asks, sensing weakness. I look to Evie and she nods.

"Okay, but not for too long."

Immediately a mad scramble commences as they race upstairs, no doubt to secure the first turn.

Evie sighs, leaning back in her chair. Her appetite is declining, but she managed to eat half a burger and a few slices of salted tomato, one of her favourites. Doctor Moxley isn't concerned, she told me after her visit last week, so I shove down the lump in my throat and stay quiet.

"We should get a dog," she says, eying her plate. "I can't stand to waste so much food."

"We already have a cat," I point out, taking her plate and stacking it on top of mine.

"We'll do those," Kat says smoothly, giving Jack a pointed look that has him on his feet and gathering up the dishes. Evie giggles as they disappear into the cool depths of the house.

"God help him," she says.

"He seems to really like her."

"She's wild about him, too." She meets my eyes and I know what she's saying.

"I love you," I tell her, as easily as breathing.

"I love you too."

Kat's face appears at the door. "Um, Nick? Your dad is here."

"My dad?"

"Yes. He looks... well, he doesn't look himself."

I'm on my feet and walking inside before she's even finished speaking. My dad stands in the front hall, shifting his weight from one foot to the other and examining the chandelier as if it's the most fascinating thing he's ever seen.

"Dad?"

He tears his eyes away from the lighting to look at me. "Nick. I'm sorry, I should have called. I didn't realise you had guests."

Evie appears beside me.

"That's okay, come on in." I catch Evie's look as we turn around and I can tell she's thinking the same thing I am. My father *never* drops in unannounced. In fact, he never drops in period. He's always working and we see him on my mother's terms.

Kat and Jack are still busy in the kitchen so we have the patio to ourselves.

"Where are the kids?" Dad asks as he settles into Kat's empty seat.

"Upstairs in the playroom," Evie answers. "They've just gone up but I can call them if you'd like to say hello?"

"Not just yet."

The silence that follows has me reaching for my beer, but Evie fixes my dad with a look I know well. "David, is something wrong?"

To my horror, my dad's face crumples like a piece of ancient paper. Evie reaches forward automatically as his shoulders heave, knocking over her glass of water. She ignores it, stumbling to her feet and curling herself around him. It looks awkward, but Evie doesn't move, and I'm frozen in place as a myriad of awful thoughts run through my head. *What the hell could've happened?*

"Is it Mary-Anne?" Evie asks.

The renewed heaving answers that question.

"Is Mom okay?" I ask. My chest has tightened and I almost don't want to know the answer.

"Your mother is fine." The words are barely audible, but enough.

"Does anyone want any...?" Kat is back. She takes one look at my dad, swivels on her heel and disappears. A moment later she reappears with a large scotch which she deposits in my hand. She gives a head-jerk toward my father and then vanishes once more.

"Here," I say, setting the tumbler on the table before him.

My dad finally raises his head, wiping at his wet eyes and promptly downs the glass. My eyes widen.

"Would you like another?" I ask, helplessly. He nods.

By the time I return with the drink Evie is back in her chair, her hand over his, and my dad seems to have recovered enough to speak.

"I'm sorry to burden you with this," he stammers. His voice is hoarse.

"Don't be ridiculous," Evie tuts, "we're family. Now, tell us what happened."

"Mary-Anne..." he curls his hand around the tumbler and stares into space. "Mary-Anne is leaving me."

"What?" I exclaim. Evie gives me a stern look.

"What do you mean she's leaving you?" she asks kindly. "Did you two have a fight?"

Dad shakes his head. "No, not at all. This is my fault. I've..." he trails off, his familiar eyes finding my own. Filled with shame... his eyes are filled with shame. "I've been having an affair, son."

The thought of my father having an affair is so unbelievable that I can't speak, but, to our collective shock, Evie starts to laugh.

It begins as a snort-like giggle that she tries to disguise, but soon her shoulders are shaking and water has pooled in her eyes from the strain of trying to appear sombre.

"Evie!" I'm horrified. I know she doesn't particularly like my parents, but to laugh, it's just too much.

"I'm sorry," she snuffles beneath the hand glued to her mouth. "It's just..." she looks at my dad and squeezes his hand with her own, the one that she hasn't removed since she sat down. "It's about time."

I look between the two of them, watching intently as my dad's lips curve slowly upward, at the way he's *looking* at her and it dawns on me that I'm the outsider here. That there's something far deeper at play, a secret that I suspect I'm the last to know. His words echo in my head. I'm having an affair, *son*. He wasn't telling us. He was telling me.

It takes a lifetime for me to find my voice. When I do, I turn on my wife. "You *knew*?"

Evie gives a guilty start. "I'm sorry, Nick," she begins to apologise, her words tumbling out over one another, "I wanted to tell you but it wasn't my place, and your dad – he was so desperate not to disappoint you..."

"To disappoint me?" I'm reeling, my brain like a tortoise wading through mud as I try to process this information overload. "Don't you mean Mom?"

My dad sits up straighter, his hand sliding out from beneath Evie's as if he needs to prove to himself that he can do this alone. "Nick, your mother and I... well, we haven't been happy for a very long time. She's a great woman and I will always love her, but we haven't been in love since... since..." he searches for the right words and draws an entirely new conclusion. "Well, I'm not sure we ever were truly in love."

"You've been married for a shit long time for two people who were never in love," I point out. I can feel my anger rising, radiating off me in waves. "And there's the fact that this opinion is one-sided. You can't possibly expect me to believe that Mom feels the same way?"

"She does," Evie murmurs softly and my eyes slice to her. "You've seen it, Nick. Your mother isn't a woman in love. She never has been. She's just too God-damned stubborn to do anything about it because she wouldn't want to lose face."

"You don't like her," I remind Evie, trying not to sound too judgemental. I don't want to lose this precious and fragile new closeness between us, but I also can't allow her to speak on behalf of my mother. "And even if it's true, Dad, that's no excuse for having an affair."

My father doesn't argue. "I know that. Evie told me to end things with Mary-Anne months ago, when I met Barbara..."

"Oh, she has a name, does she?"

"Nick, stop it," Evie snaps at my scornful tone.

"How could you condone this, Evie?"

"I didn't condone it," she says gently, with only the slightest tilt of her chin, "but I understood why and how it happened. Tell him," she adds, laying a small hand on my father's sleeve. "Tell him," she repeats when he shakes his head, no.

"Your parents haven't had sex in over eight years," Evie announces.

Oh hell no!

"Nick doesn't want to hear it, Evie," my dad mumbles, his face glowing.

"Tough. Eight years, Nick," she continues, unrepentant.

"Yeah, well... they're old."

Their dual snorts make me cringe.

"I'm old, not dead, son," Dad says, while Evie nods sagely beside him.

"I don't want to hear this," I groan, dropping my head into my hands. Neither of them speaks. "Where is Mom now?" I ask, when I finally raise my head.

"She's gone to the club," my dad replies. "They needed help with tallying the proceeds of last night's bingo evening."

"She's... gone... to... the... country... club?" I ask, each word a statement. "To count money?"

My father shrugs. "You know your mother."

"Apparently not as well as I thought."

Evie is smug but sympathetic. "She doesn't love him, Nick. She never has. This is a good thing – now they both have the chance to be happy."

"How do you even know about this?"

"That's my fault," my dad intervenes quickly. "Evie was... um... she..." he seems to have second thoughts about whatever it is he was going to say so Evie fills in the blanks.

"I went over there a few months ago to spray more glyphosate on your mother's petunias," she admits with a flash of contrition. *No wonder those petunias never grow.* "I saw your dad's car in the drive, which was odd because it was the middle of the morning, so I went in through the back door and..." she shifts a little in her seat and my dad's face blazes crimson. "Anyway," Evie waves her hand and, most likely, the mental image, away. "It all came out."

"Evie didn't judge me," Dad tells me proudly, as if this proof of just how wonderful my wife is shouldn't go unnoticed, "but she did tell me to make a decision one way or another. To end things with Barbara, or ask your mother for a divorce."

Evie gives me a look that's clearly supposed to say I told you so, but I'm already speaking. "But you didn't do either of those things, did you?"

"No," he admits. "I didn't. Not then."

I take a giant swig of my beer. "How did Mom find out?"

"Barbara told her."

"*Barbara?*"

"The woman your dad's been seeing," Evie explains quickly.

"I know who she is," I cannot believe I'm having this conversation, "what I want to know is why she's the one who dropped the bomb on my mother."

"She didn't do it to be cruel," my dad says. "Just the opposite, in fact. Barbara knows how difficult it's been for me to tell your mother the truth. She's a good woman, Nick, and she didn't mean for any of this to happen. Neither of us did. Anyway," he hastens to add when I fix him with a cold look, "I've been growing more and more desperate to have it all out, but your mother – well, you know she's not the easiest person to talk to. When Barbara realised my nerve had failed me yet again, she took matters into her own hands and she contacted your mom."

"How convenient for her. No, I'm sorry Dad," I hold up my hand as he opens his mouth, no doubt to defend her, "but you expect me to believe that Barbara told Mom to help you, when it conveniently gets her exactly what she wants? Leaving you free to continue your relationship with her, unencumbered? I'm not buying it."

"Barbara left me."

Evie recovers first. "Oh, David, I'm so sorry!"

"She told your mother about the affair after she'd broken things off with me," my father says. "And I'm ashamed to admit it, but I'm glad that she did."

"How did Mary-Anne take it?" Evie asks.

My father laughs, a horrible, sad sound. "She's worried about what the bridge ladies will think, but she wants me out of the house."

"Do you think she'll give you a divorce?" Not 'do you think she'll divorce you', or 'can you work it out'. Again, I get the eerie sense that Evie knows something I couldn't possibly understand.

His face crumples again. "Oh God, Evie, I hope so."

CHAPTER 34
Evie

"You should've told me." Nick is more disappointed than angry, which makes me feel worse. We're finally alone. Kat and Jack left discreetly during our conversation with David, and David himself left a few minutes ago. I'd invited him to stay the night in Julia's old room, but he'd declined. He's staying with one of his business partners whose wife is abroad visiting their daughter.

I give Nick an apologetic look. "I know. I'm sorry, but I didn't feel it was my secret to tell."

"Have you met her?"

"Not officially," I say, recalling the sight of Barbara's pink, wobbling backside disappearing down the hall the day I caught them *in flagrante*. I would never tell Nick they were on Mary-Anne's Persian carpet. He'd never let the kids play on it again. "But I hope to."

"How can you say that?"

"Because it's the truth. I know this is a lot to take in, but deep down you know this is the best thing for all of them. Your mother included."

He knows I'm right. His face tells me so, but he's not ready to admit it yet, so, instead, he changes the subject. "Did you really poison her petunias?"

I nod, sheepishly.

"She's been on the phone to every botany specialist in the state about those fucking flowers."

"I know."

"Do you feel even a little bit guilty?"

"Not really."

His eyes are sparkling now. "You're worse than the kids."

'She started it."

"Because she didn't like your T-shirt?" he's teasing me now.

"Please don't be too harsh on him." As much as I want to drop the subject I feel the urge to protect David. I need to know that he and Nick will be okay. "He never wanted to hurt her."

"I believe that," he sighs. "And I know my mom hasn't made his life easy." He ponders this for a minute. "Do you think Barbara will give him another chance?"

"I hope so." I draw in a deep breath and add, "He loves her."

"My mother isn't equipped to cope on her own."

"Your mother will be *fine*. We'll help her through this, just as we'll help David. We're family, and that's what family does."

"Will you stop poisoning her plants?"

"I'll do one better. I'll buy her some new ones."

It turns out I was right. The following morning we pay Mary-Anne a visit. Nick is all smiles and gentle coaxing, pussy-footing around her as though she might shatter into a million pieces.

"I take it you've spoken to your father," she snaps, after about five minutes of tolerating it.

"We have," I say. "And we wanted to know if there's anything we can do."

"Actually, there is," Mary-Anne sniffs primly. "Firstly, Nick, you can stop walking on eggshells. I'm a grown woman, I can deal with whatever life throws my way. And second, you can take those revolting plants with you when you leave." She eyes the peace offering Nick insisted I buy her with disdain. "Petunias are far too much work. The bloody things just don't grow and, if I'm going to be spending most of my time at the club, I want a low maintenance garden."

Nick is struck utterly dumb. "Close your mouth," Mary-Anne snaps. He does and she continues more gently. "I know this might be hard for you to understand, sweetheart, but sometimes people grow apart. I know divorce sounds scary, but it's not as if you're losing either of us. Think of it as a fresh new start." She's addressing him as one would speak to a child and I stuff my scarf into my mouth to keep from giggling. "Your father and I will always care for one another, but this is for the best." She pats his knee and misses the fact that his mouth is agape once more. She turns to look at me and I mould my face into a suitably attentive expression. Mary-Anne rolls her eyes – *rolls her eyes* – and turns back to Nick, saying, with the utmost sincerity, "After all, not every couple is fortunate enough to have what you and Evie do."

I don't have time to react before she's on her feet. "Now, if you two will excuse me, I'd like to spend some time with my grandchildren. Which reminds me, Evie, dear, Grace Fawcett sent me an article the other day about the dangers of children spending too much time on these iPads and things. They're calling it digital heroin; would you believe it! You will keep an eye on Jesse, won't you?" And with that, she walks away, her crisp trouser suit barely shifting, without a thought for the fact that she's the one who bought him the iPad in the first place.

I slide across the sofa and close Nick's mouth, gently pressing up against his jaw with the tip of my finger.

"What just happened?" he asks.

"It was her way of letting us know she's okay."

"She can't. I can't..."

"Nick?"

"Hmmm?"

"It's really none of our business."

Together, we stand and walk outside, arm in arm, to join Mary-Anne and the kids in a friendly game of football. "I can't believe she paid you a compliment," Nick whispers, just before we come within earshot of the others.

"Don't worry," I whisper back, "I won't let it go to my head."

I fall asleep in the car on the drive home. I only played one game before my strength gave out, but I still made sure we won, carrying Casey, who clutched the ball to her chest, until we had passed the goal-posts. Nick had given us the goal and I'd even high-fived Mary-Anne, although, in truth, all she did was stand around in that white trouser suit and avoid any contact with the ball. After I had pulled out, she'd made slightly more effort, but I'd still keeled over laughing when the ball, kicked by an avenging Jesse, had hit her in the gut and knocked all the wind out of her. After that we were both benched, leaving Casey to valiantly face the heavily-manned field on her own. Being Casey, and much adored by her bigger brothers, she still won by two goals.

"We're home," Nick coos in my ear, rousing me from my dream memory. I smile and open my eyes to find the car empty, the kids already inside.

"Do you need any help?" Nick asks as I get out. I shake my head, stretch my arms and walk toward the house. The ache in my bones is getting harder to ignore. The pain subsided substantially after my hospital visit, but it's been almost a month and I should've known it wouldn't last.

"Come here, you three," I call the kids as I go upstairs. In my room, I beckon them onto my bed, filthy feet and all, and feel the warmth of them sinking into my bones as we huddle together. Jesse's back is pressed up against my stomach, my arms holding him tightly against me, while Dylan and Casey peer over my back and my butt respectively. "What was your favourite part of today?" I mumble sleepily.

Dylan liked the soccer, Casey the chocolate-chip ice-cream cones May-Anne had made, which we enjoyed sitting on the grass while the sun beat down and melted it faster than we could eat. "And you, Jesse?" I ask into the thatch of his dark hair. I breathe in the scent of grass and apple shampoo and the faint tang of stinky boy simmering beneath.

"I don't know," he mumbles into my arm.

"I bet you liked it best when grandma told you that you needed a haircut." He shifts in my arms and I lean closer to his ear. "Oh, no wait. Was it when she told you to stay off your iPad because it'll kill your brain cells?"

There's a breath, a pause, and then: "When is Julia coming back?"

"I'm not sure, baby."

"Could we go and visit her?" Jesse obviously didn't buy the vacation story.

"We'll see," I reply, not able to commit. To my surprise, he lets the matter rest.

I must have dozed off, because when I wake, the children are all asleep, their limbs entwined in mine. I manoeuvre myself through the labyrinth as carefully as I can before I wander downstairs. I find Nick on the lounger outside, a whiskey in hand, staring up at a blanket of stars. He is so deep in thought he doesn't hear me until I'm right beside him.

"I thought you were sleeping."

"I was. I'm not anymore."

"Come here." He sets the glass down on the flagstone paving and opens his arms. I curl into the space beside him. I've lost so much weight I fit easily. With my head resting on Nick's shoulder and his arm draped lazily around me, we watch the night sky.

"If you had one wish, what would it be?" I ask him. Nick cuts me a wry look and I shake my head. "Okay, that was a stupid question. What else?"

His chest rises and falls beneath my ear as he considers the question.

"I'd like to go back to Harbour Bay and find that stone," he says eventually.

Perfect answer. "That would be something," I murmur, my voice thick with emotion.

"What about you, what would you wish for?"

"So many things. I want Jesse to let go of this burden he's carrying, for him to be a kid again and to stop worrying about me, for Casey to stop sucking her thumb, for Dylan to make pitcher for once and not be the only kid left on the bench. For you..." I trail off, knowing I've ventured into dangerous territory.

"For me to what?" Nick prompts. "What do you wish for me, Evie?"

"So many things," I repeat softly.

He doesn't push it. "That's a lot of wishes. You're only supposed to get one, remember?"

I focus on one star above me, a small, insignificant little star that is barely noticeable amongst the others. *You matter*, I want to tell it. *I pick you.* I think of the red bag in my vanity and how desperately I need it, but I don't move. Instead, I focus on my breathing, on the fabric softener scent that still lingers on Nick's shirt, despite the sweat. On that little star, still burning, still twinkling even though it hasn't a hope of outshining the others.

"A puppy," I say, only half-joking. "If I had one wish right now, it would be that we had a puppy."

CHAPTER 35
Julia

It's been over a month since I left, but I cannot get the Danvers out of my head. It's not just Nick, although he is the one who haunts my dreams, dreams that I wake from shame-faced, and yet I still cannot suppress that moment of despair when I realise it was only that: a dream. I miss Evie, too. I miss her quick wit and easy smile – the way she always knows exactly what to say. At least ten times a day I find myself reaching for my phone to call her, but I stop myself, because the love I feel for her is overshadowed by the guilt at my feelings for her husband. I miss the children so badly it hurts. Somehow, in the few short months I had with them, they wormed their way into my heart and I'm only now starting to realise that no amount of time will diminish the place they hold.

I take my frustrations out on the potatoes I'm mashing, pounding so hard into the pot that my wrists ache.

"You're going to break that," my dad remarks wryly from his spot at the kitchen table. I glance up to find him peering at me over his newspaper.

"I don't want any lumps," I say.

He lets it go. "How was work?"

I drop the masher into the pot. "It was fine."

It wasn't fine. I'd managed to get a job downtown serving drinks at a pub which is over ten miles from the house. The bus fare alone is eating into most of my wage. I wouldn't mind so much if this particular establishment didn't cater to a very select group of fifty-somethings who are mostly single, or keep their wedding rings stashed in their pockets and find it highly amusing to try to charm the pants off the female staff.

Who are you to judge? my subconscious murmurs. Or is it simply that these married men are not the *right* married man?

I set the mashed potatoes down on the table next to the fried chicken and fall into my chair.

"How was *your* day?" I ask, desperate for a distraction. My dad folds the paper and sets about filling his plate.

"It was good, actually. Archer's Bow broke the yard record and Graham's Pride is competing in his first graded race next weekend. I told Kat those horses weren't getting enough fibre."

I can't help but smile at how assertive he's become. His confidence trickled back, slowly at first, but then in leaps and bounds, until somehow, the man sitting across from me suddenly became the father I grew up with. His grey pallor is long gone, replaced by a deep, even tan from hours spent outside, and his eyes have regained some of the sparkle he lost after my mother died.

"How is Kat?" I ask, masochistically. Kat is close to Evie and Nick, and even the mention of her name is like a punch to my gut.

"She's seeing someone," my dad mumbles through a mouthful of chicken. "Seems like a nice young chap, and she certainly seems happy."

I pick at my peas. "What's his name?"

"Jack. Nice strong name, Jack." He pauses, his fork halfway to his mouth. "Have you spoken to Nick or Evie at all?"

"No."

The fork clatters against his plate. "Juju, please. Can't you just tell me what happened?"

"Nothing happened Dad. I told you, it wasn't working out. I needed to find something else."

"Working in that pub?" he raises his brow.

"It's only temporary."

"Look there's obviously more to it, but I'm not going to press you. If you don't want to tell me, I'm sure you have good reason, but right now you're in a slump. You miss them. Even if you're not working there anymore, you can still visit. You were friends, weren't you?"

"Yes." My voice has shrunk.

"Then go and see them. They're good people, they're good for you. You shouldn't cut ties with them because you don't work there anymore."

"Yeah," I say, only to get him to drop it, "maybe I'll pop around this weekend."

"That's a good idea. It beats hanging around here day in and day out. You should take your costume if the weather's nice. And please quit that awful job. I'm earning again, I can take care of you. You could even resume day classes."

He so desperately wants to fix things and I hate that I'm falling apart now, just when he's getting back on his feet. I pull myself together and force a smile. "I missed registration, but I'm definitely going to start up next semester. And I won't quit yet, but I'll cut down my shifts so I can look for something else."

"That's my girl," he smiles. "Now eat up, will you? You're going to fall through your own backside if you don't put some meat back on those bones."

The next day I tell Georgie, the owner of the pub and its most frequent customer that I need to cut down my shifts.

"But I've already fixed the roster for the whole of next month," she whines.

"I know, and I'll work all of those shifts, but on the next rotation could you cut me down to three shifts a week?"

"That's not fair on the other girls," she points out.

"I'll speak to them, see if anyone wants to pick up a few extra shifts."

"If you don't find anyone, I'm going to have to look for someone to replace you, Julia. You're a great worker, but the job is five days a week."

I bite my tongue to keep from screaming. "I know. I'll... let me see what I can do."

She nods curtly and wanders off to socialise with a few of the regular customers. A new table has just come in and I force a smile.

"Hi!" I say brightly, "what can I get for you?"

"Julia?" The sound of my name draws my attention to the man sitting at the far end of the table.

"Ian! Hey! What are you doing here?" I splutter. *Why, oh why did they sit in my section?* I sneak a glance over to where Lydia, the other waitress on duty, is picking her nails, her lone table's drinks having just been refilled.

"Our office is just a few blocks from here," Ian replies, indicating the three men sitting with him. "We thought we'd grab a quick lunch." His eyes narrow. "Do you work here now?"

I nod. "Yeah, for a few weeks now."

"You're not working for Nick and Evie anymore?" There's genuine confusion on his face.

"No." Something very strange is going on. "Didn't they tell you?"

"I... we..." he stops, remembering he has company and then he shakes his head. "No, they didn't."

I don't frown. I don't react at all, but I know that something must have happened. I secretly hope that Nick punched him in the face. Whatever it was, the fact that Ian hasn't seen Nick or Evie sets me at ease. He wasn't good for either of them.

"Okay, well, what can I get you?" I ask, and this time my smile is genuine. "I can recommend the rump."

CHAPTER 36
Evie

THE AGONY ROILS AROUND IN MY BONES AS IF SEARCHING FOR A place it's never visited before. I throw back two pain pills even though it's only been an hour since the cannabis, and wait, every second stretching into an hour of torture.

"Breathe," Kat says again, and I slowly draw the air in through my nose and let it escape through my mouth. "Again."

I do as I'm told, focusing only on my breathing, until, finally, mercifully, the pain begins to ease. When I sit up, I'm white and shaking.

"Better?" Kat asks. I nod, waving away the glass of water she's holding out and wrapping my arms around myself. "They're getting worse."

"No need to state the obvious," I tease, then grimace as a vengeful spasm shoots through me.

"You should go to the hospital." It's the first time she's ever encouraged it, and it terrifies me.

"No, I'm fine. The pills are kicking in, although you might want to order take-out for the kids – I'll be high as a kite in no time." I've been increasing my cannabis dosage faster than my body can build up a tolerance.

Kat snatches up her phone as I lie back on the sofa. Her voice sounds disconnected as if she's speaking underwater. "Jack, I need you to pick up some food on your way over to Evie's. No, not pizza, something healthy." A pause. "Yeah, that'll do, thanks babe." She ends the call. "He's going to stop and get something. He said he'll cook."

"He doesn't have to do that."

She rolls her eyes. "Right. What else do you need?"

"Nothing." She makes to stand, but I seize her hand. "Where are you going?"

Kat's eyes widen as she recognises the expression on my face for what it truly is. Fear.

"I'm just going to get you a blanket, Evie." Her voice is soft, fragile. "I won't leave you."

I squeeze my eyes shut against the tears. "Thank you."

Five minutes, I tell myself sternly. *You have five minutes to feel sorry for yourself and then you pull yourself together.*

The pain on its own wouldn't be so bad. It's what it represents that tears me up inside. The pain I can live with, it's the fear that's begun to claw at my chest, growing, ever-growing, that is sending me into a tail-spin.

I don't get five minutes. It takes only three for Nick to walk into the house carrying a squirming bundle of creamy silken fur that drives the fear away.

"Oh!" I shriek as he deposits a baby Labrador on my lap. "Nick! You didn't!"

"You see," he smiles, as the puppy jumps up to lick my face, "wishes can come true."

"Where did you get him?"

"Her," he corrects. "She's a girl."

"Oh God," Kat drawls, coming to a standstill a safe distance away.

"Isn't she cute?" I laugh, scratching the puppy's ears.

"She's probably riddled with fleas."

"Oh, shut it." I tease, so fixated on the wriggling ball of fur that I miss the look between Kat and Nick. "She's perfect."

"What do you want to call her?" Nick asks, coming to sit beside me and petting her sweet head.

"I'll let the kids decide."

"Speaking of which, where are our children?"

"Emily took them to the park," Kat interjects smoothly.

"Emily?"

"My assistant. Don't worry, she's perfectly capable."

A furrow appears in Nick's brow. He looks from Kat to me and I try desperately to look fine.

"What happened?" There's no ignoring that tone.

"I had a bit of a bad spell," I admit while Kat glides out of the room. "Coward!" I yell after her, hoping to get a smile out of Nick, but he isn't in the mood for jokes. I slump back, keeping one hand on the puppy. "Kat came over and she brought Emily to take the kids off my hands for a while."

He keeps his face impassive, but the tendons in his clenched fists are strained, bulging.

"How bad?" his eyes cut to the table, to the red bag and the blister pack of pain pills.

"Bad," I admit.

His arms are around me, holding me, warming me, loving me, and the fear that only just surrendered is replaced by a wave of sadness. The puppy squirms out from between us and hops down off the sofa, making off with one of my slippers.

"Kat!" Nick calls. She appears, as if summoned by magic.

"Could you take the puppy down to the park and make sure the kids stay there for an hour or two?" I don't raise my head to see Kat's response to having to spend time with the dog, but a second later I hear Nick say, "There's a leash in the bag in the hall," so I assume she's done as he asked.

"Look at me," Nick murmurs when she's gone. I shake my head against his chest, the tiny buttons on his shirt scratching my sensitive scalp. "*Look* at me."

I do.

"You're okay," he croons, taking my face in both of his hands. "I love you, and you're okay."

He pulls me back into his chest and I hold onto his arm, shutting my eyes against the world and pretending that everything is going to be all right. I don't know how long we sit like that, but long enough that the sun dips lower in the sky and the night chill creeps up on me. Kat must have re-routed Jack to the park.

Slowly, I pull away from Nick's arms. My throat bobs. "I'm better now," I say.

"You sure? Any pain?"

"No, but have those pink leprechauns always lived in the fireplace?"

Nick laughs. "You're not that stoned." Then he turns sombre. "When is your next appointment with Doctor Moxley? Surely there must be more he can do for the pain?"

"I haven't actually told him yet," I stammer, "but I'll do it tomorrow, I promise."

"Do you want me to call him?"

"No! I'll do it."

Nick nods his acceptance. "Tell him it's becoming debilitating, that might help."

"You think he reserves the strong stuff until we say that magic word?" I smile, but Nick isn't listening.

"Evie, we have to replace her," he says suddenly.

I know who he's talking about. I knew he'd bring it up the second he found out I had to call on Kat to fetch the children from school because I couldn't make it to the kitchen, let alone the car, doubled over as I was with pain. In the wake of the divorce, Mary-Anne has thrown herself into the Country Club with even more fervour and I don't like to call on her at the last minute. That, and she still annoys me.

"I don't think we can," I say. "It took me so long to find the right..."

"There's no right or wrong person!" Nick snaps. "We just need a nanny. Any nanny will do, but you can't do this alone anymore."

"Mom?" Oh God. Neither of us had heard Jesse enter the house.

"Hey Jesse Knight!" I can only pray that my red eyes aren't too noticeable in the fading light.

My prayer falls on deaf ears.

"What's wrong?" Jesse asks.

"Nothing," I say, my voice coming out a croak. I clear my throat. "Nothing's wrong. Where is everyone?"

"They're coming now, I ran ahead." He's staring, that uninhibited, intent look that only children can get away with.

"Did you see the puppy?"

Thank God for the dog. The mention of it is the perfect distraction and Jesse's face relaxes slightly. "She's so cute."

"Did you guys think of a name?"

A semblance of a smile. "Guinevere."

I fall back onto the sofa cushions with a chuckle.

"Do you like it?"

"Jesse, it's *perfect*!"

He comes over to sit beside me. Nick leans toward the table to pick up my glass of water and when he hands it to me, the pain pills have vanished. Jesse doesn't notice.

"You owe me big time!" Kat announces, far less sophisticated, as the puppy hauls her inside. She's holding the end of Guinevere's leash in one hand and a brown paper bag in the other. As she looks at it, she gags. I giggle, and so does Jesse.

Guinevere spends the rest of the evening chewing four cushions, both of my slippers and the straps off Nick's laptop case, before flopping down at the foot of the sofa with a contented sigh.

"Can she sleep in my room?" Dylan asks, when we finally call bedtime. Kat and Jack stayed only long enough to eat the dinner Jack had cooked, which was delicious.

Nick looks to me. Jesse isn't fazed, so I nod. "Don't let that one wake up, though," I murmur as he lifts a sleeping Casey off the floor, where she had curled up next to the puppy, "or it'll turn into an argument over who gets to have the puppy in their room."

Dylan scoops the puppy up and follows Nick up the stairs before anyone can change their mind.

"You too, Jesse, you've got school tomorrow," I say.

Jesse comes over to me, his arms slipping around my shoulders. For a second, I feel like the child, tiny and fragile in his arms. His dark hair tickles my face and I breathe it in, inhaling him into my chest, into my soul.

He stays that way for a long moment, his fingers stroking my back. "I love you, Mom."

I feel the familiar pinch in my chest.

"I love you too, Jesse Knight."

CHAPTER 37
Nick

I PULL INTO THE SWEEPING DRIVE OF ARCADIA – A residential estate that Danvers Inc. was fortunate enough to secure the interior design contract for – and feel a familiar thrill. The development is still in its infancy, nothing but bare structures and tarmac, fake lawn and sapling trees, and my mind reels with the creative possibility. I love what I do – or, at least, I love the part of it where I'm presented with a blank canvas to fill with colour and texture. This development is a massive undertaking, one that will pour a vast profit into the business, but it's also the most excited I've been about a job in forever. The financial investor is a delightful man, nearing retirement, who wants to leave a legacy behind. He and I have similar ideas, a rustic, not-too-stylised approach, much to the dismay of the chief developer, who's a prize prick.

I get out of the car to find them both waiting for me at the main doors of the lifestyle centre.

"Nick!" Old man Hadley greets me warmly, his dry, mottled hand encasing mine. Greg, the developer, has a handshake like a limp fish.

"Did you bring them?" Mr Hadley asks, rubbing his hands together as he eyes the laptop bag in my hand.

"I did. I'm hoping you'll like what you see, but please remember this is just a starting point. Everything is open to change and your opinion is my priority." I follow them through to the open- plan office that is being used as a base and boot up my laptop on the desk. I can feel Greg bristling beside me as I open the design files. I've poured so much of myself into this project, but, without Evie beside me, offering her silent support and approval as she has so many times in the past, I feel the self-doubt trickling in.

Mr Hadley and Greg remain silent while I talk them through my presentation, explaining the reasoning behind the design, the overall feel of it. I'm starting to get into my stride, my confidence returning, my passion for the work overcoming everything else, when my phone rings.

"My apologies," I mutter, pulling it from my pocket. "I thought I'd set it to silent."

I glance at the screen and frown. It's Evie. She and Kat were fetching the kids from school so I didn't have to rush and taking them to see a movie. They should all be in the cinema right now. She shouldn't be calling. Greg clears his throat but Mr Hadley waves his hand at my concerned expression.

"By all means, Nick, take it. We can wait."

Greg opens his mouth to contradict that statement but I've already lifted the phone to my ear. The first words out of Evie's mouth send a jolt of fear through me.

"Jesse's missing!"

It's so unbelievable that I'm incapable of speech.

"Nick!"

Her panic jolts my tongue into action. "Evie, what do you mean he's missing? Where are you?"

"Still at the school. We thought maybe he had been delayed or that he had practice and forgot to tell us, but we've searched everywhere. He's not here."

Time seems to slow down as my heart-rate speeds up. I can hear Greg's fingers drumming on the table, hear Casey's crying down the line, Evie's rasping breath.

"Nick?"

"Nick?"

Evie and Mr Hadley speak as one. I drag my eyes upward to find the old man gazing at me, his eyes shimmering with compassion.

"Go," he says.

I stand there, helplessly, not moving, until Evie's frantic voice calls my name again. I don't need any further prompting. I snatch up my laptop, nod once at Mr Hadley and rush for the door, the phone still pressed against my ear.

"I'm on my way," I say, yanking open my car door. I toss my laptop unceremoniously onto the passenger seat. My precious designs no longer seem to hold any value. "Have you checked all the bathrooms?"

"We've looked everywhere. He's not here, Nick."

"Okay, look, let's not panic yet. Maybe he got a ride home. Go home, check the house. I'll meet you there, I'm only twenty minutes away."

I make it home in fifteen minutes. Kat's car is in the drive, the passenger door open, and, even from here I can hear Evie's voice calling through the house. She collides with me at the base of the stairs, her knuckles white as she clutches my arms.

"He's not here."

"Where are Casey and Dylan?"

"Kat's got them out back."

I look over her shoulder, through the patio doors. "Stay here, I'll be back in a minute."

My heart is hammering and my mouth has gone as dry as chalk, but I keep my face composed as I walk out onto the patio to face my children.

"Hey guys!"

Dylan is slumped on Evie's lounger, his eyes red-rimmed, his jaw trembling. Casey, who is easier to distract, is sitting at the edge of the pool with Kat, her feet trailing in the crystal water. She only waves when she sees me, unperturbed, and I give Kat a discreet nod before I move over to crouch beside Dylan.

"Hey champ."

"Where's Jesse?" he asks, his mouth twisting in an effort to fight the tears.

"I'm not sure buddy, but I'm sure he'll be home soon. He's probably gone home with a friend and forgotten to tell us about it."

Dylan nods, jaw still slightly clenched.

I spare the time to give him a hug, long enough to make it count, not too long that he unravels. "Your mom and I are going to find him, okay, buddy? You stay here with Kat and we'll be back soon. Can you do that?"

Another stiff nod. It's the best I'm going to get. My eyes meet Kat's and she gives me a reassuring smile, letting me know that she's got this – that she's got them.

Back inside, I find Evie bent over the kitchen table.

"What are you doing?" I ask. Long gone are the days when Jesse used to hide under there while Evie and I pretended we couldn't find him.

She straightens, her eyes narrowed, then walks around the island, her eyes scanning the floor.

"What is it?" I ask. Something's bothering her, and I know her well enough to trust her instinct. If she's not rushing from the house to continue the search, she must have a damn good reason.

"The dog," she says eventually, after a cursory peek into the living-room. "Where the hell is the damned dog?"

Discovering that Guinevere is missing is both a relief and a conundrum. There's no doubt that Jesse and the pup are together, but where the hell are they?

We search the park, hoping that perhaps Jesse took Guinevere for a walk, but other than the exhausted mother pushing her twins on the swings to a chorus of "Higher, Mommy, higher" the park is empty.

Evie's hands are in a state of constant movement, ceaseless fidgeting that only gets worse as we drive with no destination. "Where is he, Nick? Where the hell is he?"

CHAPTER 38
Julia

I HOVER MY MOUSE OVER THE SUBMIT BUTTON ON MY COMPUTER screen. I'm not sure why I even hesitated in the first place, but now that I have, I can't seem to bring my fingers to perform that final click, the one that will enrol me for the upcoming semester. *This is what you want,* my brain urges. My heart stays my hand, frozen in limbo over the mouse.

I don't know why I'm hesitating, but it probably has to do with the fact that this commitment will mean the end of any hope I may have of returning to work for the Danvers, of going back to being their nanny, which is ludicrous considering everything that's happened. I couldn't go back now even if I wanted to, even though the pain of losing them has become bad enough to send my traitor's heart to purgatory. I could bury my feelings for Nick so deep inside of me that I would never again be at risk of betraying his family.

I am so lost in thought that I almost fall of my chair with fright at the sudden knock on the door. I open it, part-relieved and part-annoyed at facing yet another distraction to keep me from pressing that button. My eyes find only empty space, and then, as they trail down toward the ground, I discover a mop of unruly dark hair, a pair of guilty blue eyes and a wriggling yellow Lab at Jesse's feet.

"Jesse, what are you doing here?" I ask, ushering him and the puppy inside.

"I wanted to see you," he replies, "to show you our new puppy." He lifts the Lab and shoves her toward me. It's another distraction, one cleverly disguised, for an almost eleven-year-old, but I'm not fooled.

"Do your parents know you're here?"

He blushes. Shakes his head.

"Oh, Jesse!" I glance at my watch. "How did you get here?"

"I caught the bus."

"From school?" I frown. I don't recall a bus service that comes all the way out here direct from the school.

"I... I went home first to fetch Guinevere."

"Guinevere?" I take in the puppy's adorable, sad face, and a moment to appreciate the name before I'm brought back to reality. "You walked home from school?"

He nods. "Do you like her?" Another delay tactic, but I'm not biting.

"Jesse, your parents must be worried sick about you." I deposit the puppy on the floor. "I'm going to call them."

His face falls as I find Evie's number in my contacts list.

"Could you... could you ask them if I could stay for a while?"

"Let me just let them know you're safe," I say. "We can talk after."

I leave him in the kitchen and step out into the garden, sliding the door closed behind me. The garden fence isn't secure and I don't want the puppy getting out onto the road.

My hand trembles in time with the monotonous dial tone in my ear. Evie answers on the third ring, her voice breathless, panicked.

"Julia?"

"Hi, Evie..." I don't get any further.

"Is he with you?"

"Yes."

"Oh, thank God." Her relief is palpable, even over the phone. I hear Nick's deep voice in the background as Evie relays that information and then she's back. "We're coming over."

I boil the kettle and fix Jesse a sandwich while we wait. He slumps over his plate, absent-mindedly feeding bite-sized pieces of his crust to Guinevere, who runs in circles around his chair. I'm mopping up her second accident when I hear the car pull up outside and my heart forgets how to beat.

Evie erupts into the room like a mini-hurricane. She rushes right up to Jesse and pulls him off his chair, half-strangling him in her arms as she clutches him to her. I'm glad she's not looking at me because I feel my face drain of colour at the sight of her. She's thin – so thin, and her face is grey, a washed-out version of the woman I last saw only a little over two months ago. I am so focused on Evie that it takes me a while to register that I'm being watched. Nick is standing in the doorway, his eyes on me, a smile, so infinitely sad, on his beautiful face that my heart slams against the bars of the cell I sent it to.

And then he turns to where Jesse is being held in a vice-like grip by a sobbing Evie. He crosses the room in two determined strides and wraps his arms around them both. I feel like a stranger in my own home, an intruder on this private moment, so I slip through the door again to wait in the garden.

Evie finds me first. I wait for the onslaught that I'm expecting, for her to take her anger and her fear out on me, but she doesn't. Instead, she walks right up to me and pulls me into a hug that is far too strong for someone so frail. I hug her back, a sob rising in my chest. God, I've missed her.

"I'm sorry," I mumble into her shoulder.

"It's not your fault," she half-laughs while her hand rubs my back. She couldn't possibly know that I'm sorry for so much more than Jesse coming here without permission. I'm sorry for kissing Nick, I'm sorry for abandoning her when she needed me most, and most of all I'm sorry that she's sick, that she's going to die and there's not a damned thing any one of us can do about it.

"Can we talk?" Evie asks, after a time.

I nod and lead her to the peeling garden chair which is slowly disappearing into the sea of weeds that have taken advantage of my dad's new job to lay claim to our tiny garden.

Evie doesn't waste any time. We've barely sat down when she speaks. "I want you to come back."

"Evie..."

"No, hear me out, please. I'm not above using my condition to blackmail you, but I'd rather you came willingly, so let me speak." It's such a remarkably Evie thing to say that I laugh, but her next words wipe the smile from my face. "You're in love with Nick."

My mouth works but no sound comes out.

"I'm right, aren't I?"

I cannot deny it, but my eyes fill with new tears.

"That's why you left?" she prompts gently. She fixes me with that intent glare until I dip my head in confirmation.

"I'm so sorry. I never meant to..."

"Of course you didn't."

"For what it's worth, nothing happened. Nothing... we didn't..."

"Sleep together?" She's trying to be nonchalant but I can see it, the pain shimmering below the surface.

I nod again, my cheeks flaming.

"I know."

"You see, then, why I can't come back?"

"No."

"No?" I blink in confusion.

She picks at the flaking paint on the bench. Beneath it the wood is faded and lifeless. "Whatever happened, it wasn't your fault. Not yours, not Nick's."

"How can you say that? It *was* my fault. I let myself fall for..."

"No!" Evie insists, her eyes clouding over. "You didn't do anything." I rear back, hurt and confused and more than a little concerned about her mental state of mind, but Evie continues, her eyes holding mine. "It wasn't your fault, Julia, because it was mine."

CHAPTER 39
Evie

Telling Julia the truth is both cathartic and crippling. Admitting what I've done was always my last resort, and doing so now forces me to accept that it's almost time. My body is failing, slipping away from me without care or consequence and there's nothing I can do to stop it. I feel like I've spent the past few months on a rollercoaster which has finally begun its last descent, hurtling downhill, gaining speed and momentum. I have no brakes. There's nothing left to do but crash.

Julia listens, pale-faced and trembling, like a leaf that could be swept away by the wind at any second. It's impossible to tell what she's thinking, what she's feeling, because she has completely shut herself down, her face betraying nothing, giving nothing away.

When I'm done, I rest my hands in my lap, take a deep breath and wait. There's nothing more I can say. I've bared my heart and soul. It's up to her now.

"You..." Julia's voice breaks. She licks dry lips, releases her tongue, starts again. "You did all of that?"

I nod.

"Why?"

I smile. "Because I love them." It really is that simple. "Just like you do."

She presses a hand to her forehead. "I don't know what to say."

"Say you'll come back?"

"I don't know if I can."

"I need you, Julia. My family needs you, now, more than ever. Please," I trail off, a lump forming hard and fast in my throat. "Please come back."

She doesn't reply, doesn't commit. Instead, she gets to her feet, brushing imaginary dust off her skirt and holds out her hand to help me up. Thoughtful, despite everything she's learned.

"I need to think about it."

"Fair enough." It's not the answer I want but I certainly didn't expect anything less after the bomb I just dropped on her. All things considered, she has every right to kick me out of her house and never speak to me again. Still, I press her, because this is my family we're talking about and I am running out of options. "But please don't take too long. Time's not on my side."

A smile – faint, but reassuring. "I'll let you know by this evening."

My heart feels lighter as we make our way back inside. We find Jesse showing Nick all of Ted's medals and trophies. There are so many of them, but Jesse pulls a lengthy description of how each one was earned from memory. Nick glances back at me as Julia and I enter the room. He gives me a questioning look but I shake my head. I'll tell him later, once Julia's made her decision. Julia avoids looking at Nick and I wonder if she sees him in a new light now that she knows the truth – whether she's trying to figure out if what she feels for him is genuine, or a product of my actions. I don't blame her, and I certainly don't have the answer.

"Come on Jesse Knight," I say. "It's time to go." I won't let him off so lightly, but his punishment will have to wait until Nick and I can think up something suitable. It's hard to keep up the boundaries of normality when you know your days are numbered.

Nick scoops up the puppy and walks to the door. "It was good to see you again, Julia," he tells her as he passes. The words are stilted, forced, but I think deep down he means it.

"You too," Julia's reply is warmer and a faint blush stains her cheeks. I don't think it's his doing. I genuinely believe that Julia is happy to see all of us again. "No sneaking off again, okay, Jesse?" she adds, ruffling Jesse's hair. Jesse doesn't reply, snubbing her for reporting him, and then he and Nick are gone, leaving only an empty doorway and Julia and I, alone once more.

"I guess I'll speak to you later?" I murmur. Julia nods, her bottom lip trapped between her teeth and, as hard as it is, I know it's time to go – to leave her be and let her make up her own mind.

We get home to discover that Kat has roped Jack in to help with the kids. She's sunning herself on my favourite lounger, wearing one of my old bikinis and Jesse's baseball cap, while Jack scampers around the garden, entertaining Dylan and Casey.

"I should've known you wouldn't cope on your own for long," I tease, flopping onto the grass beside her. Dylan is crowding Nick and Jesse, desperate for information about what happened this afternoon, and Jack joins them, much to Casey's dismay.

"She's got him wrapped around her little finger," Kat drawls, as Casey hauls Jack back onto the grass to play. Then, lowering her voice, "Where was he?"

"Julia's."

"Ah." She leans back. "And how did that go?"

"I asked her to come back."

"And?"

"And I told her the truth."

Kat whistles. "How did she take it?"

"Better than I expected."

"Do you think she'll tell Nick?"

"No." It's an honest answer. Julia is simply too good, too kind, to do something like that.

"So he'll never know?"

"Actually," I scoot closer to her, ignoring the pain in my hips, "that's something I wanted to talk to you about."

Kat doesn't interrupt while I outline my plan, but her lips purse and she heaves a pained sigh every now and again for dramatic measure, which I ignore. When I'm done, she lowers her sunglasses and gives me a hard look. "You know, you can be a real bitch, Evie Danvers!"

"I know." I grin, "But you love me regardless."

"I do," she sighs again, with acceptance this time, slides her glasses up her nose and settles back on the lounger. "Now ask Jack to get me some wine, will you. I'm going to need it."

Jack does as he's asked, bringing me a glass of iced water too. I stopped drinking a few weeks back when even a few sips of alcohol started to make me throw up. Nobody said anything, and we just transitioned into this new phase as we had with every other phase of my illness. I love that Kat didn't offer to stop drinking in solidarity. It would have made things weird, and besides, she wouldn't have expected me to do so if our roles were reversed.

Casey curls up on my lap as the sun sinks lower in the sky, her blonde hair fanning out across my legs. It's not long before Dylan joins us, curling into my side and resting his head on my shoulder. When Jesse takes his place on the other side of me, lifting Casey's legs to drape them over his own. I incline my head toward his.

"I've made my decision," I tell him. His body tenses but he doesn't raise his head. "No iPad for a week." His hair tickles my cheek as he nods without argument and I kiss the top of his head. "And if you ever scare me like that again, you'll be grounded for life," I whisper. I see the corner of his eye crease and I pull him closer.

Kat smiles at me over her wine glass and Nick pulls his phone from his pocket to take a photograph - capturing the memory. None of us know that it will be the last photo taken of me with all three of my children. Except, maybe *I* do.

CHAPTER 40
Julia

It feels weird to be knocking on the familiar mahogany door. I'd left my key behind when I walked out two months ago but the formality still throws me. It's not Evie or Nick who answers the door. Instead, it's Kat, clad only in the briefest of bikinis, her pale skin smooth and supple, and smelling faintly of coconut oil.

"Hi," I say, trying to keep the tremor out of my voice. The white-tiled hall is cool and inviting, but I don't step inside. Kat's eyes fall on the suitcase at my feet and her lips curl upward. "Welcome home," she says, stepping aside.

"Who's tha...?" Nick's voice cuts dead as he appears behind Kat. "Julia?" One look at his face and I know that Evie didn't tell him I was coming. Didn't even mention the possibility. Kat sweeps away, leaving us facing one another in the doorway.

"Hi, Nick." I begin lamely. "I, um... I don't know if Evie told you I might be coming back?"

"She didn't." I can't read his expression. He glances at my suitcase. "You're back for good?"

I nod, my throat bobbing helplessly. "I hope it's not a problem. I told Evie I would let her know tonight but I figured I'd save myself the phone call. If it's not a convenient time, I can always come back tomorrow?" I leave the question hanging but Nick doesn't say anything. I shift my weight to the other foot wondering if I've made a mistake. Wondering if shutting down my computer without pressing that button is going to be something I regret for the rest of my life. And then, Nick smiles. It's an honest and open smile, one that holds the promise of friendship and a new start.

"I'm glad you're here," he says, leaning forward to take my bag. "I'll take this to your room, you go on out back and see Evie. She's going to be thrilled."

I find Evie alone on the patio. She looks tired but smiles when she sees me. "You came." She says it in a way that makes me wonder how deeply she doubted I would.

"I did. Did you think I wouldn't?"

"I expected to have to beg. I already had my guilt-trip speech planned."

"I'm sure you did."

Evie's cheek dimples but her eyes are solemn, serious. "Do you hate me?"

"I wish I did," I admit. "It's easier said than done."

"I've heard that before but I never really appreciated it until right now." A pause and then she pats the sofa beside her. 'Sit."

I do.

"I'm really happy you're here, Julia."

I look up at the sky as I take her hand. It's a blanket of black, clouds stretching as far as the eye can see and blocking out the stars. It's an empty sky.

"I'm happy I'm here too," I say. Evie squeezes my hand so tightly it hurts, and, as the warmth of her fingers seeps into mine, the lingering hurt and betrayal falls away.

Kat must have been eavesdropping, because no sooner have Evie and I fallen into companionable silence, she breezes out onto the patio followed by a handsome man.

"You must be Jack," I say, extending my hand. His grip is firm and friendly but he barely gives me a second glance, all his attention fixed on Kat. He wears his devotion on his face like Nick does.

"Jack, would you pour Julia some wine?" Kat asks.

"I hear that's going very well," I tease her as he disappears inside.

"Your father is an incorrigible gossip." She's feigning annoyance but I can tell she's pleased. "I take it you two have worked out your issues?" she continues curtly. "I didn't hear the slap of flesh so I'm assuming you're okay with Evie's devious plotting, Julia?"

I choke on my drink. "You knew?" I raise my brow, daring her to deny it.

Kat shrugs. "Every pilot needs a wingman."

Evie chuckles. "God, I wish I could still drink. A slug of vodka wouldn't go amiss right now."

"You don't need to drink," Kat scoffs. "You get to get high whenever you want."

"It's not the same," Evie grumbles. "There's no getting off that train once it gets going."

"Here you go!" Jack announces, as he sets a glass of wine on the table before me and takes his place back at Kat's side. Evie gives the glass a longing look as Nick steps outside.

"What a beautiful evening," he says, gazing at the stars.

"It is indeed," Evie sighs softly, her eyes drawn to him. She's dressed in layers, a thick, ribbed sweater drowning her, but she looks peaceful, content.

Nick comes around to her other side and takes a seat, his arm resting across the back of the sofa, a beer in his other hand. Evie's drinking water.

"Can I make you some tea or coffee?" I ask. I haven't touched my wine and I'm quite happy to have a cup of tea with her.

"No, Julia," she teases, "you can just sit here and enjoy this beautiful evening with us."

"Yes Ma'am," I grin.

"What did your dad say when you told him you were coming back?" Kat asks.

"He was very happy, but I think that's only because I won't smell like fried food anymore."

Kat looks alarmed. "Do I even want to ask?"

I laugh. "I was working in a pub."

"Probably easier than looking after the kids," Kat murmurs. Jack pokes her in the ribs. "What? Kids are hard work."

"They're worth it, though," I say without thinking.

Evie flashes me another grin. "Atta girl," she says.

"I guess they're not so bad," Kat admits. Jack pulls her closer so she can't see the delighted look on his face. I guess Jack's not as averse to fatherhood as Kat might like.

Much later I head up to my room. I can't stop myself looking in on the kids on my way up, and my heart swells at the sight of them, fast asleep in their beds. Jesse has kicked off his covers and I tuck them around him, careful not to wake him. He smiles in his sleep. Casey is snoring and Dylan has Guinevere curled up against his back – a natural heater. She looks up as I enter the room and I pat her sweet head to settle her.

My bedroom is exactly how I left it, the bottle of perfume still on the dresser, but, as I step closer, I notice a handwritten note has been slipped underneath it. *I'm sorry*. It's Evie's handwriting. I smile as I crumple it up and throw it into the wastepaper basket. *No, you're not.*

As I unpack, I wonder at the effort she went through to find me, to bring me here. The only thing she didn't do, couldn't do, was to make me fall in love with them all. I did that all on my own.

I climb into bed, a small sigh escaping my lips as my head sinks into the familiar pillow, the smells and sounds of the house washing over me. I haven't felt this peaceful in months. I guess home truly is where the heart is.

Over the next week I slip back into my routine. Jesse has a music exam coming up and the sound of his guitar echoes through the house driving everyone demented, especially Evie, who is fading faster every day but refusing to admit it. She had told me that time was running out but I hadn't realised just how serious she had been.

"I'm going to have an aneurism," she remarks one morning at breakfast as the *dun-dun-duns* reverberate through the house, followed by a rough twang. Jesse's been learning how to pick. Evie rubs her temples.

"Do you want me to turn it down?" I ask.

Evie shakes her head. "No. He's so focused, it's good for him. My ears can bleed."

I nod, but I'm already outlining a plan that will work for everyone.

Nick's been so busy with this new development he's working on that he hasn't had the chance to clear out a space in the garage for Jesse to practice. That way, Evie can escape to her room, on the other side of the house. With the door closed, she'd barely hear a thing. On Saturday morning I despatch the entire family to the park, determined to get it done.

"Guinevere needs the exercise," I point out. The puppy is getting fat, which I suspect is because the children keep feeding her unwanted items off their plates when they think nobody is looking.

The unusual hustle and bustle ensues as the kids pull on their socks and shoes and Guinevere yaps playfully at the door. She knows what the leash means and it never fails to get her worked up.

I wave as they head out and then walk back inside with single-minded purpose. I want everything ready by the time they get back.

Evie makes it halfway down the drive before she collapses. I hear Nick's frantic shout and bolt outside to find him crouched over her. Her summer dress is hitched around her thighs, a bold splash of colour against her chalk-white legs. Her eyes are closed and, for a horrifying second, I'm convinced she's stopped breathing.

Nick must be thinking the same because he lowers his face to Evie's, trying to feel her breath on his cheek. "Get the kids inside!" he yells, as Casey starts howling. I snatch her up, drawing her face into my shoulder and grab Dylan by the hand. His lips are quivering and his blue eyes are wide, his silent tears more heart-wrenching than

Casey's screams. Jesse remains fixed to the spot as he stares down at Evie.

"Jesse!" I plead. "Come inside!"

Nick is already on his feet, Evie scooped into the hollow of his arms, her face lolling against his chest.

"Inside, Jesse!" Nick roars over his shoulder. It suddenly occurs to me that he'll need help with the car door and I take a tentative step forward, trying not to let Casey or Dylan sense how frightened I am, but Jesse is too quick for me. He's already there, hauling open the back door so that Nick can lay Evie across the seat. The slam of the door makes me cringe.

"No, Jesse," Nick lays his own hand over his son's as Jesse's reaches for the passenger door handle.

"I'm coming with you!" Jesse says.

"No, you're not." I know how desperate Nick is to get Evie to the hospital, but he stays, bending on one knee and turning Jesse to face him. He doesn't want Jesse to see her, I realise, but he doesn't want to make it obvious. "I'll come back and get you, Jesse, I promise," Nick continues. How he's keeping his voice so calm is beyond me. "But you can't come with me now."

"She's my mom." The break in Jesse's voice cuts through me like a knife and a sob rises in my chest. I clutch Casey closer as Nick places his hand on Jesse's shoulder.

"You need to stay here and be brave for Dylan and Case." Nick's face twists in a grimace of pain before he can stop himself and then his eyes find the window behind Jesse. I don't know what Evie must look like, don't want to know, and I know that Jesse can't witness this either. If it's time... if Evie's going to... I stride forward, prepared to drag Jesse inside if I have to, but then Nick speaks again. "I have to go, son. I need to get your mom to the hospital, now."

Desperate tears stream down Jesse's face but he nods and takes a step away from the car. I hear Nick's relieved exhalation as he sprints around the front and vaults into the driver's seat. I reach for Jesse and he takes my hand as Nick pulls away, the tyres emitting a faint squeak.

"I want Mommy!" Casey is still howling and Dylan is shaking so badly I can barely keep hold of his hand.

Jesse swallows hard, swipes at his eyes with the sleeve of his T-shirt and takes Dylan's hand from mine. My eyes find his and I try to tell him, without words, how grateful I am – how strong he is, how brave, but I don't know if he sees any of it through the shimmer of fresh tears.

"Come on, you guys," I say gently, "let's go inside."

CHAPTER 41

Evie

Someone groans. Groans again. It wakes me up, dragging me from the depths of the deepest sleep. I try to open my eyes but they're heavy-lidded and uncooperative and my mouth is sandpapery, my tongue bloated.

"Evie?" Nick's voice above the groaning. *Shut up!*

"Evie?" I can feel the pressure of his hand over mine, but not the warmth of it. It's as if there's an invisible barrier keeping him out.

My eyes fly open at the same moment I retch and vomit spectacularly, all over myself. The groaning has finally stopped, and it takes only a quick scan of the clinical room to realise it was me. It had to be, there's no one else here.

Nick is holding a kidney-shaped bowl beneath my chin. *A bit late, don't you think?* I try to joke but the words can't get past my giant tongue and it comes out garbled, incoherent nonsense.

"It's the drugs," Nick tells me, sensing my distress. I follow the line of his gaze to see the drip hanging just to the left, above my head. "It's quite a cocktail."

I suck in my cheeks, run my tongue over my teeth and into the roof of my mouth. It loosens up, ever so slightly.

"I feel like I've been run over by a bus." I'm still not entirely coherent, but it's better.

Nick tries to smile and fails miserably. "I spoke to Doctor Moxley," he begins slowly, as if he's trying to gauge how this conversation will play out, "he said..."

"That he hasn't seen me?" I ask, not waiting for him to finish.

Nick nods. "He said it's been months. That you declined any further treatment?" There is so much pain on his face but he's trying to keep it together. His eyes are pleading for me to deny it. "You told me you'd seen him."

I'm too tired and this has gone on too long for me to bother denying it. "I see the cat," I say. "I named the cat Doctor Moxley."

He takes time to process this, to understand what I've been doing. Clarity follows confusion and disbelief is not far behind. His mouth opens, shuts, opens again, but nothing comes out. He throws his hands in the air as if calling on God or the purified air for answers, and then he shakes his head, looking at me as if he's never seen me before. Even I'm shocked when he starts to laugh.

And, like water bursting through a damn wall, the hilarity of the truth erupts and I'm laughing along with him. I can't help it and neither can Nick.

"Only you," he says, when he can finally draw enough breath to speak. "Only you could come up with something so devious."

"I'm sorry," I say, wiping tears of mirth from my eyes. "I know it's not what you wanted."

His smile is fading now, like the rose-gold of the sun disappearing over the horizon. "I wanted you to get better."

"That was never going to happen."

Another nod and he takes my hand. "How's the pain?"

I know how hard it must be for him to change the subject, but I can feel the warmth of his hand again and it fills me with comfort. "Bearable."

"What can I do?"

I smile. Nick's always had a driving need to make things easier, to help, but this is my burden to carry. "Stay," I murmur. "For now, just stay."

He does. He stays for as long as it takes me to fall asleep, but whether that's five minutes or five hours, I couldn't say. I slip in and out of consciousness, a combination of the drugs and good old mother-of-three exhaustion.

At some point Doctor Moxley arrives. The real one, not the cat. I keep my eyes closed, feigning sleep, until I hear Nick's amused chuckle. "Stop acting, Evie."

I half-open one eye to find him and Doctor Moxley watching me.

"How did you know?" I grumble, opening the other eye and slowly rising on my pillows.

"You stopped snoring. It was so loud you woke yourself up."

"If it makes you feel any better, you had me fooled," Doctor Moxley offers generously.

"That's very kind of you, Doc." I wince at a spasm in my back and they both dart forward to help, rearranging my pillows until I'm as comfortable as I can be, which, admittedly, isn't very comfortable at all.

"Nick tells me you named your cat after me?" Doctor Moxley is teasing.

"Don't flatter yourself." I flash him a grin. "He's not actually our cat."

"He also tells me you've been experiencing a lot of pain?"

I flush, embarrassed, though I have no idea why. "Yes."

"And these – episodes – does your medication help?"

"That would depend which medication you're referring to."

"Evie..." Nick warns.

"What? It's not as if he's going to have me arrested."

Doctor Moxley smiles. "Does the pain react to any medication – prescribed or otherwise?"

"It was, but lately... not so much," I admit with a frown. He's not writing any of this on my chart.

The doctor pushes his glasses further up his nose. "Evie, how would you describe your pain now, on a scale of 1-10."

I tap into my body, into the part I've spent months trying to ignore. "Around a four, I guess."

Doctor Moxley turns to Nick with a wry smile, and Nick mumbles something that sounds suspiciously like, *Don't believe a word she says.*

"Fine, maybe a five, or a six," I grumble. I know immediately that it's not good. For someone in his position I would really expect Doctor Moxley to have a better poker face.

"What?" I ask, fear making me snappish. "What does that mean?"

Doctor Moxley looks at the drip, checks my chart. "The medication we have you on is the best there is." An uncomfortable pause. "If it's not working..."

"It doesn't get any better than this, is that what you're saying?"

He feels bad about it, but there's no denying it. "No. I'm afraid it isn't going to get any better."

Hope is a fickle bitch. "Okay, well I guess it is what it is. I'll manage. Now, when can I go home, Doc?"

The expression that crosses his face brings the world to a standstill. Nick clears his throat, looking anywhere but at me and I realise they must have had a conversation about this at some point while I was really asleep.

"Right." I fiddle with the edge of my blanket to keep from crying and to give Nick a chance to compose himself. He's so close to falling apart. From the corner of my eye I see his back straighten, his fingers curling ever so slightly into his palms.

Nobody says anything, because there's nothing to say.

I'm not going home.

The seconds pass in absolute silence. A nurse passes the doorway, flashing me a polite and professional smile. From down the hall I hear the chiming of a call-button ringing in the nurse's station. Somewhere, a phone is ringing. Mundane, ordinary things are happening while I learn my fate. My head dips in grim resignation and then I drag my eyes upward, to find Nick staring at my blanket-covered feet.

"Hey!" I say, getting his attention. "Stop that."

"Stop what?"

"Dwelling."

Doctor Moxley takes his cue to leave. "I'll be back to check on you in a bit," he says. "I'm going to go and check on the results of your blood test."

"Look at me," I tell Nick when he's gone. He obliges. "Everything is going to be okay. You're going to be okay."

He shakes his head, slowly, side to side, as if the action might banish the dark thoughts from his mind.

"You will be," I insist. "Now stop being such a pansy."

"You have no idea," he rasps, his words thick with suppressed tears. "No idea how much I'm going to miss you."

"You'll see me again. Do you really think a little thing like dying is going to keep me from finding you again, in the afterlife?" I'm speaking quickly, forcefully, and I trip over the words.

His hand covers mine and it's still warm, so much warmer than my own. "Don't."

"Nick, you're going to be okay." I suck in a shaky breath. "I've made sure of it..." One look at his face and I know he's not ready for this. I don't think he'll ever be ready for it, but I have so much I need to say and I'm running out of time. I glance down at his lean, strong fingers, the tanned skin of his hand, with only the slightest smattering of dark hair near the wrist. Hands that drilled the holes to hang our family pictures, tickled our children until they squealed for mercy, hands which have brought me so much pleasure over the years that even now the thought of it brings a warm rush of heat to my face.

I can't bring myself to tell him yet. *Soon*, I think. *Soon, but not now.*

CHAPTER 42
Julia

Nick has been gone all day. He's checked in twice, letting us know that Evie is okay, but that she's going to have to stay at the hospital. He doesn't say for how long. The children are unnaturally subdued and I know that they won't really believe that Evie is fine until they see her with their own eyes, but Nick doesn't mention me bringing them to the hospital and I don't have the heart to ask. His voice is weary, laid-down with worry and exhaustion, and if he doesn't want them there he must have a good reason. Until then, it's up to me to keep the children distracted.

"I'm waiting up for my dad," Dylan announces when I gently prod them that it's time for bed.

"We don't know what time your dad will be back, sweetheart," I begin, but three pairs of eyes stare me down until I relent and let them fall asleep in front of the TV. It's Sunday tomorrow, it's not like they need to be up early to get ready for school. At last that's what I tell myself as I clean up the dinner mess.

Nick gets home after ten. I am dozing off on the sofa beside Jesse when I hear his car pull into the garage and I walk quietly through to the kitchen to meet him, careful not to wake the children.

I open the door that leads to the garage just as Nick gets out of the car. He slams his door, runs his hands through his hair and then, unaware of me watching, slams his fist into the wall. I cringe at the dull thud and avert my eyes. Nick growls something, low and deep, as if the words were formed in the pit of his chest and by the time they rumbled to the surface they had become twisted into something unnatural. I don't need to know exactly what those words were, because I can tell by the way they were said, that the news isn't good.

"Nick?" I say softly. He turns to peer at me through swollen eyelids.

"She's not coming home."

"For how long?" His face falls and I close my eyes for a second, letting the meaning wash over me. *Oh God, no!* I want to dissolve – to stride forward and punch that same spot, but my grief can wait. "Come inside," I tell Nick. "I'll make you some tea."

He follows me into the kitchen, slumps at the island and hangs his head in his hands.

"Where are the kids?" he mumbles, too shattered to lift his head.

"Sleeping. They're in the living-room. They didn't want to go to bed but I'll carry them up shortly."

"No," he sighs, getting to his feet. "I'll do it."

"I'll help you."

I carry Casey upstairs and tuck her in, sliding her favourite teddy under her arm. Her forehead is smooth and warm to the touch as I brush a feather-light kiss across it. Nick has already taken Dylan and is on his way back down for Jesse, so I go back into the kitchen. I set Nick's cup down just as he comes back from hefting Jesse upstairs.

"He's getting so heavy," he says, resuming his slumped position.

"I'm sorry I should have taken them up earlier, but they stayed up quite late and I wanted to make sure they were properly asleep before I did."

Silence. He doesn't even seem to have heard me. My tooth snags on my lip, but I force myself to ask: "What did the doctor say?"

"She can't come home."

"Maybe she'll pull through... she's done it before. You know how this goes, it's always up and down. She has her good days and her bad days. Maybe she-"

"She's not going to pull through," Nick cuts me off. "Not this time." He won't look at me and I suspect it's because he's using every ounce of that herculean strength of his to keep it together.

"Can the children see her?"

He nods. "We can take them through tomorrow."

I set my cup down and draw in a shaky breath. "Do we need to prepare them? Is she... are there any machines, or..."

He seems to understand what I'm asking and, to my relief, he answers before I finish. "No, just an IV, and they've seen that before."

I steel myself to ask the question I need to, the one that requires an answer – not for me, but for the three innocent little people upstairs who I need to make sure get through this.

"How long?"

The words ricochet off the walls and Nick shudders as if he feels it when they hit him. His eyes cloud over, a storm coming and his jaw is tight when he speaks. "A week, if that."

Dark tendrils flit at the edge of my vision and I blink them away, terrified that I might black out. There's no air in this room, and if I can't breathe, I have no idea how Nick can.

"Well, I'm going to go to bed," I say. I can feel my control slipping and I'd rather not be around him when it does. "Unless there's anything else you need?"

He shakes his head and I leave my cup on the counter as I head for the door.

"Julia."

"Yes?"

"Evie doesn't know. She doesn't want to know. She won't live by a clock."

"I won't say anything," I promise.

I drag my feet upstairs and curl up in my bed without bothering to get undressed or even to brush my teeth. Instead, I toss and turn, fully-clothed, all night until the rose-gold of dawn begins to filter through my curtains. Usually, I would appreciate the beauty of the sunrise, but today it only marks the beginning of a gut-wrenching countdown.

After a hot shower I head downstairs to find the children engaged in a full-out war over cereal boxes. Milk has been spilt all over the vinyl floor and Dylan and Jesse are grappling over a blue plastic bowl which, to anyone else, looks exactly like every other plastic bowl in the cupboard, but for some reason is suddenly coveted above all the others. Before I can get to her, Casey slips in the spilt milk and bangs her head painfully on the floor. There's a brief pause as she draws breath to scream and I scoop her up before she can erupt, pressing her face into my shirt to muffle the sound. There is no sign of Nick.

"Stop that!" I tell Jesse and Dylan, snatching the bowl with my free hand and holding it above their heads. "What is going on with you two?"

"I had it first!" Dylan yells, trying to jump for the bowl.

"It's my favourite!" Jesse insists. "He knows I always use that one!"

"It's only a bowl!" I snap. "And if you're going to fight over it then neither of you can have it." I set it on top of the fridge where neither can reach it. "Touch it and you'll be sorry," I add to Jesse, who's already reaching for a chair. "It's all right, Case," I say, lowering my voice and rubbing the back of her head. Her hair is coarse and knotted from being slept on. One-handed, I take two new bowls from the cupboard and set them on the countertop.

"Jesse, this is yours," I say, pointing, "and this is yours, Dylan. Now both of you are going to sit here and eat your breakfast while I deal with your sister."

"I'm not hungry," Jesse snaps.

"Eat!"

I hear the clatter as the bowl hits the floor. "You can't tell me what to do! You're not my mother!"

I whirl on the spot and Jesse has the good grace to blush. I know his words are borne of anger and fear but I'm surprised how much they hurt. At least with all the drama to distract her, Casey has stopped crying.

"I know I'm not," I say slowly, "but your mom's not here right now and she left me in charge. Also," I add, knowing his Achilles heel, "I'm going around to my dad's later. If you finish your breakfast and put your plates in the sink, I might just consider taking you with me." Jesse tries to look disinterested, but I hold his narrowed gaze levelly. He caves first and retrieves the cereal box.

"You too, Dylan," I say. Dylan starts pouring cereal into the bowl and, heart hammering, I head back upstairs.

I get Casey dressed and ready as quietly as possible and when the boys join us a few minutes later I instruct them to do the same. Nick and Evie's bedroom door is closed. I noticed this when I brought Casey up to her room and I don't know whether to knock, or leave Nick be. He's usually an early-riser and I'm a little concerned, but he was up late and perhaps his emotional exhaustion has finally caught up with him.

By mid-morning, my already frayed nerves are in tatters.

"Ginny, no!" I yell as the puppy zooms through my legs carrying one of Casey's teddies. I retrieve the bear, shut the puppy outside after checking that the net is on the pool and set up a puzzle on the dining-room table. I rope the children into helping me build it, keeping one eye on the clock above the mantle. Casey gets frustrated by the small puzzle pieces so I pull her onto my lap and place perfectly matched pieces side by side for her to put together.

"I want Daddy," she announces just after ten.

"Daddy's sleeping sweetheart. Here, can you put these two pieces together?" I slide them toward us, positioned perfectly to interlock, but it's a pitiful attempt at distraction.

"I want Daddy," Casey repeats, and this time it's less a question and more of an instruction.

"Okay, let me just go and see if he's up," I tell her. I get up and set her back on the chair. "You three stay here and keep building, I'll be right back."

I can feel Jesse's eyes on my back as I leave.

The door is still closed. I step right up to it and cock my ear toward the painted white wood, but I hear nothing. I knock gently. Nothing.

Louder.

Nothing.

"Nick?" I say softly.

Nothing.

"Nick?" Louder this time, but still no response and fear rises in my chest. I recall how he looked last night, his state of desperation and the way he punched the garage wall. I don't want to wake him if he's sleeping, but what if something is wrong? Concern and etiquette wage war in my head. Concern wins by a landslide and I grip the door handle with one clammy hand.

It's not locked. As the door swings open it bumps against something and stops halfway open. I peek around it to locate the source of the obstacle and my gaze falls on a pair of bare feet.

"Nick?" I'm already halfway inside the room when I realise he's crying. He's sitting on the floor next to the bed, dressed in yesterday's jeans and T-shirt, and his body is heaving with dry, silent sobs. I don't think he's slept at all.

The curtains are drawn and the room is dark but I push the door shut behind me anyway. I don't want any of the children coming in here and seeing him like this.

I crouch beside him, my hand finding his shoulder. Even in the dim light his eyes are hollow black as they gaze up at me. I try not to flinch. His eyes are dead, as if his very essence has been sucked out of them.

I don't say anything, not only because my grief-addled brain can't think of a single thing to say, but because nothing I could say will make any difference. Instead, I settle on the floor beside him and slide my arm around his neck, pulling him to my chest the same way I did with Casey this morning. He continues to sob, his hands clutching my forearm as the grief pours out of him. And even as I hold him and murmur soothing words into his hair, I can't help but think that this wave of despair which has been building for months, has not yet fully broken. I dare not think about what will happen when it does.

CHAPTER 43

Nick

Julia's perfume lingers in the air like a long-lost friend. There's something about the smell of her that rips my insides apart and makes me feel inexplicably happy at the same time. She left about an hour ago, taking the children and the dog to the park to give me time to pull myself together. An utterly fruitless exercise. There is no way to fix what's been broken.

A short, cold shower washes away the fear-induced sweat of yesterday and the blood from my hand. It provides temporary relief to my bruised knuckles. Judging by the excessive swelling of the middle one, I suspect I may have broken it, but I'm hoping it's just a minor fracture.

I grab a cup of coffee and head for the tiny area off the hall that we use as a home office. It's less cluttered than I remember – another sign of Julia's solid, efficient presence. My fingers ache as I boot up Evie's laptop and sign in with her password. It's 'password', which I've always thought ridiculous but which never fails to crack her up. My laptop is currently on my desk at the office and I need to let Amy know I won't be in tomorrow. I am about to click 'new email' when a message in Evie's inbox catches my eye. It's from Kat and the subject line reads: I still think this is a bad idea. Evie never uses email – not since she stopped working - and the email is a couple of months old. My hand throbs as it hovers over the trackpad and I flex my fingers, the sweet bite of pain as my tender knuckles protest the strain providing temporary relief from the incessant ache. *I shouldn't read it.* I know I shouldn't read it but it's not as though I don't use Evie's laptop. We're always swapping phones and we both have full access to one another's laptops and online accounts. If she didn't want me to see this particular message surely she would have deleted it?

I double-tap the mouse before I can change my mind and Kat's message pops up on the screen in a new window. It's short and to the point.

I STILL THINK this is a bad idea, but I know better than to argue. Questions are fine – good luck finding someone who doesn't think you're bat-shit crazy right at the outset.

P.S: Pinot Grigio is on special at Liquor Town.

I READ THE EMAIL TWICE, then a third time, but I'm no closer to deciphering it. I scroll down to find a short message from Evie, sent to Kat the previous day.

INTERVIEW ATTACHED – what do you think?

FRANTIC, I glance at the top of the mail, but there's no attachment. It would have been lost when Kat replied. Feeling more and more like a traitorous bastard, I click into Evie's sent items folder and find the initial mail she sent to Kat. Bingo! Clicking on the small paperclip icon, I feel my mouth go dry, but there's no going back now. It takes a few seconds for the document to open – Evie stores most of our family pictures on this laptop and the memory must be almost at capacity. I drum my fingers against the smooth surface of the desktop and cast a furtive glance through the window which offers a clear view of the street outside.

INTERVIEW QUESTIONNAIRE.

I STARE at the bold text at the top of the page. That's it? A cursory look at the first few questions confirms that this must be the questionnaire Evie prepared when she was interviewing nannies. I scroll down, skimming the questions out of curiosity. The first few are generic – can you drive, do you smoke, do you have childcare experience, basic first aid, have you ever been convicted of a felony? That last one makes me smile. The list goes on, the questions becoming more specific as Evie asks about ballet and music, spaghetti and meatballs. The question "Who would win in a battle – Arthur or Mordred?" has me laughing out loud. I keep skimming, part-amused, part-heartbroken.

Can you sew a button onto a pair of pants?

The question brings me up short. It's a long-standing joke between us that Evie has never once sewn any item of my clothing. If a button falls off, she buys me a new pair of pants.

I squint at the screen.

Do you know how to make Boeuf Wellington?

My pulse quickens. Evie can't stand Boeuf Wellington and neither can the kids. Well, technically we don't know if the kids can't stand it because they've never tried it. It's *my* favourite, but we never eat it.

I want to stop reading, but, like a blind man groping in the dark, my eyes are drawn back to the list. On and on the questions become more personal, seemingly nonsensical, to anyone but me. Me and Evie. *Oh Jesus.* No wonder it took her so long to find the right person. Evie was never just looking for a nanny. The words she spoke at the hospital echo tauntingly in my head.

"Nick, you're going to be okay. I've made sure of it."

I'm going to be sick. I shove my chair away from the desk and stumble back into the hall. My blood thunders through my veins, pounding in my head. I make it upstairs, but my brain is in hyper-drive, memories pushing through to the surface and demanding I finally pay attention.

"Please just try to get along with her. For me?"

"I know you don't like to talk about it, but I might not always be here. I think it'll be good for the kids to form a bond with someone else."

I cannot sit still, Evie's words washing over me, making so much sense now, and yet I was blind to what she was doing.

"You don't need to show Mommy. She saw me," Casey had said after her ballet recital. And Evie had been sad to miss it, but not nearly sad enough. A bark of harsh laughter scrapes out of my throat. Evie would never have missed it, not even if it meant it was the last thing she'd ever do. An image blooms in my mind, of Evie, huddled in the dark, watching Casey's headband falling off, watching as she brought the entire performance to a halt and reduced the audience to tears. That had been the first time Julia had taken her place but it hadn't been the last. Had she really masterminded all of it?

I pause outside Julia's bedroom. The door is open, the bed neatly made. I scan the room and my eyes fall on a bottle of perfume on the dresser. I don't hesitate. I cross the room and snatch it up, yanking off the lid and bringing it to my nose. *You didn't have to get me anything else, Evie. The perfume is more than...* Julia never finished that sentence. Evie cut her off, so quickly I hadn't given it any thought, but as the scent assaults my senses, I realise why being near Julia was so difficult. This perfume evokes memories of sex, nostalgia and bliss. Evie wore nothing else when we were first married.

I slump onto Julia's bed the bottle still in my hands.

"Oh Evie," I groan, another jagged splinter ripping through my already shattered heart. "What the hell did you do?"

CHAPTER 44

Evie

Kat's head appears around the door. I catch only a glimpse of her dark glasses and then she's slinking around the frame like a cat. It's not even close to visiting hours.

"How did you get past the nurses' station?" I'm not surprised, just curious.

"I waited until one went to the bathroom. The other took advantage of her absence to call her boyfriend. The last thing I heard when I slipped past was her telling him what colour underwear she was wearing, so I figure if she comes in here and tells me off, I'll just tell her to keep her lilac panties on."

I laugh and my chest shrieks in protest at the slight movement.

"That bad?" Kat asks, tossing her glasses carelessly into her handbag.

I nod. Kat ignores the visitor's chair and sits on the bed beside me. Her creamy-pink painted fingernails pick at the starched sheet.

"I don't think they'll kick you out," I say. "They seem to relax the rules when they know you don't have much time left."

Kat doesn't contradict me. Instead, she pulls out her phone and shows me a picture of a white Honda Civic. Someone has drawn a perfect cock and balls on the rear windscreen. I don't need to check the registration to know that it's Mary-Anne's car and I clutch my chest as I start to laugh again.

"She came to see me this morning," I say. "She and David – together."

Kat's perfectly shaped eyebrows disappear into her fringe. "Are they reconciling?"

"No," I shake my head. "But I think, for the first time, they're actually getting along. I don't think either of them has been happy for a long time." I give Kat a sheepish look. "She's actually not that bad."

"Are you saying I should stop pranking her?"

"No. To be honest, I think she enjoys it. How did she take the cock and balls?"

"She didn't notice at first. I watched her drive up the street toward Grace's house. I can only imagine what the bridge ladies must have thought."

"Probably turned them on, the stuffy old goats."

Kat picks at the sheet again. "I'll miss having you as my wingman."

"You have a new one," I point out.

"I admit you did well," she concedes. "Better than I ever expected. Julia's great." A pause. "But she's not you."

"She's the new and improved me. And she looks better in a bikini."

"Yeah, but you have better hair."

We both laugh at that, but somewhere in the middle it all goes wrong. Tears spill from Kat's eyes and cut a trail through the foundation on her cheeks. I don't think I've ever seen her cry. Not when her first company went into liquidation, not when she went through her first break-up, not even when her father died, although granted, they hadn't spoken in over a year because he'd borrowed money from her for rehab and blown it all on the bottle.

I reach for her hand. "Kat."

She squeezes my hand so tightly I wince. "I'm fine," she sniffs, turning her head so I can't see her face. "Just give me a minute."

It takes a little longer and her grip doesn't relent. Eventually, she swivels to face me again, her eyeliner smudged, a watery smile fixed on her face.

"I'm sorry to abandon you like this," I say.

"You should be."

"We had a good ride."

"The best."

There's nothing left to say. Kat stays, her hand still gripping mine, but more gently, letting the blood flow back into my fingers. I want to stay with her, in this moment, but the pain is rising, rearing, and my free hand itches to reach for the small button connected to my IV which will release a fresh dose of morphine into my system. I fight the urge, knowing the oblivion will pull me away from her, even as the agony becomes unbearable. Kat smiles, sadly, and leans over to kiss my forehead. When she pulls back I see the white box in her hand.

"I love you, Evie," she whispers, before pressing the button.

I HAVE no idea how long I sleep, but I wake to the sound of rain. It's a cheery drumbeat, my favourite sound in the world. For a moment, I think I must have fallen asleep outside, on the patio sofa, but then reality reasserts itself and I feel the scratchy hospital linen across my legs. I open my eyes to Nick's beautiful face. My gaze drifts down to his fingers, drumming on the side of the visitor's chair. It's not raining.

As if he senses my eyes on him, he raises his head to look at me. "Hey."

I try to speak but my tongue is once again thick and clumsy, my mouth stiff and unresponsive. For a moment, I know a moment of pure, unadulterated terror, and then a bout of coughing frees my lips.

"Hi," I manage to croak.

"The kids are waiting down the hall," he says. He's holding a piece of paper in his hand. It's creased, as if it's been folded and unfolded a hundred times while he waited.

"I found this." He holds it up for me to see. I only need to read the first two words to know what it is. And what he knows.

My cracked lips sting as they stretch into a smile. "I would say I'm sorry but I'd be lying."

"I figured as much." A pause. "Were you going to tell me?"

"Yes."

He regards me intently, searching my face for any sign that I'm being dishonest, but he finds none. "You really are a stubborn wench, Evie Danvers." He's letting me off the hook. I can see how much he wants to say, but we both know it would change nothing.

"I know," I whisper. "And you love me for it."

"I do." He lets the paper fall and gets to his feet. Strong, familiar arms reach for me, and I breathe in the smell of him, the smell of my past and my present, the smell of a life well-lived. "I love you," he murmurs into my ear, his breath hot against my cheek, his words deep, filled with emotion and sincerity. "I have loved you since the moment I laid eyes on you and I will love you forever, long after this shitty world is done with both of us."

I cling to him, pouring out my very soul and a piece of my own heart, and praying that it will be enough. I don't ask him about Julia, about whether or not my plan worked, because it doesn't matter anymore. I underestimated him, all along, this man – this lion-hearted, courageous man, who will be more than enough for our children and who will be strong enough to weather the storm all on his own.

"I love you, Nick," I whisper, feeling the hot tears on my face. "Don't you ever forget that."

The children are almost my undoing. Almost, but I keep it together because I'm also strong. Like calls to like, and I married a man who was my equal. It's not easy, but I call on every ounce of strength within me not to cry. Casey and Dylan settle on either side of me. Dylan is more subdued than usual, but Casey is determined to tell me exactly what I've missed – at once, and without interruption. I listen, letting the sweet lisp of her voice wash over me as I run my hand up and down Dylan's back. Jesse hovers near the bed, his bruised eyes taking in every tube, every piece of daunting electronic equipment and every laboured breath I take.

"Come here, Jess," I beckon. He doesn't move. My throat chokes up and I try again. "There's room for one more."

He shakes his head, lips trembling.

"Give your mom a hug, Jess," Nick is pleading, but I shake my head at him, telling him to let it go.

"I need a wee," Casey announces eventually when she's run out of stories to tell. Nick takes her from me and Dylan hops down off the bed to tag along. I wait until the bathroom door shuts behind them before turning to Jesse.

"You can stand over there, Jesse Knight," I say, casting a sceptical look at his feet, "but there's something you should know." A puzzled frown, but it erases some of the fear etched on his face. I know my son and I know what this is doing to him. Jesse cannot heal because he hasn't had to face his worst fear yet. He cannot slay the dragon of despair until he actually has to face it, and as long as I'm here, he's living in a perpetual state of grief. Jesse will only begin to heal when I'm gone. It's time for me to say goodbye, to let go, so that my family can grieve. So that they can grieve and then finally begin to heal.

"What?" Jesse whispers, rousing me from my heart-breaking revelation. "What do I need to know?"

"Oh, nothing," I shrug, ignoring the stab of pain it induces. "Just that the floor's lava."

Without thinking, Jesse bounds forward, not toward the door, but away from it, right onto the bed, right into my waiting arms.

CHAPTER 45
Epilogue

"NICK!" JULIA'S VOICE IS BREATHLESS, CARRIED TO ME ON THE wind. I jog over to her, my feet digging into the warm wet sand. "Is this it?" she asks. Her eyes dance with excitement.

I glance down and smile at the rock at her feet. "No," I shake my head. "That's not it."

The fire in her eyes fades as she scowls at the harmless stone. "It looked... I really thought..."

I cock my head to one side. "It actually looks a bit like a..."

"Goat!" Casey announces, appearing between us. "That looks like a goat."

"Or a dog," Dylan adds, his wet hair clinging to his forehead.

Jesse frowns, walking a tight circle before his blue eyes rise to meet mine. "It's a cat," he says. "Definitely a cat."

My lips part, a smile tugging up the corners of my mouth and my heart swells with emotion.

"It is a cat," Julia agrees, pulling Jesse against her. Dylan and Casey have already lost interest, and they race away flicking up sand as they go. The sound of their laughter fills me up inside.

"Dad, do you *wanna* play ball?" Jesse asks.

"You think you can take your old man?" Jesse gives me a knowing look. "Okay," I tease, "but don't cry when you lose."

He sprints back toward our basket, a short way down the beach.

"I really wanted to find it," Julia says softly, her eyes downcast.

I drape my arm around her shoulders and she smells of salt, and sea, and Julia.

"I know you did. But she wouldn't have wanted you to."

She peers up at me through dark lashes. "She would've wanted you to find this one," I explain. "Because this one is yours. Only yours."

Evie's final gamble didn't pay off the way she planned. It's been a year and Julia and I are not together – not in that way – but she is my best friend in the whole world and she still lives in our house. She drops the kids at school on the way to college and she makes Boeuf Wellington every Friday night. The kids eat it too. She's a mother and wife in every way but one. We haven't laid a finger on one another, but, looking at her now, her pink lips pursed in an adorable pout, the swell of her breasts above the modest cut of her bathing suit, I feel a flutter in my chest and wonder if perhaps Evie did know best after all.

I pull my phone from my pocket and Julia smiles, stepping to the side so that our feet are perfectly spaced beside the cat-shaped rock as I capture the moment – a brand new memory.

Dylan and Casey are back, circling like a pair of hysterical vultures, and Jesse is throwing the ball up into the air and catching it, taunting me as only a pre-teen can.

"Uh-oh," Julia warns suddenly, her voice low and meaningful. We all freeze. Jesse lets the ball drop to the sand, his face splitting in a grin and I toss my phone down beside it. Casey and Dylan look like they've just stepped up to the starting-block.

"The floor's lava!" Julia yells, but we're already running, all five of us, hurtling toward the surf.

Acknowledgments

As always, there are a number of people to thank. No book is created in a vacuum and I am blessed to have an amazing team who travel this journey with me.

Catherine Eberle, my editor, who has worked with me since *The Legacy*. Without you, I would be lost.

Wendy Bow of Apple Pie Graphics, cover number 14! Your talent astounds me daily. Who would've thought we'd get this far without tearing each other's hair out! Not me...

To my husband, Murray, and my three gorgeous babies, this book was without a doubt the hardest I've ever had to write. You know why.

And finally, to my readers. This book is for you.

About the Author

Lissa Del is a pseudonym for award-winning author, copywriter, and lover of the written word, Melissa Delport. She is published in both S.A and the U.S.A and offers professional copywriting services and author coaching.

For ten years she owned and operated her own specialized logistics company until she woke up one morning and decided it was time to put her English degree to good use.

Melissa lives with her husband and three teenagers, none of whom take her seriously.

She also writes romantic suspense as Lissa Del and contemporary romance as Rachel Rhodes.

For more information, visit www.melissadelport.com

Also by Lissa Del

CONTEMPORARY WOMENS FICTION (AS LISSA DEL)

Rainfall

Riven

A Life Made of Lava

ROMANCE & ROMANTIC COMEDY (AS RACHEL RHODES)

Awkward in Print

Awkward Abroad

Awkward Infidelity

Awkward in Trouble

URBAN FANTASY

GUARDIANS OF SUMMERFELD SERIES

The Cathedral of Cliffdale (Book 1)

The Fight of the Fallen (Book 2)

The Hope of Hawkstone (Book 3)

The Balance of the Blood (Book 4)

Full Series Boxed Set (Books 1-4)

SHADOW MAGIC SERIES

The Witchborn Curse (Book 1)

The Shadow Huntress (Book 2)

The Charmed Quarter (Book 3)

The Rogue Coven (Book 4)

The Darkest Realm (Book 5)

The Hybrid's Fate (Book 6)

Full Series Boxed Set (Books 1-6)

THE TRAVELER DUOLOGY

The Traveler (Book 1)

The Survivor (Book 1.5)

The Saviour (Book 2)

TIME TRAVEL FANTASY

The Clock Keeper

DYSTOPIAN

THE LEGACY TRILOGY

The Legacy (Legacy Trilogy Book 1)

The Legion (Legacy Trilogy Book 2)

The Legend (Legacy Trilogy Book 3)

ANTHOLOGIES

The Space Between Dreams & Chaos

The Space Between Magic & Mayhem

www.ingramcontent.com/pod-product-compliance
Lightning Source LLC
Chambersburg PA
CBHW020913310726
48980CB00011B/865/J

* 9 7 8 0 6 3 9 8 4 4 7 5 6 *